VIOLINS OF AUTUMN

VIOLINS OF AUTUMN

Amy McAuley

Walker & Company
New York

First published in the United States of America in June 2012
by Walker Publishing Company, Inc., a division of Bloomsbury Publishing, Inc.
www.bloomsburyteens.com

For information about permission to reproduce selections from this book, write to
Permissions, Walker BFYR, 175 Fifth Avenue, New York, New York 10010

Library of Congress Cataloging-in-Publication Data
McAuley, Amy.
Violins of autumn / by Amy McAuley.
p.   cm.
Summary: When World War II breaks out, seventeen-year-old Betty, an American studying in
England, trains as a spy and parachutes into German-occupied France to join the Resistance,
but after meeting a young American pilot she begins to realize fully the brutality of the war
and their dangerous position.
ISBN 978-0-8027-2299-7 (hardcover)
[1. Spies—Fiction.   2. World War, 1939-1945—Underground movements—
France—Fiction.   3. Americans—France—Fiction.   4. Air pilots, Military—
Fiction.   5. France—History—German occupation, 1940-1945—Fiction.]   I. Title.
PZ7.M478254Vio 2012   [Fic]—dc23   2011034634

Book design by Regina Roff
Typeset by Westchester Book Composition
Printed in the U.S.A. by Quad/Graphics, Fairfield, Pennsylvania
2 4 6 8 10 9 7 5 3 1

For the daring women of the Special Operations Executive.
May their heroism never be forgotten.

VIOLINS OF AUTUMN

PROLOGUE

The shackles binding my arms and legs to the chair scour my blistered skin to a bloody mash.

Firm hands clasp my hair and forcibly lower my head.

Ice water envelops my face, flowing up my nose, devouring my head whole. A thousand pinpricks of pain spark across my raw cheeks. Panic wrings the air from my lungs, and it climbs my throat, claws of desperation sinking deep.

Fingers wind tighter through my tangled hair, raising me to the surface.

Above me, my interrogator shouts in French, "You are a spy! You are an agent of the Special Operations Executive! You are the American, Betty Sweeney!"

"*Non*," I gasp, catching my breath. "*Je m'appelle Adele Blanchard.*"

"You worked with the British agents Denise Langford and Timothy Bishop! Where are they?"

"*Je ne connais personne de ces noms.*" I know no one by those names.

"You do! Who is assisting them?"

"*Je ne sais pas.*" I do not know.

My head plunges, displacing jagged chunks of ice. The sting becomes excruciating, as if my face has been turned inside out.

"You do know them! You will give us their locations! You will tell us where the weapon drops take place!"

I spit a mouthful of water on the floor in the direction of the shiny pair of army boots I see there. I draw a long breath. Down I go again.

Garbled voices bounce back and forth above me.

I strain against the chains, screaming on the inside. Fear eats what little oxygen I have left.

I am about to drown. There is nothing I can do about it.

ONE

May 1944—Somewhere over France

I sit at the edge of the plane's trapdoor, feet dangling into the abyss of the moonlit night. The plane wobbles, unstable at such a low altitude. My hands press to the metal on either side of me, gripping tighter. My parachute is too big for me, and with the added bulk of the million francs stashed in the back of my jump overalls, I have to sit closer to the edge than I would like. But I can't fall. Not yet, anyway.

When the time comes, Denise and I will jump first. If we girls have the courage to jump, there will be no good excuse for Bishop and Shepherd to stay in the plane. They can't be upstaged by "the weaker sex."

From the day my training began it seems as if I've been carried along on a swiftly moving conveyer belt. I've reached the end with expectations of parachuting into Nazi-occupied France, and I'll go through with it. I've come too far to turn back now.

I sneak a peek across from me at Bishop's fearless demeanor. He's already completed one mission in France and is about to drop back in for more. When we prepared to board the *Halifax,* the pilot took one look at the rest of us and jokingly referred to Bishop as Grandpa. What a mistake to be fooled by his silvery sideburns. If only boys my age had this same kind of rugged strength and maturity I secretly swoon over.

Shepherd, on the other hand, looks hardly old enough to shave, with his baby-smooth skin. I couldn't believe my ears when he told me he was twenty-three. The great pains he takes to keep his boyish haircut neatly combed only makes me want to run my hands through and muss it all up.

Again the plane wobbles. My queasy stomach wobbles with it. Sandwiches and rum were supposed to have been served on the flight. We got nothing, which is okay with me. They might have ended up raining down on some Frenchman's rooftop.

Next to me, Denise dreamily stares forward when I try to catch her attention, as if she doesn't have a care in the world. If her hands weren't covered by leather gloves, she'd probably be inspecting her polished nails, even as we wait to jump onto death's doormat.

Denise and I met at the Special Operations Executive's paramilitary school in Inverness-Shire, Scotland. I went to the school after the preliminary stage of having my character and potential assessed, without knowing much about what would go on there. They purposely kept us volunteers in the dark, in case we didn't make the cut. The deeper we went in our training, the more secrets we learned.

Incompetent trainees were weeded out and sent to a detention center called "the cooler," where they were encouraged to forget about the cloak-and-dagger stuff going on in the English and Scottish hillsides before being dropped back into regular life. I wasn't one of those incompetents sent off to the cooler. I passed and continued on. Just to be set apart like that, placed in the worthy group, was motivation enough for me to stick with the training. The funny thing is I don't know what I said or did to impress them. I suppose it doesn't really matter.

The lamp above our heads continues to glow scarlet, warning us to stay put. Waiting on pins and needles for the lamp to flash green, I press the silk lining of my gloves between fingers that tingle to the point of numbness.

At Ringway airport, near Manchester, they did their best to prepare us for this moment. On ropes and swings, we learned to coordinate our jumps and land properly without injuring ourselves. They had the old fuselage of a plane set up, where we practiced correct jump techniques. It took me a while to get the hang of it, but with so many of us looking gawky and ridiculous all at once, it wasn't too embarrassing.

The instructor said my face looked white as a sheet before the two practice jumps from a real plane. The scariest part was that first step into thin air several hundred feet off the ground. I was convinced I wouldn't survive. Once there was nowhere to go but down, the fear of dying was suddenly replaced by a new kind of fear that made me feel more alive. I imagined free fall felt like a roller-coaster drop, but instead it was like flying. I wished my instructor could have seen the smile I wore, lips and cheeks contorting like rubber in the wind, all the way to the landing.

Thanks to horrible weather my third required jump was called off. Would my confidence have been higher tonight with one more jump under my belt? Doubtful. German soldiers weren't waiting on the ground during the practice run. Botching tonight's jump would have far more serious consequences.

After a few moments the red lamp switches to a jolly green, giving the go-ahead to plummet into danger.

"I don't think I can go through with this. It's madness," Shepherd says.

No one else appears to have heard him above the roar of the engines. It's the worst thing anyone could say before my jump.

Full-blown panic replaces the butterflies in my stomach. He's right. Leaping into black nothingness is crazy. My heart races.

The dispatcher roars, "Go, go, go!" The words fire out of him like cannonballs.

Denise leans against me. A thin lock of auburn hair has escaped from under her helmet, and it lays coiled over her mouth like a dashing mustache. "Let's give 'em hell, Adele!" she shouts. Then she's gone, vanished through the hole in the *Halifax*'s floor.

Adele.

When we jump we leave our real names behind. As a matter of security we'll refer to each other only by our aliases. I have to be Adele, through and through. My name, Betty, never really suited me anyway.

"Go, go, go!" the dispatcher continues to roar.

It's now or never. And never isn't an option.

I swallow one last time to clear my ears, aching hard from the plane's lack of pressurization. If I wait another second, whatever fumes of courage I have left might evaporate. I need to separate action from thought and just go.

I inch forward until I'm seated at the edge.

Go out straight to avoid the slipstream. Don't bash your nose on the other side of the hole.

I push myself up on my hands and drop through the hole in the plane's fuselage. I fall through empty space. Alice through the rabbit hole. Above me, I hear my static line quickly unraveling, segment by segment—*pop, pop, pop*. Even though they showed us we were well hitched to a hook in the plane, a voice breezes through my mind saying, "I hope your line is really attached." It comes to me with a flood of cold sweat that I might die in this position. Feet together, soaring through the silent night without another word to anyone. But then, after a few seconds of free fall, the static line yanks my parachute open. The shock jolts my entire body, as if I've jumped feet-first into a pool of cold water.

As I drift, claiming a piece of the sky all to myself, the overwhelming joy I remember from my practice jumps rushes through me.

I search the sky, unable to see Denise's parachute anywhere. We're to be met on the ground by members of a local Maquis—a cell of the French Resistance. They should be marking the landing area with red-capped flashlights. I see no lights. The full moon has slipped behind a cloud. Everything beneath me is black.

"Don't panic," I whisper to myself, as if that might help.

I realize just then that this mission won't be "like dropping into an easy chair," as I was told. Somehow I fell for that line at the time. Now it sounds like pure nonsense. All I have to do is drop into foreign country, aid and train members of the ever-growing Resistance movement, sabotage railways, travel the country on a bicycle while concealing top-secret information, blow things up, and try not to get killed. Sure, easy as pie. Things already seem to be going wrong, and I haven't even reached the ground yet.

I continue to fall toward a wide-open field. And while I know logically that I'm soaring through the air at an insane speed with only a rubber helmet for protection, the descent somehow feels slow and peaceful. Like I'm a tuft of dandelion fluff. That all changes in a snap. I reach a certain height and suddenly the ground speeds up to greet me. It doesn't seem possible that we can come together without one of us getting severely crushed, and I'm pretty sure the earth will hold up better than I will.

Most girls my age are fresh out of school, working in typing pools and factories. And here I am, seconds from touching down in enemy territory.

There are no brakes to pull. No going back. I brace myself for the hard landing.

It isn't until my feet collide with the first branches that I realize the expanse of shadow beneath me isn't a field at all. I'm crash-landing into a forest.

Two

I cover my face, not because I remember that instruction, but because vanity takes charge. I also don't want to lose an eye. That's just common sense.

Other instructions come flooding back. I keep my legs together and fall freely into the trees. My parachute catches, bringing me to a bouncy stop. Right away, I move my arms and legs. I wiggle my fingers and toes. Only a small spot on my right side hurts. I breathe deeply in relief.

For a while I hang suspended, listening for the drone of the plane's engine. The sky is silent. Where is Denise? Where are the Maquis members?

In the distance, a dog barks. My muscles tense. Barking dogs are never a good thing. Where there are dogs, there are people. I don't have contacts in France yet nor a sense of who to safely trust. People who are nice to your face can easily turn against you behind your back. I learned that at boarding school long before joining the SOE.

I twist in my harness, gauging the distance to shades of gray and black ground. I didn't come all this way to die or injure myself within the first hour. I swear under my breath, hoping Denise and the men are searching for me.

I look up to the parachute hopelessly entangled in the tree-top. What to do? My gloved fingers fumble with the buckle of my harness. It refuses to budge.

I go back to hanging and listening.

The snowcapped mountains of France were visible from the large window in my dormitory room at boarding school. How much time did I fritter away daydreaming about life on the other side of those mountains? More than the headmistress approved of, I know that much. I'm finally in France, where I've longed to be. But I'm no tourist.

The SOE offered me the experience of a lifetime, an adventure more daring than most people can ever hope for, and I willingly accepted. Nobody forced me into this. At seventeen, I'm plenty old enough to take charge of my life.

As I hang from the tree, the reality of my adventure starts to sink in. I'm stuck in a strange country, in the dark, without supplies. Agents don't last long here. I could be killed or find myself in the kind of circumstances my emergency cyanide pill is meant to rescue me from. None of that seems romantic or exciting now.

I press my gloved hands to my face, feeling foolish for getting swept up by the recruiters' enthusiasm. The coolness of the leather against my warm cheeks helps to clear my head. I close my eyes and take a deep breath. I can't hang around in the forest until dawn. I have to get myself out of this mess.

I grab my knife from a pocket in my overalls. The blade slices through the harness with a freeing *zip*. I fall through the air, hit the uneven ground hard, and collapse in a clumsy heap. For a good half-minute I lie there with my hand clamped over my mouth, moaning away head-to-toe achiness. I crawl to the base of a thick tree to catch my breath.

To my left, the trees are sparse. I've landed near a country road. I wait, my heart thumping like a kick drum. Huddled small and out of sight, no one will ever find me. I listen for signs of life but hear nothing. What if the rest of the group has banded together and left me behind?

Just as I decide to dart for the road to find help, the rhythmic footfalls of a solitary person puncture the cool night air. Arms wheeling, I scramble backward. Gripping my knife, I sneak to the thick undergrowth near the forest's edge. The approaching footsteps close in on my hiding place. Within the shadows I raise my head, shocked to see Shepherd marching down the country road, arms purposefully swinging at his sides. He's a civilian volunteer, not a military man, but that's exactly what he looks like: a British officer on a parade square and nothing like an ordinary Frenchman. Did he completely lose his mind between the plane and the ground?

I don't know what to do. Dressed in my jumpsuit, I risk capture if I join him on the road or call out to him.

Time to consider my options runs out. Four men leap from the ditch on the other side of the road. Gendarmes—the French police. They're on Shepherd before he has time to react. He struggles and puts up a good fight, but against four armed men he has no chance. I hold my breath as he gives up and they lead him away down the road.

The police were waiting. They know about our drop, and now they're looking for us. They're looking for me.

I return to my ensnared parachute. I'm supposed to hide it, along with my overalls, except I can hardly see it, much less retrieve it. The parachute will have to stay where it is, sure to be found in the morning. But I guess Shepherd's capture has done more to give us away than my abandoned parachute will.

Under my jump overalls I'm wearing a dull-as-dishwater blouse and skirt that will help me hide in plain sight behind enemy lines. But if I'm captured in the civilian clothes rather than a military uniform that would protect me under international law, the Germans can legally execute me as a spy.

My suitcase of belongings is inside a one-foot-by-six-foot metal cylinder that was dropped from the plane before I jumped. Each piece of clothing made specifically for us by the SOE has no labels, no wrappers or tickets in the pockets—no markings or signs that the clothes actually come from Britain. Without proper clothing, I won't fit in. And not fitting in is one of many things that can blow my cover.

I tug my helmet off. My sweaty cap of hair breathes again. I bend over and comb my hands through, separating the loose dark-brown waves. My hair is the one thing I truly love about myself. Girls at boarding school got permanents to have wavy hair like mine. Not that they would have been caught dead admitting it; that gossip came to me through the grapevine, when a group of bullying seniors ended up looking like badly groomed poodles. Perfect punishment, I thought, for making my first year so miserable. My best friend, Sylvie, and I practically wet ourselves laughing.

As I stuff the helmet into my overalls, a beam of moonlight glints across the silver knife blade in my other hand. Without realizing it, I'd been flashing out my position all along. I sheepishly return the knife to its proper pocket.

Heel to toe my feet silently roll forward, avoiding fallen leaves and branches. I stick to the shadows, like an owl on a nightly hunt for mice. But the longer I walk, the noisier I seem to get. I can't help but focus on insignificant sounds. My body betrays me by pumping blood too loudly, forcing each breath to travel a bumpy road—whistling wind through a voice-box cave and nose-hair trees. I swallow. I blink. I can't help any of it.

"Adele."

Frozen in place, I stare at the spot where the voice came from, unable to see any telltale human outlines.

"Adele."

There's no mistaking that springy British whisper. I haven't been left alone, after all.

"It's me," I say, so quietly I doubt Denise heard. "Come out."

Seconds later, from behind a bush not five feet away, she appears, still in her jumpsuit. I jerk back, surprised to see how close she really is.

I point to the bush. "How did you get there?"

"Quietly," she says.

Denise closes the distance between us in three soundless steps.

"Where'd you land?" I ask.

"Not in the proper place, apparently. I saw your chute on its way down. I had a rough idea where to find you. So, you landed in the trees. How's that for a welcome?"

"I'm okay. No broken bones. My parachute is stuck in the trees, though."

"Mine's tucked in a hollow log, near the field I came down in. And I found a couple of our containers."

"Where are they?"

"Near the road." Her outstretched arm shows me the way.

Near the road. They may as well have landed on the steps of a gendarmerie. Sunrise is a few short hours away and curfew ends at five o'clock. The gendarmes know about our jump, and if they find our personal items inside the containers there will be no doubt that female agents were dropped into the area. As spies go, ordinary girls like Denise and me are unexpected. We need to use that to our advantage.

"We need to move the containers, Denise. I think we might have fallen into a trap. Shepherd's been taken. I saw it with my own eyes."

"Bloody hell." She sighs. "I had a feeling something wasn't right. What happened?"

"Four gendarmes came at him from a roadside ditch. We could be next."

Denise pauses while taking this in.

"We won't be next." She pulls out her pistol. "Follow me."

We slink through the woods. Each time the full moon goes into hiding Denise all but disappears from sight, only to reappear out of the darkness in front of me like a ghost taking form in the eerie moonlight. After a clumsy close call with an exposed tree root, I somehow recover my balance quietly. I speed up to shorten the space between us, trying not to crash through the forest like a rampaging bear.

Through a break in the trees I see the field Denise must have landed in. She signals a message to me with her hands. We were taught not to use the same trail twice, to avoid a possible ambush. At the next fork in the path, she heads down the left branch.

The trail meanders along a narrow riverbed. I kneel to roll a pebble over the edge. It bounces a short distance through the deepening black of the gully and skitters to a stop.

"No splash," I whisper.

I climb to the bottom, checking the softness of the bank with my knife as I go, a trick I picked up playing cops and robbers with my brother, Tom, and his friends. I always played the part of beautiful bank robber Bonnie Parker, and my brother's friend Nick was Clyde Barrow. The two of us got so good at being on the lam that sometimes Tom and the other boys couldn't find us for hours. But after Bonnie and Clyde really were gunned down by police, the game didn't seem as fun anymore.

Denise joins me and we follow the dry riverbed, out of sight, without leaving behind a map of footprints on the bone-dry earth. At an old bridge in the country road, she motions for us to leave the riverbed. We climb to the top, concealed by the bridge.

No matter how hard I squint, no unusual forms stand out among the shadows. The soft moonlight can't locate our containers. Neither can I.

We skirt the field and come to a shallow ditch alongside the country road. Denise stands next to me, silent, as she scans the darkness. Eventually she puts her mouth to my ear and says the words I don't want to hear.

"The containers are gone."

THREE

The containers are gone. After everything else that's gone wrong, I get a terrible sick feeling in the pit of my stomach, as if it's another sign of things to come.

I eye up the surrounding forest. Any number of sly German soldiers or French police like the ones who nabbed Shepherd might be hidden there in the pitch black. I shiver at the thought of them slipping out from the cover of those trees like boogeymen.

Maybe someone should have done a better job of talking me out of this.

"What should we do?" Denise asks. "They told us the safe house would be no less than a mile from the drop zone, but we can't wander aimlessly in the middle of the night. If no one finds us soon, we'll have to stay put and wait for first light."

I don't like the idea of sleeping outside on the cold ground without a fire, but it's looking like our only option.

"Besides, we were dropped in the wrong place," I say. "Who knows where the safe house and reception committee might be. I can't wander around with a million francs stuffed into my jumpsuit."

"True." Denise quickly ducks. She points toward the trees to our left. Three men walk onto the field from the forest at the roadside. I crouch, ready to withdraw my knife. "When I make a run for it, stick with me."

"Denise, wait—it's Bishop," I say.

He runs toward us, waving his arms above his head. "Don't shoot."

"However did you find us out here?" Denise asks.

"We heard the two of you talking." Bishop doesn't sound at all happy about that, and my relief at being found turns to embarrassment. "Voices carry greater distances at night, girls, don't forget that."

"Our containers," Denise whispers. "Where are they?"

"We have them. Your radio is safe, Denise, no need to worry."

"Shepherd has been captured," I say.

"Yes, we know," Bishop says. "It's unfortunate. We'll discuss it at the safe house."

He and the two other men, part of the group that was to have met us on the ground, lead us through the woods. The long walk seems to take even longer because no one speaks. We come out near a stone farmhouse. Comfort is only steps away. How has it been hours, and not days, since we left England? It doesn't seem possible.

We were forewarned that the people of France are starving. The occupying Germans strictly ration most foods and restrict the diets of every French man, woman, and child to the calorie.

The first thing I see when I enter the farmhouse is a long wooden table set for dinner.

A petite woman rushes around the table to greet us. Her round cheeks remind me of pink lollipops. "*Bienvenue. Bienvenue. Entrez.*"

The woman reaches around Bishop to fish me out. She throws her arms around me as best she can. My arms hang lax at my sides. I'm not sure what to do about this stranger's eagerness to show me affection. Able to see clear over the top of her upswept graying curls, I count eight place settings at the table and wonder who will take up the extra one.

"I am glad to have you here," she says before moving on.

Denise endures the woman's enthusiastic squeeze until her steely British reserve wins out. I almost laugh when she squirms away and redirects the hug toward Bishop.

He diverts the hug by politely extending his hand. "How do you do?"

The exposed wooden beams framing the slanted ceilings far above my head make the room seem grander than I would have expected. After introductions, the woman, Claire LaRoche, leads the way to a cozier adjacent parlor.

"Take a load off your feet, ladies," Bishop says to Denise and me, gesturing to two matching side chairs.

Denise jumps to take up the offer. "Don't mind if I do."

I don't want to take a seat simply because I'm a girl, but I'm as sore and tired as anybody else now that the aftereffects of my jump and hard landing are catching up with me. That padded chair looks mighty comfortable.

From a walnut curio cabinet, Madame LaRoche removes a seemingly endless stream of family photographs. She sets a photo of a wiry little boy with tousled brown hair in my hands. Even in the grainy photo, the mischievous gleam in his eyes is obvious. It's that look boys get when they're about to do something they probably shouldn't.

The front door swings open, and Madame LaRoche says, "Here is my handsome boy, Pierre, now."

Expecting to find a child in the doorway, I first notice Pierre's battered military boots and denim trousers. My gaze moves higher and higher, past his gray woolen sweater and rugged shoulders. I stare directly into the face of the most handsome man I've ever seen outside of a movie.

In the photograph, Pierre's eyes hint that he's ready for trouble. Now they make him appear dark and brooding. Maybe even dangerous.

The door slams.

"They sent us more girls? Girls. Again. My God." Pierre's pointed French words burst my bubble like tiny arrows. "How do they expect us to get our country back when all they do is send us these flimsy little girls?"

"Pierre, you don't mean what you say. These beautiful girls are guests in our home."

He clomps across the wooden kitchen floor, yanks a chair out from the table, and flings himself into it. Maybe he isn't so far off from the child in the photo after all.

After we're seated, Madame LaRoche serves dinner. We eat our cold potato-and-leek soup in awkward silence. I reach the bottom of my water glass. The urge to get some much-needed sleep has snuck up and wrapped me in a woozy cocoon. Head heavy, eyelids heavier, I struggle to stay upright and alert as Madame LaRoche begins to explain how life in France has changed.

Between the two world wars, France took drastic precautions to ensure that Germany could not attack again. Along the shared border, a massive fortification was built—large fortresses nine miles apart that housed one thousand soldiers each, and smaller forts in between that housed a few hundred men. This Maginot Line was vast, impressive, and impenetrable. Or so it was believed.

Rather than attack through France's stronghold, Germany went around the line, successfully invading Norway, Denmark, Luxembourg, and Belgium along the way. In early May 1940, armies invaded France through the unprotected—though thought to be impassable—Ardennes Forest. That France surrendered so easily came as a major shock and a blow to the pride of the people. They were assured that the Maginot Line would protect them and their country.

"Premier Reynaud resigned, refusing to surrender to Germany!" Madame LaRoche exclaims. "And the new government dances for the Germans like wooden-headed puppets as they Nazify our country. They are imprisoning and killing our people. It makes me ill to think of it!"

She downs several mouthfuls of wine.

"One day they announced that Jews must sew a yellow star on their clothing. 'Don't do it, Hannah,' I told my dearest friend. 'They are making you stand out.' She was such a good woman. She only wanted to do what was right. She thought that if she obeyed their rules, they would leave her alone. Then one day she went away. They took her." Openly weeping, Madame LaRoche says, "What if I never see her again?"

Pierre covers her trembling hands with his to steady them on the table.

"And your poor papa, sent to his death. For what? Daring to

speak out? It is a crime now, to tell the truth? They intend to comb all of France until they have done away with everyone who looks, acts, and thinks differently than they do? It is insanity!"

I shrink down on my chair, as if that might help me disappear. As I pick at a loop of thread in the seam of my skirt, I notice the brief shake of Pierre's head to his mother.

"I apologize for my outburst," she says.

Bishop tears his bread into halves. "Please don't apologize, Claire. In your shoes, none of us would accept what the people of France have been asked to accept."

"Some of us were not content to sit back and watch the Germans take over our country," Pierre says. He gestures around the table. "Say one day you find strangers have moved into your home. They eat your food while you go hungry, sleep in your bed, hurt your family, steal what is rightfully yours. Would you give up and allow them to stay? And not only that, you find out you must *pay* for them to stay. Pay them to control your life? Bullshit! We risk prison and death to stand up and fight because we have to. Because it is the right thing to do!"

I catch myself staring at Pierre in wonderment and quickly put an end to it. Abrasive and insulting people aren't supposed to say things I agree with. I'd already made up my mind to dislike Pierre.

While Madame LaRoche tells us about day-to-day life, how to use our ration coupons and identity cards, the gentle singsong of her voice does me no favors for staying alert. I pinch my leg.

"Remain vigilant, always," she says. "One slip, something as insignificant as ordering black coffee, will give you away. Milk is rationed here in France. No choices are available to you, so there is no need to specify. All *café* is black."

A burst of nervous tension sends my heart thumping. The potential for slipups extends beyond what I've already considered, possibly right down to how I hold my knife and fork. Only so much can be taught in a training school. Our education in nitty-gritty details is about to progress to the field, where we run the risk of learning lessons the hard way.

"I'm sure lovely girls such as yourselves need not worry about this"—Madame LaRoche begins, and I have a hunch we're about to be cautioned against something we enjoy—"but you must not smoke."

We're already aware of this, but Denise groans anyway. The allure of smoking left me about the same time I moved to my aunt and uncle's home in London. Away from boarding school, the pressure to fit in with other girls my age disappeared, and I felt free to be myself again.

"Cigarettes may not be rationed in England, but they are rationed here." Madame LaRoche pats Denise's shoulder. "Most French girls can only dream of being able to afford such a black market luxury. They do not smoke, and therefore neither can you."

"*Oui, madame*," Denise says.

Pierre excuses himself from the table, and he leaves the house as quickly as he entered. The two men from the reception committee empty their wineglasses before rushing out the door after him.

A quiet descends over the kitchen. Denise and I share our uncertainty in a quick glance across the table. Neither of us seems to know what to do next.

"Girls, come with me," Madame LaRoche says with a kind smile. "I will show you to your room."

She leads us from the kitchen and up a wooden staircase. Through an open bedroom door at the end of the hallway, I spot our suitcases on the floor. Madame LaRoche points to a low dresser below the room's window. "There is warm water in the jug and basin. And a chamber pot beneath each bed."

We wish each other a good night, and Denise claims first dibs on the wash basin.

I remove my watch and withdraw my one and only piece of jewelry—a silver charm bracelet—from the pocket of my skirt. I set both on the dresser and practically fall straight into bed. After tonight, who knows where I'll be sleeping, possibly under the stars or inside barns. I can't waste a moment in such a comfortable bed as this one.

My unwinding mind wanders to thoughts of Shepherd. Better him than me. I have to watch out for myself. But still, I'm worried about his safety and wonder what this mission might hold for me.

When Denise finally blows out the candles, I close my eyes and curl up in the crisp blankets. The faint scents of fresh country air and flower gardens instantly remind me of my childhood home in Connecticut. I usually fight hard to forget those memories. It hurts too much to think about my life before the accident, a time when my mother and brother were still alive. To my father, their deaths were all that mattered, and not that I survived.

Soon after the accident, he introduced me to a wealthy woman named Delores. Her movie-star beauty and glamorous clothes obviously impressed my father. I hated the way he looked at her. When we met, she coldly shook my hand, as if I were an adult and not a grieving ten-year-old.

Delores had studied at a private boarding school near Geneva,

Switzerland. My father assured me I would love the school as much as she had. I deserved the best education money could buy.

The day he dropped me off at the school was the last time I saw him. I thought he would stay by my side while I settled in or walk me through my strange surroundings so I wouldn't get lost. I didn't want to be there. I was frightened to be left on my own.

As I rested on the bed in my new room, still sick and exhausted from travel that seemed never ending, I tearfully watched my father button his coat and put on his hat.

He patted my hand in the same no-nonsense way he did everything else, and said, "Be a good girl, Betty. Write to us often."

After he left, I began to wonder about his final words. *Write to us.* Much later, I learned he meant the beginnings of his new family. A family that didn't include me.

And here I am in a strange place, in a strange country all over again. This time I'm too exhausted to care. I drift off to sleep with Madame LaRoche's sun-dried blankets clutched to my face, not wanting to let go.

fOUR

The morning gets off to an early start. I'm sure I closed my eyes for only a moment, but dusty rays of sunshine are streaming through the room.

"Wake up, girls," Madame LaRoche says, with a knock on the door.

Denise pulls the blankets over her head. "I guess she's never heard of beauty sleep."

I didn't get much sleep, beauty or otherwise. I don't really know Denise well enough to tease her, but I say, "At least I didn't keep you up half the night by snoring."

"That's a load of codswallop. I don't snore."

I roll out of bed already dressed in my gray outfit. "Well, it said so on your SOE file."

Denise's covers fly to the end of her bed. Her legs swing over the side. "You're lying. I can tell because your face is twitching."

I'm too good to let anything twitch. "I'm kidding around. I only looked at my file."

Denise pops open her suitcase. One item at a time, she removes a comb, a brush, some hairpins, and a tube of lipstick, and lines them up on the wooden stand next to her bed.

"Did you really look at yours?" she asks. "Those files were confidential."

I take my own comb from my suitcase. From the feel of things, my sweat-drenched hair dried in an unflattering mess, as if I dunked my head in glue and stood in a hurricane. Roughly tugging on the comb to free it from a whirl of hair, I say, "I broke into the safe."

"Really? All that time they spent teaching us to pick locks and burglarize, and it never occurred to me to put those lessons to good use." Denise uncaps the lipstick. Partway through one lip, her puckered mouth flattens. "Like what you saw in your file?"

I give up and return the comb to the suitcase. "They said I rebel against authority. Among other things."

The report also said I show great potential as an agent. I figure they must be right, since I successfully broke into a safe to find that out.

After tightening my watch around my wrist, I notice Denise's curious glance as I return my bracelet to the confines of my pocket, but I pretend I didn't.

Early morning sunlight illuminates the house's deterioration. Peeling wallpaper, yellowed with age, frames a cracked bedroom window, a bare bulb hangs from an ornate ceiling fixture, and the wood stairs and floors are stripped and scratched. Still, the house shows signs that it was beautiful once, before the war.

At the end of the hallway, I stop in front of a nine-paned

window that resembles a tic-tac-toe grid. Through the center pane, I watch a barn swallow swoop across the sunlit grass like a tiny bomber plane before soaring away over the wooden rail fence. Thick forests, brilliant green with new leaves, surround the pastures and a small pond. In the yard, a pair of triangular ears pokes up through a patch of weeds next to the water pump. I laugh when a calico kitten springs out, paws ready to pounce.

"I hoped there would be cats here," Denise says as she squeezes in next to me. "My, what a lovely sight that is."

When we arrived during the night, the farm was tucked away in the darkness, a shadowy shape in the middle of nowhere, with a single candlelit window showing the path to the door and little else. That dark and gloomy atmosphere was what I expected. After all, we had geared up to face a dangerous and unfamiliar country, where life is so different than what we're used to. But now, looking at the peaceful scenery outside Madame LaRoche's home, it seems as if I dreamed last night up.

"I know we need to lie low," Denise says as we descend the staircase, "but I am positively itching to get going."

Not me. I'm not in such a hurry to lose the security of the farmhouse.

We enter the kitchen as Pierre walks in from outside.

"Which one of you is the wireless operator?" he asks without so much as a hello or good morning.

With an offhand wave, Denise says, "I am."

During the final bit of training, we were assigned specific jobs to perform in the field in addition to whatever side work is thrown at us on the fly. Denise showed a knack for code and transmission, so she received special training to be a wireless radio operator. I taught myself Morse code when I was young, but

I don't have a technical bone in my body. What I do have going for me are "unassuming looks." Sadly, that means I'm plain enough to fly under the radar. I also have a sharp memory, good gut instincts, and trustworthiness, which makes me a good fit for the courier job. Apparently when large sums of money are involved, the temptation is too great for some people.

Courier work is dangerous, but what could be more thrilling than scooting around the countryside on a bicycle, carrying top-secret messages between cells of the Resistance, right under the noses of oblivious Germans? I know I can do the job, and I don't care if the occupying forces underestimate me. In fact, I'm counting on it. They can go right ahead and think I'm just a "flimsy little girl" as Pierre put it. I'll show them.

At the opposite end of the kitchen, Pierre pushes a cabinet away from the wall. From a hidden compartment accessible only from the back, he removes a piece of luggage that came in with our drop. The components of Denise's wireless set—the transmitter, receiver, power supply, and accessories—fit perfectly snug inside a modest brown suitcase. Of all the SOE's clever devices, that radio is the one we can't do without as it's our only safe way to correspond with headquarters in London. The Nazis listen in on telephone calls. Mail sent through the post is liable to be intercepted. The French are cut off from the rest of the world. And without Denise's radio, we would be too.

"I wish we had a transmitter receiver like this one," Pierre tells Denise. "Our radios receive messages from the BBC, but we can't use them to respond or request supplies."

Each day, the British Broadcasting Corporation broadcasts the *messages personnel*s, phrases that sound, to eavesdropping Germans, like innocent communication between friends and relatives in France and Britain. Really, they're coded messages to the Resistance. In preparation for our night drop, the reception committee would have heard two messages, one to put them on standby and another to let them know whether the drop would take place. The *messages personnels* phrases I learned in training were surprisingly silly. I wonder if Resistance members ever have a good laugh when they hear ones like "The rabbit drank an aperitif" or "Yvette likes big carrots."

The British government discourages civilians from listening to long-range European service broadcasts since they contain propaganda and coded messages. Of course, the order to not snoop on coded messages zooming across the airwaves only made me want to snoop more. But no matter how hard I tried to find a radio with the long wave band, I never had any luck. My aunt told me they stopped manufacturing them.

Now the coded messages are part of my job. Listening to foreign broadcasts is illegal in France, but that won't stop me. Those Germans have some nerve, banishing free speech. I can't imagine facing fines, imprisonment, or even death for something as simple as listening to a radio. I bet most French people feel the way I do, and they listen to the BBC's radio broadcasts *because* they're not supposed to.

"We are grateful for the Sten guns, pistols, and demolition packs the SOE has supplied us with," Pierre says. "But our situation is about to become dire. Everyone, even Hitler, knows the Allies intend to cross the Channel and invade within months. We don't know when or where it will happen, but our time to act is now."

Like the Pied Piper's entrancing flute music, his heartfelt patriotism has a hypnotic pull. I give my head a slight shake to focus.

"German troops have been occupying and fortifying our country for four years. They will not scatter out of the way and let the Allies roll through France to Germany. They are entrenched. They are waiting, eager to fight. The northern coast may as well be a vast brick wall. It is up to us, the Resistance, to weaken the strength and morale of that wall. The Germans must not have the upper hand when *le Jour J* arrives."

Le Jour J: D-day.

Only the Allied planners of the invasion know when and where it will take place. I'm used to hearing about this future "D-day"—the day the invasion will begin—but the way Pierre speaks of it grabs my attention, like a sharp tug to my arm. He doesn't take the word lightly. I sense just how strongly he feels about the invasion, how much it will mean to him, and it reinvigorates my excitement to be part of such a monumental day.

"We urgently need heavier weapons," he says. "Before you leave, can you transmit that request?"

"I'll pass it along," Denise says. "I need to radio headquarters today to let them know we've arrived safely."

"Thank you. The last radio operator we used to communicate with London left for Paris. She was never seen or heard from again."

Pierre makes it sound as if her disappearance were more an inconvenience than anything else. And why mention her in the first place? To purposefully frighten Denise and me right before we embark on our missions?

Denise's eyes narrow. "Radio operators perform incredibly dangerous work in the field. Hopefully that woman hasn't been captured or killed."

He gives her an offhand nod and says, "I'm taking a load of supplies to the men. Bishop said you two can help with that. Since you're the only agents here, I guess I have no choice. Come with me."

My mouth drops open after Pierre abruptly walks out the front door with the radio.

"No choice?" I say to Denise. "Doesn't he realize we had to pass the exact same physical and psychological training as the men in our group to get here? The SOE didn't pluck girls from the market and drop them into France to look pretty. Where would he and his men be without us?"

Denise crosses her arms. "If he's expecting us to cook breakfast for them, then he should think again. That is not what I signed up for. And he carted off my radio. Who exactly does he think is going to operate it to pass on that list of requirements he just mentioned?"

Denise has good reason to be in a huff. Anyone, even a child, can easily use a home radio. Denise's radio requires training and skill. The first time I saw the lid lift open on a suitcase wireless set like hers my mind boggled at all the tubes, switches, meters, plugs, and sockets packed into such a small space. Not to mention the fluency with Morse code necessary to operate such a piece of technology.

Switching back to the required French, she says, "Let's go."

We stuff our feet into shoes and follow Pierre along a well-worn path to a stone barn, where a horse-drawn cart waits.

Denise stops to stroke the white blaze between the horse's huge chestnut-brown eyes. "Look at you, you beauty. You look just like my Gingersnap."

The horse's nose twitches up to reveal a toothy smile.

Pierre turns at the waist. "You—" he says. "What's your name again?"

I glance side to side, supposing he means me, since Denise is still getting acquainted with the horse.

"Adele."

"Adele, the bags of clean laundry go in the cart," he says as he enters the barn.

I wander closer. Beyond the doors, two bulging duffel bags sit propped against each other on the cement floor. I struggle to lift one, wondering if it's filled with rocks. Together, Denise and I carry the bags to the cart and heave them over the backboard.

"I'll go tell him we're finished loading the bags," I say.

Even with the double doors wide open, the interior of the barn dims within my first tentative steps. The containers and supplies we dropped are nowhere to be seen. Everything appears normal, giving no sign of Pierre's involvement with the Resistance.

He isn't in the main section of the barn, so I walk farther inside.

"Don't touch that!"

I spin around with my hand over my pounding heart. Through a trapdoor in the floor, Pierre emerges. At the top of the ladder, he effortlessly hauls himself out of an underground chamber. He fits the door into place and covers it with a hay bale.

"I wasn't touching a thing," I say.

He points to a grimy canvas sheet draped over what looks to be, from its lumpy shape, an unusually big bicycle.

"You weren't touching that?"

"N-no, I wasn't," I stammer. "I came to tell you we've loaded the laundry."

"You managed to get the sacks into the cart?"

"Well, yes," I say warily. "Do you need us to load anything else?"

"No, that's all. You and the other girl climb into the wagon. You can sit on the hay."

I trudge back and meet up with Denise at the cart.

Pierre tosses two more burlap sacks into the back and takes his place up front. He steers us down a laneway that runs the length of the property between the barn and the road. I hold tightly to the side rail to keep from bumping around.

"Should you be traveling in broad daylight, Pierre?" Denise asks. "What if you're caught transporting supplies?"

"This area is very remote," he says. "That's why men who escape the compulsory labor service are drawn to these forests. We rarely see Germans pass through anymore, and usually they are on the move to somewhere else. The towns and cities are risky, yes, but not here. That will change when the invasion comes, of course. Then all the major roadways will be clogged with Germans heading north."

I can't blame anyone for running away from the compulsory labor draft, the *Service du Travail Obligatoire*, created in response to Germany's employment woes. With the majority of their workforce at war, they need replacement workers, and France has plenty of people. Problem solved. Does the injustice of taking men and women against their will not matter to the Germans? Do they even see it as an injustice to begin with?

The horse plods down the country road. I could outpace it on my bicycle.

Denise laughs. "Pierre, your vehicle is literally the one-horsepower model. She's a beauty, but not very speedy."

He hunches further in on himself, clutching the reins. "I had a car before the war. A sleek metallic-gray Simca. I held on to it for a while, but at what cost? My mother was going without laundry soap and sugar, and standing in line for hours for a lousy fifth of a pound of butter. With fuel rationed, the pumps drying up, and no petrol coupons to be had, I was left admiring a car I could not even drive. When the war is over, I'll have another car. I'll drive it fast and whenever I choose."

The cart rolls to a stop on a secluded side road. Pierre leaps down and strides to a mass of overgrown brush. On either side of his mud-caked boots, I spot the faint indentations of wheel marks in the grass. The tracks disappear into the woods without circling back, as if the cart usually lifts into the air and flies away.

Pierre wedges his hand through the tangle of leafy branches. A latch clicks. An entire section of the woods swings open on hinges.

"How fun! A camouflaged gate," I say.

I turn to share a grin with Denise about the secret opening to the forest, but she gives me an odd look. I quickly glance away, wondering what I said to make her react that way. But then again, maybe it wasn't so much what I said, as how I said it—as a seventeen-year-old tomboy she doesn't know rather than a professional grown woman named Adele. I'll have to be more careful about slipping into my old self.

Beyond the gate is a fairy-tale forest, with mossy rocks, yellowed autumn leaves still scattered over the ground like gold coins, and slender sunbeams sneaking through the treetop canopy. Reins in hand, Pierre leads the horse-drawn cart through the gate. After securing it again, he climbs back into the driver's seat.

Moments later, Denise taps me on the shoulder. "Can you

smell that?" She wraps her arms over her stomach. "A cooking fire. And I am so hungry."

I close my eyes and sniff the air for one of my all-time favorite scents. Every Sunday afternoon during the dreary winter months, my aunt sent her boys to collect whatever small logs and branches they could find. As a special treat, they were allowed to toss them into the coal fire. I loved how wonderful it made the front room smell, like pine or applewood. We sat around together, huddled under blankets, listening to radio shows and singing songs like "Roll out the Barrel" and "It's a Long Way to Tipperary."

The forest opens into a clearing. At least twenty-five men mill about in a camp of tents and thatched huts. A patchwork of canvas tarps, strung up in the trees like a giant moth-chewed blanket, protects the camp from bad weather and hides it from view of the German scout planes.

Pierre steers the cart around until the supply-laden back end faces the camp.

A stocky man stirring something in a metal bucket atop the fire gets to his feet. Pointing a long-handled spoon at me, he says, "You brought the potatoes, I hope."

"We brought your clean laundry," I reply.

"Well, we can't eat laundry."

As he hops down from the driver's seat, Pierre laughs. "Leave her alone, Gus. We brought the potatoes."

Pierre lowers the back of the cart. Propping his elbow against the wooden slats, he says, "These men are the reason you are here in France."

I stare in disbelief at the scruffy bunch dressed in a hodge-podge of drab civilian clothes, leather jackets, and bits and pieces of old uniforms. Wooden peasant clogs and dilapidated field boots are the norm. Their hair, at least on the men who haven't tucked it under a beret, catches my attention the most. Some have slicked it into a long shiny plume from forehead to nape. Others let it hang loose and defiant.

This isn't what I was expecting. My chest tightens with irritation at being dropped into this place. I'm not sure if any amount of equipment or training can whip this camp of disorganized, amateurish men into a force capable of harassing an elite and powerful army. Even with our help, can they sabotage trains carrying German troops and supplies, or demolish telephone lines so the enemy can't coordinate attack plans? Do they honestly have what it takes to weaken the Germans in time for the Allied invasion? The man at the fire, Gus, can't even muster up the energy or discipline to tie his bootlaces and shave. If all Resistance members are like these, France is in big trouble.

Denise scoots to the end of the cart and dangles her legs over the edge. I wrap my skirt around my knees to copy her.

"It must be awful to live hidden away, separated from their families," Denise says.

"They do miss their families. But every one of these men would rather be living among his buddies in the woods than toiling in some German factory or work camp. They became *maquisards* by choice for a cause they believe in." Pierre hauls a bag of laundry from the cart. "I'm sure you noticed already that my mother is a generous woman. She does so much to make this hard life easier for them. When they change into clean clothes today, it will boost morale more than you might imagine is possible."

Pierre observes the camp with obvious pride. How does he not see what I see?

Denise lands feet together on the dirt. "Will the men mind if we look around?"

"They won't mind. Although, steer clear of that guy by the tents, the one whittling what he likes to call a 'gouger.' He'll steal anything that's not tied down."

I gasp. "He's a criminal?"

"Sometimes he is. Are you frightened?"

"No."

Pierre smirks at me. "You should be."

Denise fetches her suitcase. She lugs it the length of the cart, gripping the handle with both hands.

"Set up your radio at the desk. André will advise you of our requirements." Pierre gestures to a long wooden board laid across the tops of two oil drums, where a man sits listening intently to a small radio through a pair of headphones. "There should be plenty of space for your aerial. You will need to use battery power, though. I know power for the radios is hard to come by, but we've been unable to hook into the main supply."

"I'll transmit quickly," Denise says with a frown as she walks to the desk, the suitcase swinging like a heavy pendulum at her side.

I have only seconds to worry about being left alone with Pierre before he marches away with a sack of laundry thrown over his shoulder.

Everyone seems to have a job to do. I'm the odd person out and I'm not sure what to do about it. I watch my legs sway in slow circles. How is it possible to feel so alone surrounded by so many people?

As I sit within the Maquis camp it hardly seems real that only a few months ago I was working as a barmaid. Two British officers,

Charles and John, were among the pub's regular customers, and one day John called me to their table. I could never have imagined that our conversation would fling open the door to a brand-new life.

"We were mulling over your age. Charles says twenty. I say twenty-two. Let me be right to win the pint, Betty. I'm a thirsty man."

"I'm nineteen."

Once the lie escaped my mouth there was nothing to do but stand behind it and hope I didn't get caught. Switching my answer would have made me look awfully stupid.

"Nineteen?" John said. He looked to Charles, who nodded.

"That's an odd American accent you have," Charles said.

"Well, I've lived here a few years now. And I went to boarding school near Geneva."

"You speak French?"

French was the main language spoken throughout the day at school. I was fluent.

"*Je parle français très bien.*" And then I offered my slightly rusty Swiss German. "*Ich spreche auch Deutsches.*"

John looked to Charles, who nodded more vigorously this time.

"Do you like adventure?" John asked.

He might as well have asked if I enjoyed breathing. "Sure. Who doesn't?"

Charles swooped in close. He smelled waxy and fresh, and a tad spicy. "Go to 64 Baker Street. A captain will be waiting. They're in need of girls just like you." Noting my skepticism, he smiled and added, "Trust us, Betty. Give it a go."

Well, I gave it a go, all right.

A man I recognize from last night's reception team rides into the clearing on a bicycle.

"Pierre, I've come from my brother's," he calls, leaning the bike against a tree. When he reaches Pierre outside the doorway of a thatched hut, I listen in as he says, "The factory is producing military equipment for the Germans, but my brother doesn't know what is being made there. Propellers for the Luftwaffe, perhaps? The factory is fenced and patrolled by guards. No one can get near it without arousing suspicion."

I stare at my lap, straining to hear Pierre say, "Any disruption must look like an accident or else there will be reprisals against the townspeople. We'd need blueprints of the factory to locate the building's access points. This might prove too difficult and time consuming to arrange. Perhaps we should scrap the whole thing."

"I don't think we should give up on this. What if we sent someone to scout out the factory first?" His voice grows louder and clearer. I don't have to look up to know he's facing me. "Someone like her?"

"Marcus, you're crazy."

"Think about it. It makes perfect sense."

"Look at her. She's a girl. And a small one at that."

"Exactly," Marcus says, drawing the word out to make his point. "No one would ever suspect her of spying on the factory. It's perfect."

"It's dangerous is what it is. Too dangerous."

"But it isn't," Marcus insists. "Who are the guards more likely to ignore? A girl like her? Or men like us?"

"Marcus, no. We'll figure out another way to sabotage the factory. Besides, we don't know how much time we have left. Could be weeks, could be months. The girl has orders to report to Paris, and we may never see her again. We can't rely on her for something this important. If we don't take these matters seriously, we will fail. Let the girl ride away on her bicycle."

I set my hands on the backboard of the cart. My teeth clench. I dare him to call me a girl. Just once more.

"Taking our country back is a job for men," Pierre says. "Not for girls."

I push off. My skirt flutters away from my legs as I drop and plant my feet firmly on the ground.

"I'll do it."

FIVE

Marcus lets out a whoop. "Did you hear that, Pierre? She'll spy on the factory."

"I heard, yes." To me, he says forcefully, "You have not received any details, and yet you have already agreed? You don't know the risks involved. You don't even know where the factory is located. Don't you think you're being a little hasty?"

Hasty? Yes, more than a little so. My mouth loves to get me into trouble.

"It doesn't matter where the factory is," I say. "I'll do it."

Pierre shakes his head and holds out his hand to Marcus. "Let me have the map."

Marcus digs a crumpled square of silk from his pocket, grinning. I get the feeling things like this don't often go his way.

Pierre stretches the map across the cart backboard. "The factory is here." His finger jabs a patch of silk. "It is five kilometers south of that village."

Those directions aren't specific enough. I fish out the notebook and pencil the SOE supplied me with and eagerly flip to the first page. "Aren't you going to give me the coordinates?"

He sighs but gives me the numbers, which I scribble down.

"Thank you," I say. "Is there anything else I should know?"

"Take notes and report back to me."

For such an important sabotage mission, those are suspiciously lean instructions.

"How often should I report back to you?"

He turns away, shrugging. "Oh, I don't know. Whenever you're able."

I angrily cram the notebook into my pocket, knowing he only agreed to let me spy on the factory to shut me up. He doesn't expect me to report back. He expects me to ride away on my bicycle, never to be heard from again.

I'll show him. I'll do a better job than any of his men ever could.

After we return to the farm, Denise and I polish off a breakfast of hot porridge and warm milk straight from the cow.

Madame LaRoche sets two cups of steaming coffee on the table, one for me and the other for Denise.

"Fantastic," Denise says, and she greedily fills her mouth. Her cheeks bulge. Widening eyes send me a frantic plea for help.

"I should have warned you—" Madame LaRoche begins.

Denise plugs her nose and forces the liquid down her throat, the way my cousins swallow foul medicine. With a shiver, she says, "Good Lord!"

Madame LaRoche quickly crosses herself.

"I'm sorry," Denise tells her. "I assumed this was coffee."

"That, Denise, is *ersatz* coffee, a fake substitute made from chicory. It is as close as you will come to real coffee for the remainder of your stay in France. Now you know what to expect. Imagine if you had reacted that way in a crowded bistro?"

Denise blushes. "I suppose you're right about that."

"You would be surprised by what you can grow accustomed to over time. Eventually you might well enjoy chicory coffee."

"I'll drink the stuff if Adele will."

The dare leaves me no choice but to drink the coffee to the last drop. Near the end I run short of breath, but I pull through. Fake coffee isn't as unappetizing as Denise made it out to be, but for all I know it tastes like the real stuff. My aunt and I are tea drinkers.

"Wonderful. Adele likes ersatz coffee already," Madame LaRoche says.

The door to the outside opens. Bishop and a few other men come in with supplies. I wait for Pierre to join them, but the door swings closed and stays that way.

"Ladies, are you prepared to leave for Paris? You will report to your SOE circuit leader there and follow his instructions. Do you have his contact information?"

"Of course," Denise says. "But when will I get to fire my weapons? Winston Churchill himself ordered the SOE to 'set Europe ablaze.'"

"Concentrate on your radio duties, Denise." Bishop scratches the crook in the bridge of his nose, a memento from his early boxing career, as if to shield an out-of-character smile. "And don't be so trigger happy."

She grumbles, "Oh, bother—," and my immediate thought is

of the Winnie the Pooh stuffed bear at the end of my cousin's bed, his arm forever held in a cheery wave that greeted me on my way to and from my bedroom.

Bishop says, "Take a few moments to study the devices on the table. Be prepared to employ any or all of them during your time in the field."

"These little lovelies are mine." Denise reaches for a pair of clunky women's shoes that aren't little or lovely. From the wedge heel she removes a small, hidden blade. "I could kick some arse with these. Quite literally."

During our training we were introduced to some of the SOE's gadgets. I loved the ones with a surprising twist. Explosives disguised as Chianti bottles, or cigarettes, or lumps of coal. Shaving cream and toothpaste containers with secret compartments that hid codes or microprints. Tins of "foot powder" filled with an irritating itching powder.

Bishop hands Denise and me our identification papers and ration cards.

"Oh, would you look at my photo. It's dreadful!" Denise says, waving her identity card in my face. "How's yours?"

Cameras usually capture me at my worst. In the final group photo before I left school, every girl in the front row wore her prettiest smile. And there I sat at the end of the line, my face contorted unattractively in a sneeze. My *carte d'identité* breaks the photo curse. With my head tilted just so, and a perfect blend of highlight and shadow, I look sophisticated. Like a film star.

"I like mine," I say.

When I show Denise, she clicks her tongue in annoyance. "Yours is much nicer than mine. I should have asked for a retake."

In my hands I hold a new identity. Physical proof that I've

become someone else. The cards are forgeries of course, but fingerprinted, stamped, signed, and dated, mine looks so official. So real.

Bishop ushers us outside.

Things are stepping up fast. Are we really about to be cut loose, to ride away on our own, with no supervision or support to fall back on? A pang of guilt comes over me. Somehow I fooled a bunch of high-ranking people into believing not only that I'm older than seventeen, but also that I'm capable of playing a real role in this war.

The horse-drawn cart, driven by Pierre, bumps down the lane and stops outside the gate. Pierre leaps down with ease, his brown hair fluttering back from his handsome face.

"Pierre will take you as far as the nearest village," Bishop says.

Madame LaRoche runs at us, a half-empty basket of eggs swinging from her hand. "Girls, have a safe trip. Promise me you will take care."

After loading our bicycles into the cart, Bishop extends a hand to help Denise climb to her seat. She swats him away. In one graceful motion she steps up and into the cart, flaunting her obvious horse-riding talent.

Pierre steps closer. Uncomfortably close. The slight breeze stirred up when he kneels brings his earthy, manly scent to me.

I stare at his cupped hands so long he finally says, "Step up, Adele. I'll help you."

Accepting his offer of help means I'll have to touch him. My mouth goes dry. My heart pounds. In movies, handsome men make women weak in the knees, a silly made-up ailment that doesn't affect girls in real life. I'm wrong about that. It does.

I set one foot on his hands and push off with legs as wobbly as a gelatin salad. With nothing to hold on to, I'm thrown off-balance. Flailing, I grab a fistful of his woolen sweater. His strong arm protectively reaches around my back to catch me, and he lifts me to the runner board.

"Thank you, Pierre," I say.

As he climbs into the cart he nods. "I wouldn't let you fall."

This sentiment flusters me even more. There's no hope for regaining the strength in my weak knees now. I drop into the empty space next to Denise.

Madame LaRoche waves as we leave. "Our door will always be open to you."

At the end of the laneway, I shield my eyes against the bright sun to catch one last glimpse of Bishop, Madame LaRoche, and the others. I have no way of knowing if I'll ever see any of them again.

For a long while we ride in silence. The rhythmic clomping of horse hooves down the dusty road calms my nerves and whirling thoughts.

"One of your men was captured last night, Adele?" Pierre asks.

I jump, not expecting him to be the one to speak up.

"Yes, he was arrested by four gendarmes," I say.

"The French police obey all German orders like obedient little children. They're in charge of rounding up the Jews, you know. French Jews, their own countrymen. It's unforgivable. Two years ago, the police rounded up more than thirteen thousand Jews in the *Vélodrome d'Hiver*, a cycling stadium near the Eiffel Tower. They were held there for nearly a week, in vile conditions. All of them were sent to camps. My sister and her husband were able to hide only ten people before the raids."

I cover my mouth with my hand.

"They are committing unspeakably evil atrocities in Germany, and in Poland."

"What do you mean?" I ask, as fear of the answer grows in my chest.

"I don't want to tell you. It's worse than you can imagine. My sister's friend runs an underground newspaper in Paris. They have photographs of the true story and eyewitness accounts from those who have escaped. My sister, her husband, their friends, they do what they can to expose the lies. The Germans are terrified of the truth getting out. They know that if one person reads an underground paper or listens to Churchill or De Gaulle on the BBC, they will tell someone else what they saw or heard. The Germans can't allow that to happen. They justify every action they take to prevent it. It is considered a brave act now just to print a newspaper."

"Pierre, when you say it's worse than we can imagine—" Denise turns away, her body nestled into the corner of the bench. "They're not hurting children, are they?"

"They are."

She holds back a whimper with her fist, and stares at the grassy fields for the remainder of the ride.

Adults are purposefully harming children rather than protecting them. That seems almost too horrific to be true. What if I'm incapable of handling the atrocities I might witness here?

When the town comes into view on the horizon, Pierre brings the cart to a stop.

He points to a nearby road dividing the fields. "That road east is the one you want."

Denise and I hop down after Pierre. We meet him around back of the cart as he retrieves our bicycles.

Giving us an upward glace as he fastens Denise's suitcase more securely to her bike, he says, "You know where you're going?"

Denise shows him what appears to be a small button pinned to the waist of her trousers. "We have compasses. And a map."

"Good," he says, returning to the driver's seat.

"I'll be seeing you soon," I call up to him as he pulls the cart around.

The bewilderment on his face doesn't shock me. He's already forgotten our plan to spy on the factory.

"Yes, okay. Good-bye," he says. "And good luck to you."

With a brisk nod and a wave, he rides off for home.

"Well, this is it," Denise says.

"I guess so."

We push our bikes along, down a long, winding hill and up the other side. The road curves, and as we're about to hop on our bicycles, I hear approaching vehicles.

I hurriedly grab our map, cleverly printed on a square of silk, and tie it around my neck like a pretty scarf. Denise's suitcase radio will fool the eye, but not an inspection.

A convoy of trucks comes toward us from the other side of the bend.

"Keep going," Denise says. "Act normally. Everything will be fine."

She can't quite fool me into believing she isn't as frightened as I am.

We walk on, nonchalantly pushing our bicycles. I go over my cover story in my head. I prepare myself for the inevitable handing over of my papers.

The first truck rumbles past. Then another. All the trucks continue down the road. A handful of German soldiers march by on foot. Still no one asks for papers or questions what we're doing. I raise my face. A boy at the tail end of the group catches me looking and he smiles. He can't be a day over eighteen.

In passing, he speaks, tossing out a remark the same way a school chum would. I don't react and I don't look back. Neither does Denise.

"I wonder what he said," she whispers.

I put one leg over my bicycle and settle onto the seat. Denise does the same.

My shaking hands grip the handlebars. "Roughly translated, he said, 'Hiya, babes.' "

Our journey into an unfamiliar land, into all its wonders and dangers, has begun.

Six

I push the bicycle pedals through another cycle of pain. Our trip has become all about mindlessly pedaling our feet in circles to make round gears turn and wheels go round.

Beyond the wooded valley and the patches of brilliant yellow flowers and deep-green grassy wheat, the clouds skim the hills on the horizon like meringue on a cake. The bright sky reminds me of summers in Connecticut, fishing with homemade poles and catching frogs with Tom in the muddy creek behind our house. If we were riding in a car or a train the past hours would have seemed more like a holiday. It would be easy to forget that a war is on. Too easy to lapse into a sense of safety and let our guard down.

"Susan B. Anthony said the bicycle did more for the emancipation of women than anything else," I say, "since women wore pants to make riding more comfortable. If not for the bicycle, you'd probably be in a frilly dress right now."

"If you ever catch me in a dress, don't look down. I haven't any ankles. My legs go straight into my feet, like tree trunks. I'm surprised Mum didn't sell me to the circus."

"One of my toes is much longer than the others."

"Like a monkey toe." Denise giggles quite loudly over my long toe, even though I didn't say a thing about her deformity. "Does it help you swing through trees?"

"I don't find that very funny," I say, but I crack up anyway. "Can you picture me going vine to vine, upside-down and holding on for dear life with my toes?"

"What a sight you'd be. Pierre could be your handsome and noble Tarzan."

"I don't think so!" I say, laughing even harder as I imagine Pierre stripped to the waist and wearing only a small loincloth.

We travel through a wooded area and I begin to suspect the dense walls of trees might squeeze shut on us like a vise. When the forest gives way to meadows, I breathe easier. In the open we have no cover, but nothing lurks out of my sight.

Denise points past my shoulder. "Look over there."

The metal steeple of a church in the valley gleams with late-afternoon sunshine. Behind it, appearing to have burst straight out of the hillside, is a magnificent buttery-yellow stone castle. Storybook princesses don't live in the dank, dark castles found in England. They live in castles like this one.

Before leaving Madame LaRoche's, we were instructed to travel as far as her brother's farm, outside of the town of Chevreuse. We're ten kilometers away, if that. A drop in a deep bucket compared to a full day of cycling.

We come to some sparse woods and clatter onto a bridge. A river quietly burbles through the stone arches, carrying a family of ducks. The babies swim behind their mother. The father duck charges ahead in the lead.

"Aren't they sweet?" Denise gets right off her bike to take a look.

I get off my bike as well, but one glimpse into the expanse of deep water below sends me clutching for the railing. As a child, I nearly drowned in our pond out back. Even after all these years, the feeling of terror, the intense panic of being trapped underwater, unable to breathe, hasn't left me. I've been terribly afraid of water ever since.

"Let's take a break," I say, heading for dry land.

We wheel our bikes to a short slope of grass at the river's edge and park them between two evergreens. I don't know how something as ordinary as sitting on grass could delight me, but it sure does. I've never been so happy to take a seat.

I untie the map at my neck and smooth it flat on the soft grass.

"Please excuse the extra features I've sweated onto the landscape," I say with a laugh.

Denise and I hover over the map, button compasses in hand, and plot a route we both agree on. Once again the map becomes my scarf.

The ducks waddle out of the river, babies in tow. Father duck stands at attention in such a threatening way I wonder if he's about to plod over to quack a warning in our faces. *Keep your distance from the ducklings! Quack!*

"Do you know what I miss?" Denise says. "Sundaes from the Woolworths counter."

Eyes closed, she tilts her head. From the dreamy smile on her face, I'd guess she's thinking about a boy, not ice cream.

All that's left of her dark lipstick is a faded rim, as if she rubbed a cranberry around her lips. For the first time, I notice the copper-brown freckles that dot her cheeks. In spite of dirt, sweat, and sunburn, she's quite pretty. I rake my fingers through my hair and wish for a damp washcloth.

Denise's eyes pop back open. "So, Adele. What do you miss?"

What do I miss? I miss listening to Yankees games with my brother. I miss my friend Gayle, who I haven't seen since I went to boarding school. I miss slobbering over Clark Gable at the movies and doing crossword puzzles with my aunt. I miss oranges and chewing gum and toothpaste.

"I can't think of a thing," I say with a shrug.

"You know what I don't miss? The blackout. Summers were horrid. No air in the house at all. What did they expect us to do in a stuffy, muggy house with the windows shut and covered like that? Not breathe until the end of the war? I couldn't even wake up half the time; it was so bloody dark in the morning I mistook it for night."

Exhausted from the miles of riding, I'm not really in the mood to chat, especially about the blackout. All I want to do is eat, savor a few minutes of peace, and give my aching legs a break.

"And the Air Raid Patrol warden," Denise says. "What a twit, swaggering around, checking our blackouts. Living under constant watch made us feel no better than common criminals."

The entire time I lived in Britain, everything I ate, did, and said was watched and judged. Everyone, not only the wardens, kept tabs on everyone else. One of our neighbors was turned in for feeding birds in her garden. For wasting bread, she was fined a whole ten pounds. I didn't want my aunt's family to get into trouble because of me, so I followed the rules. Even the ones I found stupid or unnecessary.

The blackout was awful and inconvenient, but whenever I complained my aunt reminded me of the poor farmer in a town south of London who stepped outside to watch German bombers during a late-evening air-raid. He foolishly lit a cigarette, and all it took was that tiny red glow to pinpoint him. Needless to say, that cigarette was his last. I hated the blackout, but I would have hated being bombed even more.

"When the war is over, I hope to never again hear the words *make do and mend.*" Denise wiggles her fingers. "These hands will never darn another sock or sew another mismatched button. I won't even wash my clothes. Once they're dirty, I'll toss them in the rubbish and buy something new."

"My aunt would have a fit if she heard you say that."

"Oh, is she one of *those* women, like my mum? Rationing and mending everything in sight is like a game to them. A game they're too competitive to risk losing."

"Yes, that sounds just like my aunt!" I remember the matching jackets she sewed us from old curtains. I suddenly feel very guilty about being too embarrassed to wear mine. "She shined our shoes with half a potato and sewed patches on the knees of my cousins' new pants before they even had a chance to wear them."

"My mum combed our dog and cat for wool." Denise laughs. "I think I had fleas for a while."

All of us agents are under orders not to discuss our personal lives with each other. But it feels so nice to be having such a regular conversation.

I cram my cheese into the bread to hide the moldy bits, saying, "My aunt would make a delicious sauce out of this cheese. She was so good at taking what she had and turning it into something else."

I squeeze the bread into a tight wad and chomp on it, lost in thought, until my jaw aches. Even though my aunt is a wonderful cook, I never saw her eat much of anything. Whenever the air raid sounded during dinner, she rushed us out the door to the corrugated-iron-walled Anderson shelter in the garden with our plates but without serving herself.

"So what do you suppose we'll do after this?" Denise says. "When we get back home to regular life. What does one do, exactly, after they've been a spy?"

"I never thought about it, really."

My future, beyond my time in France, is a blank slate. What I had wished to someday return to no longer exists.

"What did you want to be when you grew up?" Denise asks.

"You'll think it's silly."

She draws an imaginary cross over her heart. "I promise I won't."

"I wanted to make movies."

"No fooling? That's fabulous!"

I grin. "How 'bout you?"

"A mum." Denise settles onto the grass and lays an arm over her eyes. "That's all I've ever wanted to be."

I take out my notebook. While Denise rests, I turn out a quick sketch of the ducklings fast asleep with their beaks tucked beneath their wings.

"Well, time to stop piddling about." Denise gets to her feet, smoothing the wrinkles from her pant legs. "We have a farm to get to before dark."

Before I have time to flip my notebook closed, she peeks at my drawing.

"You drew that? Just now?"

"It's nothing. Only a doodle," I say, tucking the notepad and pencil into my pocket. "I like to draw animals."

"My goodness, you're talented."

I turn away, squirming beneath her praise. "Thank you."

Back on our bicycles, we follow Madame LaRoche's directions, which we coordinated with our map, along a path of minor roads. The route to the farm isn't well traveled. The roads aren't roads at all, we find, but wide dirt tracks through the forest.

Denise leans out over her handlebars. She cranes her neck. "Do you hear that?"

My ears snag a subdued drone out of the peace and quiet.

"It's coming down fast," Denise says. "Hear the sputter?"

The sound screams toward us like a runaway locomotive careening through the sky, and we hurry to the side of the road. Our heads tilt back to watch as a damaged fighter plane buzzes the treetops. Thick smoke, the plane's dying breath, billows out behind it. Time stretches like warm taffy until we hear the inevitable crash. I can hardly believe that what happened right above our heads was real. It's a startling reminder that in spite of our bike ride through an idyllic countryside, we're not here to play.

Denise whistles. "That was a Mustang, a real stunner of a plane."

"Think the pilot made it out?"

We scan the sky, but our view is limited, since we're nearly surrounded by forest.

"There he is," I say. Low in the sky, straight ahead, sunlight glints off silk. "He's about to land in that meadow down the road."

Denise taps her thumb against a handlebar. "That crash is a beacon to every gendarme and Nazi soldier around for kilometers."

"Yes, I know."

"Should we go get him, then? Before they do?"

I nod, already pushing off.

We ride standing, our full weight pressing the pedals, and set a quick pace. Denise leans over her handlebars, pushing the bike to go as fast as possible. I do the same, rapidly running out of breath. We're in a race against an unseen opponent who won't let a downed airman slip through its fingers, lest he escape death or hell on earth, and there's no way of knowing how much or how little time we have.

Once past the trees the hulk of the plane becomes clearly visible, its smoke signals boldly broadcasting the location of the crash. What we can't see is the pilot.

"All he has to do is stand. Wave an arm. Anything," I say.

"They don't waste time, do they?" Denise draws my attention to the horizon. "Look there on the hill, past that field of yellow colza flowers and that small stand of trees in the middle of nothing, to the left of the grass but not quite to the wheat."

My eyes zig this way and zag that way, until I see two trucks coasting down the hillside, so far off they look like my cousins' toy automobiles rolling through the pretend cardboard scene they painted.

"Eagle Eyes, you're supposed to be looking over here!"

Denise surveys the proper side of the road. "Right, then. There he is. Do you see the spot of color near the dilapidated wire fence?"

"I see him now," I say, hopping off my bike.

At the side of the road, we jostle our bicycles into the hedgerows, past the cover of new leaves to the brambly branches beneath that tug at my clothes and hair.

When I stand upright, I say, "I guarantee you, Denise, the Nazi soldiers in those trucks do not suspect they're about to be outfoxed by two girls."

In the stillness before we spring back into action, Denise looks to me, grinning like mad. She quotes a line from *King Kong,* one of my favorite movies I watched with Tom.

" 'Oh no. It wasn't the airplanes. It was Beauty killed the Beast.' "

In this one surprising moment she becomes my friend.

SEVEN

"Should we slap him?"

"No," I say, heart racing. He lies on the ground at my feet, eyes closed, looking like a high school quarterback who's been knocked out cold. "Okay, maybe we should."

Denise leans over the pilot with the back of her hand poised to strike his clean-shaven cheek. *Whack!*

The pilot's eyes open with a start. He stares through his goggles at the two female heads hovering over him.

"Am I in heaven? Are you angels?"

"We don't have time to be your angels right now," Denise says. "Later on maybe."

Denise grabs one arm, I grab the other, and we pull him up. We let go and he wobbles, unsteady on greasy joints, but doesn't fall over. That's one good thing. We need to get him somewhere safe, and quickly.

"Keep his parachute," I say. I run to gather it up. "It might come in handy."

The pilot lets out a moan that reminds me of a bawling moose. "They killed my Bessie Lou! Bessie Lou's dead!"

I turn around to check the road, convinced the trucks are about to materialize out of thin air. We don't have time for talking, much less crazed babbling.

I push the bundled parachute into the pilot's arms. "Listen, you need to come with us."

"I hurt my hip something fierce when I landed." He takes three halting steps. "I can walk, but not real well."

Denise grips a handful of his leather and marches him away. "In minutes, German soldiers will be here. Would you like to wait around to give them a proper welcome?" She turns to me as I run to catch up. "There's nowhere to hide. Let's get the bicycles."

At the bushes, the pilot sets the parachute down. "Allow me."

He mightily pushes his way through the branches. The rustling bushes give birth to my bike first. I wheel it up to the road to stand guard.

"The road is clear," I say. "Hurry up, you two."

With a splintering crack, the bushes spit out leaves, twigs, and Denise's bike. She and the pilot topple into each other in an effort to keep the bike from crashing over.

"Come on now, then," she says, simultaneously righting her bike and her hair.

She trudges toward me, clenching the handlebars of her bike. Behind her, the pilot bends, red-faced, to collect his parachute.

"Ditch your uniform," I call out to him. "It'll give you away."

He stares at me, sapping precious time, before hesitantly removing his goggles.

While checking the road, I call, "Off with everything but your pants and undershirt."

"I can't part with my flight jacket," he whines, and I half expect him to start bawling.

"Leave the jacket or we'll leave you here," Denise says. "Have a .45 in your boot, by any chance?"

"A revolver? In my boot?"

"Yes, do you have a sidearm?"

"No, ma'am, I do not."

She gets him moving again with a flick of her hand. "Well, at least you still have your boots and didn't lose them when you bailed."

Bit by bit, the outer authoritative pilot falls away, leaving behind a bashful young man. He stashes his gear in the bushes and runs with the parachute and a slight limp to the road.

"I'll take him with me," I tell Denise.

She winks, and my face grows even hotter. I hold the bike steady while the pilot climbs on behind me. In one hand he clutches his parachute. His other hand gingerly rests on my shoulder.

"You can hold on. I won't break." I forcefully push off to get momentum going before lifting my feet to the pedals.

The bike lurches, swaying from his weight. I will myself to stay balanced and not dump him off. His bare arm snakes around my waist, leaving so much space between us that he's not really holding on at all. As I ride upright the only part of me that comes in contact with his arm from time to time is my chest, and I wish that he'd just grab hold of me already. German soldiers are in hot pursuit. This is no time for either of us to be embarrassed. Next thing I know, a bump in and out of a pothole jolts him into gripping so tightly I'm struggling for air.

The parachute presses into me when his arm clamps down.

A flurry of hot breaths batters my neck. I keep my focus only so long before reflexively swatting at my hair, as if his breaths are pesky flies that won't shoo.

The road dips into a steadily sloping arc. We zip further into the valley. Open fields now behind us, sparse forests return, the tree line broken by an intersecting road that we're approaching fast.

Over her shoulder, Denise says, "I have an idea. We'll have a picnic."

"But I have a gut feeling that the trucks are practically on top of us."

"We'll stop there, by that brook, like we did before." As I pull alongside her, she says, "We can't speed past the German trucks without arousing suspicion."

We veer off the road and continue across rough ground. The handlebars bounce in my hands, jarring my entire body. Denise, the lucky one with a bike all to herself, speeds ahead of me. I grunt and groan my way forward, desperate to catch up. That's what I get for trying to be a hero.

At the brook, Denise runs with her bicycle to a nearby cluster of squat evergreens, and then she hurries back to a shady patch of flat ground near the water. I drop the pilot off there and I hide my bike with Denise's. By the time I get back to them, they've laid out the parachute like a picnic blanket on a carpet of velvety moss.

We sink onto the silk and sit ramrod straight, looking nothing like relaxed picnickers.

"Why are we waiting for the Germans?" the pilot asks.

An uneasy giggle prickles up inside me. Why *are* we sitting out in the open and not hiding? The plan that made perfect sense a few seconds ago is falling like one of my aunt's cakes when her boys stampede through the kitchen.

The pilot inches away from me. "Why are you smiling?"

Denise and I snatched up a perfect stranger, ranting about Germans and trucks that he hasn't seen any evidence of, and carried him off on our bicycles. For all he knows, we're setting him up to be captured. And here I am, grinning at the poor guy like a lunatic, when in truth my nerves are unraveling a little.

"Places, everyone," Denise whispers. "We're relaxed, we're having a brilliant good time, we are on the lookout for fun, not Germans. Ready, and . . . action."

We fall into laid-back poses just as the trucks speed into view.

Without turning my head, I keep one eye on the trucks. "They've spotted us." The stiff smile at my lips barely moves when I say, "I sure hope they keep going."

The trucks slide through my peripheral vision.

"They're not leaving," the pilot says, in English, and far too loudly. He might as well wave a sign that reads I'M THE AMERICAN YOU'RE LOOKING FOR! "They're coming back."

His trembling legs jerk. I grab hold of his flight trousers as his seat leaves silk and yank him back to earth.

"If you run, you'll get us all killed. Calm down."

"That's easy for you say."

The trucks reverse and come to a stop. The driver's door of the second truck swings open. A soldier steps down to the road. Pebbles crunch beneath his heavy boots. He straightens his glasses, carefully analyzing each member of our group.

Unless by some miracle he stops walking, we are finished. I chew the inside of my mouth, counting each crunching footstep.

Standing tall, arms stiff at his sides, he calls out to us in perfect English. "Have you seen an American here?"

Fear clangs through me. We all speak and understand English. While Denise and I are trained to gauge our responses to the unexpected, I'm not so sure about the pilot. If he falls for the soldier's trap and shows a hint of understanding or fear, the jig is up.

"Watch yourself, pilot," Denise whispers out of the side of her mouth. "And bloody well keep your mouth shut."

"Have you seen an American here?" the soldier repeats. "An American pilot?"

Denise shrugs and calls back, *"Pardonnez-moi?"*

"Vous avez vu un pilote américain?" he says, in the same calm monotone he's used since he first spoke.

From inside the truck, another soldier is keeping an eye on us. I watch him reach for the door handle.

Without saying a word, Denise scrambles to her feet and sashays to the soldier. I pick up the odd muffled word as they talk, but it's not enough to get a good read on their conversation. The soldier's knotted expression slackens. The rigid contour of his back slumps. Unbelievably, he waves good-bye to Denise and boards his truck. On a surface level, I notice the trucks pull away. The core of me is stunned, overcome with relief.

Denise marches back, arms swishing back and forth. She plunks down next to me and promptly falls over.

"Oh my gosh, are you all right?" I ask.

"Yes."

"Are you sure?"

"I just need to catch my breath." She lays an arm across her eyes to block the sun. "I'll bet you thought his English was spot-on. He went to school in New York City."

The German soldier and I were relative neighbors once. I can't help but wonder about his life in America. Does it weigh on his mind that he now hunts American men like the pilot? And girls like me?

"We had a close call with that soldier," Denise says. "He kept looking at you two over my shoulder, so I took his attention away by asking all sorts of questions about Radio City Music Hall and the Roxy Theater, even though I've only read about them in magazines. We made plans to meet in town this afternoon for a drink, and then off he went."

"Thanks, Denise," I say. "It was really brave of you to do that for us."

I let her rest a few seconds more; all the time I feel we can safely spare.

"If they find out we've tricked them, they'll come back," I say, standing to leave.

She extends her arm and I help her up.

"Pilot," Denise says. "Aren't you coming? Up you get."

He stares at his lap. His fidgeting fingers twist and pull at each other.

"Are you crying?"

The pilot wriggles backward onto the bed of moss. He goes about gathering the parachute, head bowed.

"What do you have to be crying about? I didn't see you promising to go out on a date with that German."

He hobbles away without us, quick even with the limp, in the direction of the road. We don't have our bicycles ready. Off he goes anyway, without knowing where he's headed or what he's storming off to.

Denise chases him down. "C'mon now, pilot, toughen up. I'm

trying to protect you. Behaving like a six-year-old child will only get us captured or killed."

"You're right, I'm not six." The pilot's out-of-kilter stomping slows to shuffling steps. "Not that it's any of your business, but I'm sixteen years old."

Denise slowly spins around to face me. "Bloody hell."

EIGHT

Our shadows, three dark spires against the dusty road, loom large ahead of us, as if impatient with our decision to walk the rest of the way to the farm. We're nearly there, having passed an out-of-place stone fence that severs two barren pastures, the final landmark Madame LaRoche told us about.

Out of the corner of my eye, I watch Denise scan our surroundings. I'm still in disbelief that she had the guts to make a date with the German. She pulled personal information out of him in less time than it typically takes me to lace up my shoes. If I have to, if it means life or death, can I put so many stars in an enemy's eyes that he won't notice I've gotten away until it's too late? If not, which tricks will I use?

"What did you say to that German?" I ask her. My curiosity always gets the better of me.

Denise shoots a sidelong glance at the pilot. "I told him he *must* be more exciting than my boyfriend. And I complimented him. Flattery works every time."

He fell for flattery. That might be true, but it isn't the whole story. Denise is pretty, and pretty girls know their power. The beautiful girls at boarding school got away with a lot more than the rest of us.

While I'm at it, satisfying my curiosity, there's plenty I don't know about the withdrawn pilot.

"If you're only sixteen, how'd you get to be a pilot?" I ask.

"I lied about my age."

So, the pilot and I have two things in common. We're both Americans and we're both liars.

"Then how'd you learn to fly a plane?"

"Crop dusting."

No matter his age, his ability to fly impresses the heck out of me. He might not be winning any points with Denise, but he sure is with the girl who grew up admiring Amelia Earhart.

"Ever dream of soaring through the air like a bird? Does flying a plane feel like that? Is it ultimate freedom?"

"Sometimes."

"Who was Bessie Lou, anyway?" I ask. "You said they killed her."

"My plane."

"You named your plane *Bessie Lou*?" I start to laugh. "*Bessie Lou.* It's an unusual name for a plane, don't you think? It isn't very jazzy."

"It's my mother's name."

"Oh." I stop laughing.

"You love your mum enough to paint her name on a plane," Denise says, "but then you left her to run off and play war. Do you have any idea how she would feel if she never saw you again? Do you know how devastated she would be? You're just a child."

Trapped between their glares, I slowly wheel my bike forward out of the line of fire.

Denise isn't much older than I am. I didn't consider that my age might be an issue with her. If she finds out the truth, will she refuse to work with me? Will she turn me in to SOE headquarters?

I feel bad for the pilot. If not for him, it could be me on the receiving end of Denise's anger.

Madame LaRoche warned us that her brother's farm has become run down in the five years since his wife's death, but that didn't prepare me for what I see when we reach the end of his stone laneway. Curtains hang askew behind cracked windows, a graveyard of rusted metal litters the property, and a scrawny goat has free range of the yard, which is wildly overgrown in some places, chewed to the nub in others.

Denise says, "My mum would throw a wobbly if she saw the state of this place."

"Bonjour!" The voice booms out of thin air, like the Wizard's in Emerald City. I certainly feel as if a twister whisked me out of Kansas and deposited me in Oz.

We glance around, searching for the speaker's hiding place.

"There he is, in the loft," I say, with a triumphant smirk.

Denise snaps her fingers in defeat, putting her whole arm into it, the way my friend Sylvie used to, especially when I scored higher than her on a test.

We follow a worn path through the tall grass to the barn.

Madame LaRoche's brother calls from above, "Who has sent you here?"

I crane my neck and stare straight up at the bulbous belly hanging over his pants. "Your sister, Claire."

He leans forward to peer down at me, surprisingly steady with all that weight thrust out in front. He and his sister share a code phrase, and I forgot to give it to him.

"She said to tell you that the orchards are beautiful in bloom," I say.

"That they are." He reclines against the wooden frame. "I am Louis. I bid you welcome. You must be in need of food and rest."

Denise and I peek at each other, apparently spooked by the same thought. We've heard nearly identical words before, spoken by Dracula in one of the most spine-chilling films of all time. The sun is sinking ever closer to the horizon, and we have to spend the night at the home of this chubby man who speaks like a blood-sucking, undead Count.

"Park those bicycles in the barn. Rat is around somewhere; he will help you with your things." The rounded belly contracts and Louis bellows, "*Rat, où es-tu?*"

From around the corner of the barn, a wisp of a boy appears, silent and light on his feet, like a feather carried on a breeze. He must have been standing out of sight listening, the little sneak. A boy after my own heart.

"There you are, Rat. All is secure, I take it?"

Rat gives a vigorous little nod.

"Rat is from town," Louis explains. "I pay him to watch for those German bastards. The boy is a damn fine warning system."

Rat grins and blinks at us excessively.

"Bring your things up. Rat will help. He's stronger than he looks."

We enter the barn and I nearly keel over from the stench of goat droppings.

"*Mmmeeehhhhh!*"

In the hay-strewn stall next to my bike is a large brown-and-white goat with a flowing beard. Standing on his back, as if that's the most natural place for him to be, is a baby goat. His back end is black, his front is white, and his face is a mix of the two. Just looking at him, I know he's trouble.

Denise gently scratches him under the chin. "Oh, aren't you darling."

"*Mmmeeeehhhh!*"

Even goat kids sound like they're complaining.

When our bikes are set at the side of the barn, Rat scurries around to take Denise's suitcase. The pilot takes mine.

"Thank you—" Up to that point, I've been content to call him only Pilot.

He takes his time sparing me from further embarrassment. Finally he says, "Robbie."

"Robbie. Thank you for taking my suitcase."

"You're welcome."

The rickety wooden ladder creaks under his weight. "You should feel right at home here, Denise," Robbie says. Near the top, he sets my suitcase on the floor of the loft and continues to climb. As his foot clears the last step, he adds, "Judging from your manners, I'd guess you were raised in a barn."

———

The interior of Louis's home looks nothing like the depressing pigsty outside. If not exactly clean, it's tidy enough. By outward appearances, I would guess the house contains nothing of value. How wrong I'd be. When I bring that up at dinner and point to the gorgeous piano in the sitting room, Louis says, "Hopefully the Germans will think like you, eh? Nothing to loot here, they will say."

I think that's pretty ingenious, but next to me Denise groans and continues to roll peas around her plate with her fork.

After dinner, she mumbles something about goats and then conveniently slips away while the rest of us clean up.

Louis puts water on the woodstove to heat, so I offer to wash the dishes.

"*Merci,* Adele," he says. "I read people well. I can see you're a good girl. The one out there, she's a strange one. *Oui*?"

I smile. "Being strange comes in handy in our line of work. I think it's a requirement."

Excusing himself to finish chores for the day, Louis ambles to the front door. Once alone, Robbie and I stare around the kitchen, everywhere but at each other. I press my lips together, glaring at the kettle.

Robbie has a pleasant laugh. "What do you know, my mother was right. A watched pot never boils." As he leaves the table, he asks, "Do you play the piano, Adele?"

"Yes, but poorly."

He sits on the wooden piano bench. "Any requests?"

With a shrug, I say, "I don't know. Play what you like."

His interlaced fingers crack all at once. "Here's something pretty."

The notes fade into the background. I stare out the window. Laundry, dried crisp in the hot sun, sways on the line outside. Wood will have to be brought in. The kitchen needs a good sweeping. It's the least we can do to repay Louis for his generosity.

On my way outside to find Denise, the piano melody strikes a chord in me.

I run to the parlor, saying, "I know that song. It's 'Someone to Care for Me,' from the movie *Three Smart Girls*."

Robbie's fingers pause over the last keys he played. "You're right, it is. Do you like that movie?"

In *Three Smart Girls*, three sisters living with their mother in Switzerland decide to run away to New York on an exciting and worldly adventure, to stop their father from marrying a scheming gold digger and get their parents back together.

"I love it," I say. "Deanna Durbin, the girl who plays the youngest sister, she's Winston Churchill's favorite movie star. Did you know that?"

With a boyish grin, Robbie says, "You don't say. She's my sister Sarah's favorite."

Stashed away in a bottom dresser drawer at my aunt's house is my collection of film memorabilia. Since my aunt knows Deanna Durbin is my favorite actress, topping even Judy Garland, she clipped her profile from a fan magazine for me.

"My aunt took me to a seven-day-long Deanna Durbin movie festival," I say.

"Gosh, my sister would think she'd died and gone to heaven. She fancies herself Deanna's long-lost twin. Sarah has a good singing voice and everything, but when she tries to reach high notes"—Robbie cringes through a smile—"dogs cover their ears."

The thought of a regular girl copying Deanna's operatic falsetto makes me laughingly cringe along with him. "Then why did you learn to play 'Someone to Care for Me'?"

"It was my birthday gift to her one year. Let me tell you, people wanted to clobber me for that, but it sure made her happy."

His thoughtfulness tugs at my heart.

"Robbie, that was very sweet of you."

I lean against the wall to watch his long fingers trail through the keys. His talented playing seems so effortless, as if he were born to make music.

"Water is boiling, Adele!" Louis calls out from the middle of the kitchen, and I jump, more out of embarrassment than fright.

I ditch my lackadaisical grin and get to work.

Denise's hand flops onto my face, obscuring my view of the full moon outside the open loft doors. I reposition her arm on her chest as she draws in another rumble. If I can withstand hours of her snoring, I can surely withstand torture and interrogation.

Next to me, Robbie stirs. "Adele. You awake?"

Denise didn't take kindly to being told she was raised in a barn. She refused to sleep next to Robbie, which forced me to sleep wedged between them. Not that I mind. The warmest spot beneath the parachute is all mine.

"I'm awake," I say.

For a while, Robbie lies still. Together we watch a hazy cloud cloak the moon.

"Did you want to talk?" I ask. The instant the offer is out of my mouth I make a face at the darkened loft beams.

"I saw Denise with her radio. I know you must be here on a mission of some sort, so I won't ask you about it."

"Thank you."

"Are you American or Canadian? Can I ask that much?"

I like that he expects me to keep certain things about myself private. "I'm from Connecticut. What about you?"

"All over. Birmingham, Alabama, mostly."

"You don't sound southern," I say, glancing at the soft curves of his moonlit profile.

I spot the hint of a smile as he says, "Like I said, I've lived all over."

"Do you have any siblings, other than Sarah?"

He turns to look at me and his face fades into my shadow. "I have five older sisters. I'm the baby."

The dead weight of Denise's arm crashes down on my ribs. With a grunt she rolls onto her side, as if her subconscious is wrestling with her sleeping body to give Robbie a snappy comeback. I elbow her until she concedes and rolls the other way.

"Five sisters. That must have been hell."

"Only when they forced me to dress up like a girl and play Amy whenever they reenacted *Little Women*."

Giggling as quietly as possible, I say, "You had to play Amy? Why didn't they let you be Laurie?"

"My sister Beth insisted on playing Laurie. Figure that one out. One of the March sisters had her very own name, but no sir, she had to be a boy. I had to pretend, dressed as a girl, to marry my own sister dressed as a boy." His laugh is good-natured. "I believe the word that's coming to your mind is *disturbing*."

"No, not at all," I say, and it's Robbie's turn to elbow me. "All right, it is a smidgen disturbing, but it was nice of them to include you. Don't forget, Amy was the prettiest sister. Not many girls would be willing to give that role away."

"I bet you would. You seem more like Jo."

If there's one character I hope to be like, it's rebellious, outspoken Josephine March.

"I can't decide." I become aware of every poke and prick of the straw beneath me. "I might like to play Jo."

The cloud finishes with the moon and moves on; two ships passing in the night.

"Denise was right." Robbie's breathing quickens. The parachute flutters when he turns away from me. A stream of cold air slips between us. "I shouldn't have come here."

"You shouldn't have come to France?"

"I shouldn't have left home at all. My whole life, my sisters were so protective of me. I thought I could prove something to myself. How could I have been so stupid to believe I was brave enough?"

I smile at the back of his head in the hopes he can hear it in my voice. "I bet there's a fine line between bravery and stupidity. I wonder if any of us knew what all this would really be like."

"Fellows from my squadron have been killed in action," he says. "The night before my mission I got a real bad case of cold feet, thinking about that. I couldn't sleep worth a darn. I didn't want to die. I just wanted to go back home. The sergeant came in to talk to me. By the time he left I was raring to go. I don't know how they do it. They make you think you can do anything. Full steam ahead on the mission and you'd better believe you're ready for it, even if you're not."

I understand completely. And I envy his freedom to talk about feelings I keep hidden.

"My first time out and I got shot down. This was to be an adventure. Meet some girls, get some kills. Go home and settle down with a family. I can't stop thinking that I got myself into this mess. My birthday's next month." He sighs. "I'm not putting this right."

He was nearly killed today with his seventeenth birthday within arm's reach. Here I am, practically the same age only he doesn't know it. The harsh reality he faced today resonates through me too.

"You're putting it right," I say.

"They tell you your life flashes before your eyes when you're about to die. Except after those rounds of flak hit, my first thought was that I should have eaten more of the good breakfast before final briefing. Then the plane went into a steep nosedive. I couldn't pull up. I saw wheat fields, thick black smoke, and fire. I was in big trouble. And I wasn't sure how to use my parachute. I prepared myself to die in that plane, Adele. I said good-bye—" He takes time to collect himself. "I said good-bye to my family."

I imagine him inside the cockpit of a flaming plane as it careens toward the ground, believing he might never see his mother and sisters again.

"You must have been so scared."

"I've never been so afraid in all my life. You're supposed to die old," he says. "I've never even kissed a girl."

I bring my hand out from beneath the parachute and tentatively trail down the rough sleeve of the work shirt Louis lent him, until I feel the back of his hand. He turns his palm up in approval before I can ask if he minds, and we hold hands.

"I didn't mean to burden you," he whispers. "I'm sorry."

I curl closer to his warmth and let the slow rise and fall of his breathing carry me toward sleep.

"Don't be sorry."

NINE

"The German bastards are coming!"

I blaze from a deep sleep to wide awake. The sun has just begun to rise. A chilly fog hangs in the air. I scramble out from between Denise and Robbie, unable to place the voice of my awakener. But then I have it. Rat. That mute wisp of a boy shouted in the yard with the gusto of two full-grown men.

From inside the barn comes the cry, "The Germans! They're coming!"

Denise leaps to her feet as Rat scampers up the ladder, scarcely making a sound.

"What's happening?" she mumbles.

Blinking like mad, Rat says, "The Germans have an early start on the day. If they find you here during an inspection they will take all Louis has and burn the farm to the ground. Go, go! You may use my bicycle. I have ways of getting others."

I translate the torrent of French to myself as quickly as Rat blinks. He backs onto the ladder and descends with Denise next in line. Twitchy and anxious, I wait my turn. Robbie gathers his parachute into a haphazard bundle and takes his place behind me. When I check on him, his expression makes it clear he's hopelessly confused.

"Rat says we have to leave immediately," I explain. "The Germans are doing inspections and they can't find us here. You can ride Rat's bicycle."

"Okay. I'll just follow along. I trust you."

I hustle down the ladder. He trusts me. To keep him safe. To keep him alive. The gravity of what Denise and I have chosen to take on by rescuing Robbie and bringing him with us to Paris, in a country swarming with the enemy, hits me smack in the chest. I let go of the ladder rung and drop the rest of the way, landing with a thud.

When we have our bikes we run with them, still stiff-legged from sleep, into the yard. Tiny beads of mist cling to my face and clothing. Rat and Louis are bent over a bicycle—Rat's, I guess—around the side of the house. A suitcase has been strapped to the back and another sits at Rat's feet.

Rat motions for Robbie to join them, and he runs off, swimming in the cinched-up work trousers and shirt that are loose-fitting on Louis. With the parachute packed away and the suitcases loaded up, Robbie pushes the bike to us.

"*Merci, Louis. Nous sommes reconnaissants pour votre aide,*" I call, genuinely thankful for the hospitality Louis showed us, despite being forced to live on rations and without running water and electricity.

With a curt wave, Denise says, "Yes, thank you."

We're back on the road again. At least we got some sleep.

Once we've distanced ourselves from the town of Chevreuse, we slow to a pace we can keep up over hours. By the time the sun has burned off the last of the fog, my stomach is growling for food.

"Have anything to eat in that suitcase, Robbie?" I ask.

"Yes. Louis packed some rations for us."

Denise says, "I'm not hungry, I can wait."

Not hungry? I don't believe her.

"Are you still upset that Louis served us goat kid last night, Denise?"

She shrugs without answering the question.

"You know you're here to kill people. You're upset about the death of a goat?"

"People do wrong and evil things all the time. That kid did nothing."

"Didn't you keep rabbits back home, after the war broke out?"

Denise's hair drapes over her profile. "I don't really want to talk about it."

I fall back in line with Robbie, and we continue on without breaking to eat. Luckily, Paris is only a few hours away. I know from studying our map that we're about to enter the town of Palaiseau. At that point, one-third of today's trip will be complete.

The farther we ride, the flatter the countryside becomes. We speed along.

In French, I say to Denise, "We've seen quite a few German vehicles from a distance today. There will be soldiers in town and we won't be able to avoid them." With a sideward glance Robbie's way, I add, "What will we do then?"

We round a bend in the road. The German soldiers leaning against their truck see us coming in the same instant we see them.

My automatic reaction is panic. I take a breath, pedaling slower, and force myself to relax. Looking guilty or fearful will only raise suspicions.

We appear to be ordinary young people riding bicycles, a sight the soldiers see every day, and we're not outwardly breaking any laws. If we don't give them a reason to stop us, we should be able to ride past them unprovoked.

But we can't take that chance.

"Denise, you and Robbie have to go on without me. Pretend you're a couple having a spat and ride around the truck. I'll divert their attention."

"No. I won't leave you."

"If they find the radio, they'll shoot us. And Robbie has no papers. It's the only way."

Denise lets out a slow breath. "See you in Paris."

I can't bring myself to say good-bye.

"Keep your mouth shut, Robert," she says, pushing off. "I'll do the talking."

If the Germans search my suitcase, if they realize my papers are fakes . . . I frantically contemplate calling out to Denise and Robbie. I've been too hasty. I made a mistake.

I watch them ride away and leave me behind.

Ten

"I saw you looking at that girl!" Denise shrieks in shrill French as she and Robbie shoot past the truck. "You pig! You disgust me!"

One of the soldiers steps into the road, his raised hand commanding me to stop. I swallow back sudden nausea.

"*Bonjour.*" I lower one foot to the road and keep the other at the ready on a pedal.

My best attempt at a seductive smile is only somewhat successful. The other soldier, who looks about my age, gives me a gap-toothed grin. The soldier blocking my path remains as expressionless as granite. Looking past him, I see Robbie glance back at me one last time over his shoulder.

"*Geben Sie uns Ihr Fahrrad,*" the stony soldier orders.

A well of fear in my chest overflows, trickling throughout my body.

They want my bicycle.

"*Je ne parle pas allemand*," I say, stalling for time.

The young soldier steps forward. "We need your bicycle," he explains in halting French. "We have a flat tire, you see."

I climb off the bike and begin unfastening my suitcase. They're not making off with that without a fight.

Impatience radiates from the older soldier, like scalding steam. He grasps my handlebars. My panic grows as a creeping tug-of-war goes on between us. When at last I have my suitcase, the bike goes to him.

Leaving them no time to check me further, I say, "*Au revoir*," and march off. The first steps are the most difficult. They won't let me pass without a search. They'll shout. Or fire a bullet into the back of my head and be done with it. I put one foot in front of the other, ignoring a fierce desire to run.

But nothing happens. Minutes pass, and still nothing. My relief, pacing in confinement like some caged animal, breaks free. Barely able to think straight, I leave the roadside. My suitcase falls from my hands into the shade of a gnarled apple tree. I crouch with my back against the tree and burst into tears.

I stay several minutes longer than I should. I have to get up. I have to keep going.

I dry my face with a handkerchief, knocking tiny blossom petals free from my hair. Then I continue my journey to Paris, on foot and alone.

Just when I think I'm about to melt in the heat, leaving nothing but a mysterious puddle, sweat-drenched clothes, and a suitcase behind on the road to Paris, a car pulls up. Cars are rare in these times of rationed fuel. Any petrol that goes to the French deprives the German war machine. As far as the German army is concerned, that won't do.

The car putters beside me, looking like an overgrown slug in a metal shell. The lone occupant, a man, sits huddled over the steering wheel. His twiggy build assures me he's not much of a threat. Unless he has a gun.

He leans toward the open window. "*Avez-vous besoin d'aide, mademoiselle?*"

I consider refusing his help, but then my suitcase suddenly seems to hold ten times more weight than before.

"*Oui. Allez-vous à Paris?*" I ask.

"I am going to Paris, yes. Climb aboard. Do you need help with your baggage?"

I don't like the idea of my suitcase being outside arm's reach. "No, thank you. I'll set my suitcase on my lap."

"Very well, then." Regardless, he leaves the car with the ambition of an overeager bellhop, when I'm perfectly capable of opening a car door and taking a seat on my own.

The passenger-side door squeals open on dry hinges. I settle onto the waxy-soft seat.

When we're off, he says, "I'll begin the introductions. My name is Dr. François Devereux. I enjoy reading and bird watching. It is a pleasure to meet you on this fine spring day. Now it is your turn."

I contemplate creating a second false name. In the end, I say, "Adele Blanchard. Thank you for giving me a ride. I think my arms have stretched, lugging my suitcase around. It's a hot day for May, isn't it? My hair is hot enough to fry an egg."

How did he coax so much small talk out of me?

"A young woman shouldn't be traveling alone."

"I can look out for myself," I say, guarding my words more closely. "I had a bicycle, but the Germans took it from me."

"Taking. They're quite good at that. They'll take until there is nothing left for them to take, and even then they will look for more."

I keep quiet. Expressing anti-German sentiment or any other inflammatory statements around a stranger can get me into a heap of trouble, even if the doctor supports the liberation of France. Spies and collaborators have to pass for ordinary people, so I'm not about to accept his introduction at face value. For all I know he's not even a doctor, although the car does support him being a wealthy Frenchman of importance.

As the car rolls through the countryside, all I can do is imagine how much longer this trip would take on a bicycle. The country seems so vast. How will I ever find Denise and Robbie again? The worry that we've been separated for good pushes to the front of my mind for a moment before I can shake it off. I know the situation isn't as hopeless as it feels. They're on their way to Paris. Denise and I have the address of our circuit leader's safe house memorized. Eventually we'll catch up to them on the road. And the looks on their faces when my chauffeured car drives past will be priceless.

The thought makes me laugh, more like a goose than a girl, which startles the doctor. He rights his hat.

"I'm sorry, I wasn't laughing at you," I say. "I thought of something funny."

"It's a nice change to see such a happy person. I know too many who have become dour and fearful, going from one day to the next with a grim face and a cold heart, believing the way of the past will never return. They have forgotten that we live in one of the world's greatest cities. I don't like to see it. If we all give up hope"—he winks and says—"all hope is lost. Liberation will come."

I want to promise him it won't be long until he's free again. But a long fight looms. Paris, spared destruction when France surrendered, might still come under fire. To save him, the country's beautiful towns and cities might be reduced to rubble as the Allies battle to conquer the Germans.

For the next half an hour, Dr. Devereux happily talks my ear off. I gaze out the window, distracted, gripping my suitcase. Any moment, Denise and Robbie will come into view, pedaling and arguing. Any moment, I just know it.

"We are about to enter the city now."

Robbie and Denise can't possibly have beaten me to Paris on their bicycles. The sound of our approaching car must have sent them diving for cover as we crossed paths.

At least I hope that explains their absence on the road. What if they were captured? I don't want to prepare myself for the worst, but I might have to. Apart from my own capture, it can't get much worse than losing Robbie, Denise, and Denise's radio contact with headquarters in one fell swoop.

"Is this your first time here?" Dr. Devereux asks.

"It is, yes."

"Though the city is large, you won't become lost. Paris is made for walking."

"Where is the Eiffel Tower?"

He smiles. "You will see it. Sometimes, believe it or not, you cannot see it even when you are a hundred feet away."

As we drive through Paris, I come to understand what the word "occupied" means. Soldiers crawl the city like an infestation of ants. The SOE showed us photos of the German uniforms. What a difference to actually witness those uniformed soldiers with my own eyes.

"Where would you like me to take you?" the doctor asks.

I give him the address, changing the number but keeping the street name the same.

Dr. Devereux points out landmarks as we go, but with anxiety clouding my thoughts very little he says sticks with me.

At the end of a narrow side street, he pulls up to a grand stone building.

"Thank you for the ride," I say.

"Adele, one moment." He removes a small notepad and pencil from his black bag. Scribbling madly, he says, "If you need me, this is my address." He rips the paper from the pad. "Thank you for brightening my day."

A strong gut feeling tells me to trust Dr. Devereux. He's a good person who only wants to help me.

"The trains and Metro are under constant surveillance. Your papers will be checked numerous times there. Be careful. The nightlife is fun, but whatever you do, do not stay out past curfew. Use your head. Keep your eyes and ears open. Mind who you trust."

I fold the paper in quarters and slip it into my pocket. Leaving the car, I say, "Thank you again. Good-bye."

The doctor's car putters off down the laneway. Once again, I'm on my own.

I backtrack halfway down the street. Stone apartment buildings with sloping dove-gray roofs line both sides of the road, sandwiched tightly together. Only a slight change in color, window height, and ornamental details gives away the end of one building and the beginning of the next. Between the rows of apartments towering above me like sheer white cliffs, I feel downright minuscule.

Across the street, I find the circuit leader's apartment building. My reflection in the storefront window next door looks a wreck, but not as disheveled as I imagined.

I've barely stepped into the lobby when the concierge snaps to attention. His polished shoes clack across the marble floor.

"Mademoiselle, are you here to visit an apartment on the second floor?"

"I am. Has something happened?"

"Tenants on that floor have been arrested." He glances behind his back. "*They* are waiting, anticipating further arrests."

"Have a young man and woman come in this afternoon?" I ask, taking a risk by staying around to ask questions.

"No, I don't believe so."

"I'm grateful for the information." I quickly get together some francs to pay him for his trouble.

"Mademoiselle, I cannot take your money."

"No, please take it. I'm sure your family needs it."

He drops his gaze. "Thank you. You are very kind."

Outside the building, I stand beneath the arched front entranceway. Members of the Resistance circuit I was to work with—possibly my circuit leader and fellow SOE agents—have been arrested. The Gestapo has undoubtedly done a thorough search of the apartment. All it takes is one slip of paper with a name written on it to lead to the arrest of many others. The discovery of a wireless radio or messages, coded or decoded, would be disastrous. Has the entire Paris circuit been compromised? Is there no reason for me to even be here now? I don't know nearly enough French cuss words to put me at ease.

I wander the street until I come to a café. Its sidewalk patio, crowded with young people, will be the perfect place to blend in.

I weave through the tight gaps between chairs to claim the one and only empty table in the corner, feeling curious stares on me.

The conversation between four young women at a nearby table abruptly switches off. They eye me with suspicion. I can only imagine the thoughts behind their upturned noses.

Why is she alone? Where are her friends? Her boyfriend? Her husband? What is wrong with her?

Ignoring them, I set my suitcase beneath the table. It nudges a hard object into my foot. I kick it into my outstretched hand. *The Grapes of Wrath* by John Steinbeck. I flip through the pages, excited to see English words. The book belongs to the American Library in Paris.

From the café, I have a clear view of two intersecting streets and the apartment building. When Denise and Robbie arrive, they won't get past me.

The first hour of reading flies by so quickly I wonder if my watch is broken. The second hour slows to a walk. The third hour hobbles. The fourth practically stands still. Customers come and go, and by the end of the fifth hour the sun has sunk below the adjacent building. The café is about to close for the day. I have to admit to myself that Denise and Robbie are not coming.

ELEVEN

A gentle tapping on my shoulder wakes me. Early morning sunlight glints off the train's metal window frame. I squint to block it out.

"Excuse me, mademoiselle. The train is disembarking."

In the next seat, a young mother, who looks as exhausted as I feel, and her bright-eyed toddler are waiting to leave the rapidly emptying train.

Apologizing, I lift the suitcase from my lap and groggily rise to my feet. I shuffle into the aisle to let them out ahead of me. The mother hurries to the exit, carrying her daughter on her hip.

I follow behind, rubbing the neck cramp I developed while asleep. The hotels were seized by the Germans, so following orders to avoid them I opted for the train. A single girl on a train probably won't raise as many eyebrows as a single girl at a hotel.

I turn my head to stretch and catch sight of an attractive man on the station platform—a familiar face within an unfamiliar city. I watch him through each passing window. My heartbeat and footsteps quicken. Can it be? Is that really Pierre, right outside my train?

The instant I set foot on the platform, I see him again, drawing back from the crowds. He walks with such confidence, the same way Pierre does. He has the body of a man who can handle himself in a fistfight. From another train, German soldiers begin to disembark, and I expect him to steer well clear of the rapidly swelling group. My heart skips as I watch his next move. He doesn't go around. He walks straight through.

I can't leave the station without first showing my papers. But the man who might be Pierre didn't show his papers. He went off on his own, as if he knows another way out.

Stepping back from the crowd, I try to see where he went. Throughout the station the lines of passengers waiting to show identification are becoming disorderly, snaking the length of the platform. I quickly check the head of each line. The German soldiers appear overwhelmed by the flood of new arrivals. I glance to my right. A shielded corridor has formed between the tracks and the group of new soldiers. Can I run down it unnoticed?

I put my head down and walk away, expecting to be chased down. Around the side of the building I break into a run, my heavy suitcase banging painfully against my leg. I come to a wire fence. And there he is, on the other side, walking more casually now in the direction of a bistro. How did he leave the train yard? The vicious razor wire along the top of the fence would have sliced him to ribbons.

He didn't go up and over, so I look to the ground for answers. To my right, the grass hasn't been trampled flat. I go left instead, down a dirt path too hard-packed to grow much of anything, pushing on the fence. It has no give until I reach a section concealed by a brick embankment. Then, just like that, a flap of chain link pushes outward. I crawl through the secret door and fit it securely back into place.

I trail him as he passes the bistro and rounds the corner. Almost immediately he cuts across the street. I put some distance between us, remaining on my side of the road. When he turns down an alleyway, I run to catch up. Down the center of the empty lane he continues his steadfast march. Unlike me, he seems to know exactly where he's going.

From the back, he looks so much like Pierre. It just has to be him.

Suitcase swinging, I jog the span of the sun-dappled cobblestones. As I gather my courage to address him, he knocks at the door of a ground-level apartment. A woman with flowing red hair steps outside in a silk robe.

She kisses him.

I slow to a walk.

"Christian, I have missed you so," the woman says when they part.

The gap between the man and me closes to a few feet. I can see now that he's not Pierre.

In a haze of shock, disappointment, and bewildering jealousy I walk to the end of the alley where it opens into a dingy district, as lost and alone as I was yesterday. I have no idea at all where I am. I can walk in any direction and that won't change. There's nothing I can do from here but travel the city on foot, looking ridiculous and out of place with a cumbersome suitcase in hand.

At one end of the street, a bus crammed with passengers who peer uncertainly through the dusty windows pulls up to the sidewalk. From the back of the building, German soldiers lead a group of two men, a woman, and four children to the road. One of the children stares up at the woman, his small face seized by so much fear it makes me gasp. An older girl tenderly wraps her arm around the little one's shoulder. Squeezing him closer, she whispers something in his ear.

The soldiers wave the family forward. One by one, they're herded onto the bus.

I run then, in the opposite direction, desperate to get away. At the next street, I pause to catch my breath. What will become of that family? Where do the Germans intend to send them on that bus? I picture the small boy's terrified face. Pierre said the Germans were hurting children.

A group of soldiers crosses the street, heading my way. I have to keep moving.

On I walk, impulsively switching one street for another. Above my head, in place of the French flag, red Nazi banners herald a mocking reminder from the rooftops. Faint rhythms of uplifting band music drift from a nearby park, sounding melodious until I hear the accompanying German lyrics. Every newspaper stand I pass sells German newspapers and magazines.

This place is supposed to be the city of my daydreams.

I turn a corner, clearing tears with my sleeve, and stop dead in my tracks.

The small movie house tucked back from the road stands out like an oasis in a sun-scorched desert. It has seen better days, but in those shinier, better days it probably illuminated the entire street. The marquee reads LE CORBEAU. The Raven.

A French film. Not a German one.

For the next few hours, I won't feel quite so lost.

Twelve

Through the grimy window of the train I scan faces in the crowd as we pull into the Paris station, a habit I picked up in the five days since I became separated from Denise and Robbie. I'm losing hope that they're free, that someday I'll see them again. My mind is obsessed with what might be happening to them. Imprisonment, pulled teeth and fingernails, beatings and burnings, unrelenting questioning. It pains me to imagine agents undergoing that treatment, but for us it's always a possibility. Whenever I think of Robbie, I see his bashful smile and soft, moonlit profile. It whittles at my heart.

My spirits sink lower every day, as I witness tenants kicked out of their homes to give soldiers housing, and groups of frightened people inhumanely loaded onto trains and buses. Violent arrests seem to happen at random. The Germans are siphoning away nearly everything the people work for and need for daily survival. Frustration, sadness, and loss of hope hang in the air like invisible, choking smog. It's hard to not be affected by it minute to minute, and I haven't even spent a week in France. Four years have passed since the country fell.

From the day I arrived in Paris, I've stayed under the radar by rotating through candlelit plays, warm museums, and movie theaters—a city-wide game of musical chairs. I might as well have stayed in London. I'm getting no real work done. Several times I considered riding back to the LaRoche farm, but I can only imagine the smug look Pierre would give me. I made a promise to scope out the factory for him. If I admit defeat and go back to the safety of the farm, he'll believe he was right about me all along.

There's only one person I can go to for help.

After we're allowed to disembark, I enter a line of passengers to have my papers checked. I picture the secret door in the fence, as I do after every train ride.

The soldier examining papers at the head of my line strikes up a conversation with the soldier beside him. The Swiss German I learned at boarding school is slightly different than the language spoken by the soldiers, but I usually understand them.

"I received news this morning," he says. "My wife is divorcing me. Taking our children with her. I have plans for the bitch, let me tell you."

The cold cruelty in his voice forces me to casually step from his line. Papers shaking in my hand, I pretend to fix an issue with the clasp of my suitcase before joining a different queue. Carried by the momentum of the crowd, I shuffle forward.

At the head of the line I abandoned, the disgruntled soldier barks a sharp call for assistance, waving a passenger's papers in the air. Two more soldiers dash across the platform. A man is forcibly led away through the parting crowd.

"Papers," I'm asked.

My miraculously steady hand rises. The inspection goes on for the longest time. The soldier's assistant looks on, surely eager to learn my papers are fakes.

How many times can I expect them to believe I'm a twenty-two-year-old French widow named Adele Blanchard who has come to Paris to look for secretarial work before my luck runs out? They're not stupid people, these soldiers. All they have to do is study my face for more than a few seconds.

The sergeant points to my papers. Expressionless, I await his verdict.

"This is what real papers look like," he says to the assistant.

He returns my identification. And I very nearly float away.

———

At the city's center are two islands. The Île de la Cité is home to the stunning Notre Dame cathedral. The smaller island, Île Saint-Louis, is home to Dr. Devereux.

Entering Île Saint-Louis is like stepping back in time to a seventeenth-century village plucked out of the earth and deposited into the Seine. I take my time following a shopkeeper's directions, fascinated by the shops, *fromageries*, bakeries, and the aristocratic mansions where Voltaire and Marie Curie once lived.

I dawdle outside the impressive double doors of François's home after I arrive. Will my decision to come here lead to help or to capture?

When I finally go ahead and raise my fist to knock, the door swings open. A slender woman dressed in culottes and a blouse resembling parachute silk stands before me, inches from my hand. I draw back the punch in the nick of time.

"Bonjour. Je m'appelle Adele," I say. "I am looking for Dr. Devereux."

She cocks an eyebrow, scowling as if I'm a mangy stray cat that crawled out from a trash heap and showed up on her doorstep. The door promptly slams in my face.

I stare at the door, dumbfounded and hurt. Maybe I misinterpreted my conversation with the doctor. If he's not willing to help me, I don't know who else to turn to.

The door reopens. This time Dr. Devereux greets me with a welcoming smile. The woman—I assume she's his wife, the poor man—peers out from behind him in the foyer, blatantly keeping tabs on us.

"Adele, how lovely to see you! Do come in."

The woman blocks my path. "Really, François! Why must you help each and every needy person who comes to our home?"

He looks her in the eyes to say, "Because I am a doctor."

"I am leaving to do my shopping. You *know* how I feel about strangers in our home."

With an exasperated huff she slides outside, her back pressed to the door to avoid contact with me. Reeking of expensive perfume she strolls away, one of the last women in Paris unwilling to give up the haute couture lifestyle the war stole from the city.

"Adele, please come in," Dr. Devereux says. "I apologize for my wife's behavior. She isn't usually like that."

I enter his home, cheered by how clean it smells. I could twirl about like a little girl in a meadow of pink and yellow flowers. And I'm not even the twirling type.

François closes in to get a good look at my face. "Have you eaten?"

My pride tells me to lie, but my hunger begs me to confess.

"I've eaten, but only a few proper meals. I don't have the correct ration booklets."

"There are ways to get around that."

"Yes, I know about the black market restaurants."

"Would you like to wash up?"

I look down at my arms, smudged with dirt and train soot, wanting to shout, "My God, yes! Lead the way!" I take a calming breath. "I don't want to impose on you."

"Nonsense. Come with me."

I tiptoe downstairs, combing my fingers through my damp hair.

"Adele, I'm in my study," Dr. Devereux calls. "Can you come here a moment?"

I follow the sound of his voice to a small, dusk-lit room off the front foyer. Floor-to-ceiling bookcases line the walls, filled with exotic souvenirs and books. I've never seen so many books in a home. I study the framed bird-watching chart on the wall, wondering how many of those beautiful birds Dr. Devereux has seen with his own eyes.

"Take a seat," he says, nodding toward a chair on the opposite side of his desk.

I sit and fold my hands on my lap.

"Adele, if you don't mind me asking"—Dr. Devereux leans forward, his kind eyes pinched with worry—"how old are you?"

"I'm twenty-two," I say as convincingly as I would to a German interrogator.

"Do you have a safe place to stay the night?"

I don't know what to say. His wife will never let me stay in her lavish home.

"I don't have a place to stay."

"Tonight?" he asks, settling back in his chair. "Or no place to stay at all?"

"I don't have any place to stay."

"My wife is spending the night at her sister's home. You are more than welcome to stay in our guest bedroom."

If I turn down a night of luxurious sleep in favor of the train, my aching body will never forgive me.

"Thank you. I will stay, but only tonight. You've been too kind to me already."

"There is no such thing as too kind," he says. He removes a tablet of paper and a pencil from the center desk drawer. "I can help you, Adele, if you'll let me. My good friend, Estelle, takes people in. You will be safe there. She is an extremely conscientious woman." He slides a sheet of paper across the desktop. "That is Estelle's address. I will telephone her in the morning to make the arrangements. She has many contacts. She may be able to point you in the direction of someone who can help you more than I can."

"Thank you," I say, shocked by how drastically my luck has turned. If only I had reached out to Dr. Devereux days ago.

"The guest bedroom is upstairs, the second door on the left. I laid out some clothes for you. Feel free to take some or all of them. My wife won't notice their absence."

I remember what Pierre said: clean clothes boost his men's morale. The prospect of trading my filthy skirts and blouses for a fresh nightgown thrills me.

"Thank you again, Dr. Devereux," I say, standing. "I'll see you in the morning."

"Good night, Adele, I hope you have pleasant dreams. I'm sure it must be a great relief to no longer be stranded all alone."

"Yes," I say. "It really is."

Dr. Devereux was referring only to the week I spent stranded and alone in France, of course. He barely knows me as Adele, and he knows nothing of who I really am deep down. He didn't choose his words knowing they would have an effect on me.

I climb the staircase, remembering a time years before, when I arrived in London.

After Britain declared war on Germany in September 1939, both sides stood at a standstill. It was a phony war, people said. Believing the phony war wouldn't last, my father arranged for me to leave school and travel as far as Britain to stay with my mother's sister, Aunt Libby, a woman I had never met.

One night my uncle Edward called me into the darkened sitting room. The glow of his pipe and a weak lamp lent soft auras of light to the room.

I sat in the high-backed chair opposite him, at the far reaches of the light.

"Are you happy here, Betty?"

I'd been yanked away from my friends. I didn't want to live in the home of strangers, feeling as though I had nothing and no one. No, I wasn't happy, but what was the point in telling him the truth? It wouldn't change anything.

"Yes, sir, I'm happy to be here," I said.

"Your aunt is delighted to have you with us. You are the spitting image of your mother at your age."

"Did you know my mother?"

"We were childhood friends. But after the Great War, things changed for those of us who grew up together. Some friends came home. Some friends were never seen again. I was one of the lucky ones who came back. Your mother's brother was not."

"Yes, I know. He was a war hero, like my father."

"Falling down a flight of stairs does not make one a hero. The only action your father saw was inside a hospital." My uncle's pipe flared brightly and cooled. "I do apologize, Betty. I shouldn't have spoken about your father that way."

My mother's story of how she nursed my father back to health while they fell in love was one of my favorites. Uncle Edward was wrong about my father not seeing action. That wasn't how the story went at all. My father was an admirable man.

"But I thought my mother went to America to marry him because he was a hero."

"Betty, perhaps you should talk to Aunt Lib."

"Please, I'd like to know. Really I would."

"Well, your mother wasn't the same after her beloved brother—" Seeming at a loss for words, he said, "After her brother didn't return home."

In 1917, my mother's brother died. My uncle couldn't say that outright, though, because I had lost my own brother. When people talked about death around me, they used pleasant words like "pass away" or "resting in peace." A tear dripped to my hand.

"Your mum couldn't escape her sadness here. She leapt at the chance to run away with your father because . . . she felt she needed to. To move on with her life."

Everything I thought I knew about my parents was turning inside out. Feeling sick to my stomach, I remembered the way my father had looked at Delores, so soon after my mother's death, as if she were the only woman in the world. As if my mother never mattered to him at all. Was that why he had sent me away? Because he hadn't wanted to be my father in the first place?

"Aunt Lib wasn't blessed with the daughter she always hoped

for," Uncle Edward said. "We're truly happy to have you here, Betty. For as long as you're happy to stay."

My uncle misunderstood. Their home was only a temporary stopover, like the stepping stone Tom and I had used to jump from one side of the creek to the other. I had taken the first leap from school to London. I was sure my father wouldn't leave me stuck in the middle. He would bring me home before the war started.

I refused to give up hope as days turned to weeks. Weeks turned to months. Then, in May 1940, German troops made their move, swiftly invading France. The war became terrifyingly real. And when it did, I didn't ask my aunt for the truth. I already felt the pain of it in my heart.

I'd been stranded.

Dr. Devereux must have given Estelle a dead-on description of my appearance. When I turn down her busy street, I hear a woman call, "Adele! How splendid of you to visit!"

From the steps of an apartment building a gray-haired woman comes running. Her open arms give fair warning of the hug on its way.

"Hello, Great-Aunt Estelle," I say, returning the hug.

To enter her building we will have to cross paths with an approaching German officer. I lower my head to walk past him without attracting notice.

Estelle walks right up to him, smiling, and says, "Officer Berger. This is my great-niece, Adele. Isn't she lovely?"

He lights a cigarette and says an obligatory, "Hello." Then he carries on. He couldn't care less who I am. Little does he know an SOE agent just stood within his arm's reach.

"Come with me, Adele. My sixteen-year-old granddaughter Marie has been awaiting your arrival all morning."

Estelle's sunlit apartment reminds me of a miniature version of my aunt's house. I can't pin down any real similarities, but I feel at home when I walk through the door.

"Allow me to take your suitcase for you," Estelle says. She sets it on the gray marble top of an art deco sideboard my aunt would love to own.

"Why did you introduce me to that German officer?" I ask, rubbing my achy arms.

"Now, in his mind, you are my great-niece, Adele. He will not waste time inquiring about you, as he might if we had said nothing. You will fade from his view and he will move on to someone else. If you behave as though you are keeping secrets, the Germans will suspect you are keeping secrets."

I can see why Dr. Devereux likes this woman.

The door to the apartment flies open. A young girl flings herself into the room like a wispy ballerina taking center stage.

"Is she here?" she says, bouncing on her toes.

"Be calm, Marie. Yes, this is Adele. Adele, this is my granddaughter. Take a seat on the sofa. I will get you a bite to eat."

We sit side by side on the sofa.

Closing in on my face, Marie says, "Everyone in the building will believe we are related. Look in my eyes. Like yours, they are brown. Not dark like chocolate, but like bourbon. And here"—she gathers her dark hair in a bunch to drape it over one shoulder—"we have small birthmarks shaped like Spain on our necks."

I put some distance between us on the sofa, laughing at how quickly she spotted our resemblances.

"How old are you?" she asks.

"I'm twenty-two."

She dismisses that with a coy grin. "No, no, I don't believe you."

"I am," I insist. "Although I've been told I look young for my age."

"Well, I still don't believe you." She cups her hand to her mouth to whisper, "Don't worry, I won't tell anyone. I'm very good at keeping secrets."

I hope the Germans aren't as astute as this sixteen-year-old girl.

"Soldiers are everywhere in the city," I say. "You've lived like this for four years?"

"I was twelve when they invaded, so at first I didn't really understand what was happening. Then horrible stories started to reach us. Soldiers were moving across the country, lining up men, women, and children, and shooting them dead for no reason. My mother, brother, and I had to leave our home and belongings behind to join the evacuees fleeing south. Lines of refugees filled the roads and went on as far as I could see. It was such a bizarre parade of bicycles, wagons and carts, wheelbarrows and baby carriages. But what I remember most are the noises all around me, every minute. The wheezing of men and women moving carts. The complaining and shouting. The babies screaming until I wanted to cry myself. And I lost sight of my mother once. It scares me even now to imagine what would have happened if we'd gotten separated."

"That sounds awful," I say. "Did you ever get your home and belongings back?"

"No, we didn't. We returned as soon as we heard it was safe to do so, but the Germans had moved in to our home. After that, we came to Paris to live in the apartment across from Grand-mère. I remember that time well, because it was fun. Our lives didn't really change. The horror stories we had heard didn't seem true. Very quickly after that, life became so much worse. My mother cried and cried in those days. She loved to cook us big meals, and suddenly there wasn't any food for her children. We had no heat to get us through the winter. I still hate the Germans for making my mother cry."

Estelle returns from the kitchen. Placing a small tray of grapes, cheese, and raw carrots on the sofa table, she says, "Eat up, girls."

Marie snaps off a bit of carrot with her front teeth. "For a while there were no potatoes to be had, my most favorite food gone. So instead I ate carrots every day. My skin turned orange. I ate so many carrots I started to turn into one!"

I laugh along with her.

"Marie, you said you have a brother. Where is he?"

"Like other older boys, Sebastian was taken away to work in Germany. He and his friends didn't have time to run from the *Service du Travail Obligatoire*. Soldiers pulled them from a line as they left a movie theater."

"Oh no!" I cry, shielding my mouth as I chew on a grape.

"We miss him so much. But he's smart and strong. I believe in my heart he'll come back to our family." She shrugs, but the sadness in her eyes is clear. "My friends and I used to joke that boys are too grubby and silly to deserve our attention. Now there are almost no boys left. We wish they could all come back. What will happen if they don't? Who will we marry? The decrepit old men the Germans deemed too unfit for work?"

We make nearly identical disgusted faces at the mere thought of that.

Marie jumps. "What time is it?" Before I have time to answer, she grabs my wrist to check my watch herself. "I have to leave for work at the café now. Do you want to walk with me? I can show you the neighborhood."

"Sure, I'll go with you."

Marie glides up from the sofa. "I can tell already we are going to be great friends!"

After we say good-bye to Estelle, Marie leads me to a café in another district. I learn the location of her friends, her enemies, the old man I'm to avoid at all costs, the kind baker who gives a little more than the daily allotment, several black-market restaurants, and Gestopo headquarters on Avenue Foch.

"Marie, you are a wealth of information," I say outside the café, when she finally pauses to take a breath.

"Thank you. Have a seat on the terrace. I will bring coffee to you."

I've barely settled onto the chair when Marie comes rushing back with the coffee.

"I added a tiny bit of sugar," she says in my ear. She gives me a chipper wave. "Bye for now. I'll see you back at Grand-mère's after work."

"Okay, good-bye, Marie."

I reach for my coffee. The first sip nearly splatters on my new outfit.

It takes all my willpower to not leap up, waving my arms in the air. I convinced myself that I would probably never see them again. And there they are across the street, one looking bewildered and the other looking even more beautiful than before.

Without trying, I had found Robbie and Denise.

Thirteen

Appearing to be in good health, Denise and Robbie look no different from the last time I saw them, although Denise's fashionable clothes protest loudly about being seen in public with Robbie's typical French worker outfit. She knows better than to set them apart.

Where have they been for a week? I'm afraid if I blink, they'll disappear. I can't risk losing them again.

Denise holds up one finger to Robbie, says something that makes him wilt, and then she dashes into a clothing boutique across from the café. He slouches against the building, arms crossed. I doubt it's the first time she's left him unattended to wait for her.

As I push my chair from the table, six soldiers drunkenly stagger into the daylight from the Metro station across the street, hooting and singing at the top of their voices. One soldier goes out of his way to shove the driver of a passing bicycle taxi to the street. Blood drips from a gash on his chin when he retrieves his bicycle. He halfheartedly shakes his fist at the soldiers, but not until they've moved on to their next target.

Robbie.

Ignoring the soldiers does nothing to stop them. The beret that shields Robbie's closely cropped hair from view is snatched from his head. His meek attempts to catch the hat as it's tossed through the group always miss by a hair. I helplessly watch him be made a spectacle of, the humiliation on his face nearly too great for me to stomach.

The beret spins to the ground. Finished with their little game, the soldiers step aside, laughing. I ease back in my chair to wait to them out. My trembling hands raise the coffee to my lips but it splashes like waves battering a boat. Setting the cup on the table, I breathe slowly in and out.

Robbie bends to pick up the beret. The soldier who shoved the bicycle taxi driver sneers. His boot rises. It crashes squarely on Robbie's hand, grinding fingers on stone.

I hear Robbie cry out.

My chair spins around behind me. I storm to the opposite side of the street. Blood rushes into my face. Guttural German growls up from deep in my throat. "Leave this man alone! My father is Lieutenant General Hausser. If he finds out about this, every one of you will be sent to Siberia."

The electrifying supremacy of the moment, with German soldiers staring at me as if I could whip them to Siberia myself, belching fire and brimstone from my mouth, is like nothing I've felt before.

A soldier tugs on the sleeve of his comrade, motioning for them to get away before I can take names. Every soldier but the worst of the bunch and a cohort take off running like frightened schoolboys fleeing a tyrannical headmaster after a schoolyard fight. The remaining two soldiers can give me their menacing looks all they want, it won't match the one on my face. I have reached a point beyond reason.

Our staring match goes on for what seems an eternity. Each pump of my heart, like a grenade going off in a hollow canister, sends blood and shockwaves through my limbs. I am not about to stand down first.

The soldier picks up the beret, dusts it off, and offers it at arm's length.

Robbie has yet to utter a single word. Reluctantly, he takes the hat back.

Before leaving, the soldier turns to me. With a sly grin, he tips his helmet.

"Adele, what the heck was that?" Robbie whispers.

The effects of all those grenades going off in my chest set in.

"I feel sick." I lay my forehead against the sun-drenched stone wall. "We're not supposed to know each other. I shouldn't be speaking to you in English. You never know who's watching, and as far as witnesses are concerned, I left the café to help a stranger."

Robbie grips the beret in his good hand. His wounded hand is rubbed to raw meat in places. I take his wrist to examine the seriousness of the injuries, hoping with all my heart that they aren't permanent. If that awful German made it impossible for Robbie to play the piano again, I don't know what to say or do to make it better.

"How does it feel? Can you move your fingers?"

Robbie's voice shakes when he says, "I'm fine, Adele, really. But how are you?"

"I found the most splendid chenille"—Denise bops out of the store, and we come face to face—"blouse." Her mouth falls open. "You're looking green around the gills."

"Pretend you don't know me. Meet at the Rue Montmartre station in half an hour?"

She nods.

I pat Robbie's arm and return to the café.

When I arrive at the Metro station, Robbie and Denise are waiting at the entrance. Denise leads the way past row upon row of parked bicycles to a secluded area in a park.

"Ooh la la, take a look at you," she says.

Mrs. Devereux's expensive clothing and perfume feel maddeningly foreign on me, but they reinforce claims that I'm a German colonel's daughter. Any suspicions the soldiers have now are a waste of time.

"You don't look too bad yourself," I say. "Where did you get that new outfit?"

"I bought it."

"You bought it? With the SOE's money?"

"I'm in *Paris*. I'm sure they would understand."

I don't think anyone at headquarters will understand Denise paying black market prices unless the blouses also shoot bullets and come equipped with grenades.

"Would you like to join me in getting a manicure?" she asks.

Ragged beyond help, my nails look worse off than normal, and that's saying something.

"A manicure?" I laugh, not about to let her pull my leg. "You're joking."

She points to a street adjacent to the park. The electricity is out, as usual, and two barbers and a manicurist busily groom customers on the sidewalk.

"We'll have plenty of money left. If we need more I'll send word to London."

I honestly don't want to be forced to put my foot down or reprimand Denise. In my eyes, we're equals. I want it to stay that way.

"We're here to work, Denise. Let's get that manicure some other time."

Her lips purse sideways into an amused smirk. "The voice of reason. Where would I be without you?"

A tight hug squeezes out my breathy reply, "In shops and salons?"

"I've missed you so."

Robbie quietly adds, "We both have."

Denise tugs on my sleeve, directing me to follow her to the grass as she sits. "So, you got away from the Germans and arrived here in one piece. Tell me every detail. All but the dull parts, I mean."

I tell them about giving away my bicycle and meeting Dr. Devereux, but conveniently neglect to mention my breakdown beneath the apple tree.

"A doctor!" Denise smacks her forehead. "We heard a vehicle, but I automatically assumed it was Germans coming. We hid in the ditch."

"I thought so. When I reached the apartment, our contacts had been arrested. I waited for you. Why didn't you show up?"

"Robbie got a flat tire. I insisted he could ride anyway. He insisted it would ruin the bicycle. We spent the night behind some hedgerows and walked to Paris in the morning. The concierge warned us too. We should have received an alternate address, but the concierge collaborating with the Resistance was arrested in the roundup."

"But without a contact, where did you go?" I ask.

"At first we stayed in a hotel."

My muscles and memory still ache from the time I spent on the trains.

"Then we had the great luck to stumble upon new contacts," Denise says. "Would you like to visit headquarters for the Paris Resistance?"

I make certain we're completely alone. "I would. Where is it? Which street?"

"It isn't on any street. It's in the empire of the dead."

FOURTEEN

From the inconspicuous door to the Underground, we descend a
spiraling stone staircase, as if into a bottomless pit. "Are you
taking us to hell?" I ask, and Denise answers with an ominous,
"More or less." At the bottom of the staircase, about seventy feet
beneath the city, Denise leads the charge down narrow, dimly lit
tunnels. Moist gravel crunches softly beneath our feet for nearly
a mile.

"What is this place?" I ask.

Denise slows. "Everything you see above was once down
here. All that limestone had to come from somewhere."

I shiver with panic, half expecting Paris to come crashing
down on my head.

"Come on," Denise says. "That's not the most interesting
thing about this place."

A few minutes later, as my curiosity begins to wane, Denise
points to a door between two columns. The sign above reads
ARRÊTE! C'EST ICI L'EMPIRE DE LA MORT.

STOP! THIS IS THE EMPIRE OF DEATH.

We pass between the pillars. The beam from Denise's flashlight roams around the room. Meticulously arranged bones line the walls. The gruesome pile is nearly my height and many more feet than that deep. A thick layer of leg bones, joints set outward, is followed by a row of skulls, and then another layer of bones. The neat row of skulls capping the whole thing off reminds me of the copper studding on my uncle's favorite chair. Empty eye sockets gaze into me.

"I don't understand what this is."

"The Catacombs," Robbie says. "You're looking at a few of the six million Parisians who are buried down here."

None of the remains are complete. Each body was disassembled and rearranged in the most compact way possible. I think about the chicken carcasses my aunt boils for soup. Tiny bones far outnumber large bones, and picking out every last one is a real chore. Were the small bones of six million people thrown behind a wall of skulls and leg bones like rubbish? I suddenly wish Denise and Robbie hadn't brought me here.

"Why did they do this?" I ask.

"Just imagine how full the graveyards would have been after the plague," Robbie says. "They ran out of space, so they dug up the cemeteries and moved the bodies."

The spotlight of Denise's flashlight illuminates an intact skull. In life, the faces looked so different. In death, everyone looks the same

Robbie clears his throat behind me. "Jeepers, Adele, you're jumpier than a long-tailed cat in a room full of rocking chairs."

"I am not," I say, though not half as convincingly as I'd like. "How much farther does this go on?"

"A kilometer."

"You can't be serious."

Denise's flashlight casts a spooky light across her face. "Deadly serious."

Our tour moves forward. Denise entertains us with tall tales about the bones and their owners. Some were criminals, some royalty, others paupers. Like a circus barker wowing the crowd, she calls, "Death! The great equalizer!"

My teeth clench. Her impulsive shout chips at my confidence in her professionalism. The Resistance is using these underground tunnels. Didn't she consider that maybe the Germans are using them too?

We come to a stone altar. Robbie and Denise gather closer as I translate the Latin inscription. "Man, like a flower of the field, flourishes while the breath is in him, and does not remain nor know longer his own place. In peaceful sleep rest great people."

"I don't know what that means, but it's lovely," Denise says.

Tombs link to even more tombs and limestone quarries, some tall and wide enough to fit a church, some a tight squeeze for our single file. How easy it must be to get lost down here below the surface where all the surroundings eventually look familiar. Every so often we come across a street name engraved into a tunnel wall, and I imagine the goings on above us. Water drips steadily, tapping out a nonsensical message in Morse code.

"The tunnels seem endless," I say.

"If put end to end in a straight line, the quarries would be three hundred kilometers long," Robbie says. "And Paris is also famous for its sewers. If those two thousand kilometers of tunnels were placed end to end they'd reach Istanbul. Two people could enter at separate locations and never come across each other. You could walk for months straight and not see it all."

"Someone paid attention on the previous tour," Denise says. "At least if I die of boredom we're in the right place. Robbie, toss my corpse near that lovely monument Adele read to us."

Under his breath he mumbles, "Let's go to the bunker."

"You know I'm only teasing, Robert."

Denise might not appreciate Robbie's comments, but I think his knowledge is fascinating.

"C'mon, Denise, leave him alone," I say, once he's out of earshot.

"He can't afford to be thin-skinned, Adele."

Inside the Resistance bunker, a metal-encased room within the sewer tunnels, Denise introduces me to the SOE circuit leader, a dashing man, code name Martin Cammerts.

His dapper moustache pulls up at one corner when he smiles. "I'm pleased to meet you, Adele. We've had a bit of rotten luck with the Paris circuit lately, but we're still making a go of it. You have a safe address where we can contact you if necessary?"

"I do." I gave him Estelle's address.

"As a courier, you will be expected to ride great distances on a bicycle to drop and receive messages. Have your rendezvous in the country whenever possible, and have a lookout, a sign, something to alert the other to danger. When meeting in the city, use your head. If your contact has not yet arrived, don't stand around in the open like a lamppost. The Germans will have you scooped up in one of their vans and shipped off to Fresnes prison quicker than you can bat an eye. Are you with me, Adele?"

"I am, sir. But I no longer have a bicycle. I gave it to the Germans."

"That's a lavish gift. Before the war I could have bought

myself a car for less than the cost of a bicycle now. For what reason did you give yours up, girl?"

"Well, I wanted to live, sir."

"That's reason enough, I suppose. We'll give you another. Please try to hold on to this one for more than a week's time."

"I will."

"I move quite frequently," he says. "However, I will give you the addresses of an apartment where I can occasionally be located for orders and a letter-box where you can drop messages if you need to get in touch with me."

I nod, already apprehensive about dropping off covert messages with the contact Cammerts has assigned to be his "letter-box." I'd rather keep the list of people who know my real reasons for being here as short as possible. Everyone I make myself known to is one more person who can potentially lead to my arrest down the road.

"After memorizing these addresses, please do away with the papers as you would any other message," Cammerts says. "Burn them."

"Rendezvous"—such a fabulously foreign and mysterious word—that is, until I meet Cammerts again a day later to receive the details for my first rendezvous. Then, it becomes much more than just a word.

My orders are to contact a woman code-named Anna. Blank identity cards, forged ration cards, and a large sum of money intended for the Resistance are sewn into the lining of the jacket I'm to deliver. I don't know what Anna looks like, apart from Cammerts's description of older and a little homely.

I leave the Metro in an area of Paris that was a quaint village once before the city swallowed it up. The directions to the park, our prearranged meeting place, run through my head like a catchy tune so I won't forget them.

Everywhere I look there are soldiers; a few loiter on the corner, a trio walks toward me, more sit at a bistro. I picture how I must look from their perspective, face tensed, eyes darting about, a lumpy jacket clutched to my chest. Concentrating on each and every step only makes my movements awkward, as if I've forgotten how to walk properly.

I try to ease my shoulders lower, casually slinging the jacket over my arm. Palms sweating profusely, I hold my head high.

With a smile, the first soldier in the approaching trio says, "Good day."

As if it has a mind of its own, my throat snaps shut. An unintelligible mumble replaces my greeting. My God, what's wrong with me? I simply have to act naturally, the way I do every day of my life, and now when it matters I can't even do that.

The park comes into view. I'd love to run the rest of the way, but that will draw attention to me. I have to look calm and collected while feeling like a top spinning out of control.

My orders are straightforward. Anna will be waiting on a bench near the fountain, reading a book called *Le Petit Prince*. I will hand over the jacket and leave.

When I finally reach the park's wrought-iron entranceway, relief and panic collide. In imagining how the rendezvous would play out, I created an idyllic setting—an overcast and secluded park, one bench, no bystanders, and a woman who would initiate contact with me first. If only.

The majority of the people in the park are older women. Of the women seated on benches near the fountain, only one removes herself from the running straight away by knitting. The other three hold books. Potential Annas abound!

I have limited time to choose the correct woman before the rendezvous blows up in my face like a ticking bomb. A commotion of thoughts roars through my head, refusing to line up in a logical sequence. Hot sweat trickles down my neck. I'm exposed. Thrust onto a stage. The sun bursts out from behind the cloud cover, beaming like a spotlight.

This rendezvous is serious business. Anna awaits an agent with maturity and experience. The kind of agent who wouldn't have second thoughts. Is she watching me, dismayed to realize the immobile girl gripping a jacket isn't at the park to gossip with friends or pour her heart out to a diary—she is, in fact, the contact? I feel as though I owe her an apology.

I edge closer to the fountain. I have to be sure of her location. One chance is all I've got. I can't swap benches and seatmates until I get it right. It's practically impossible to study a person at close range and be inconspicuous about it. My head pounds from the stress of it all.

A woman to my right raises her book higher as she reads, exposing the cover. We make eye contact over the binding.

Taking in the sights, as if I'm out for a leisurely day at the park, I stroll to the bench. My roaming gaze locks on the book for a split second. There are the words I'm looking for, *Le Petit Prince*.

This will soon be over.

Anna makes room for me. I sit with the jacket between us, overlapping Anna's own belongings, an umbrella and a handbag. With that out of the way, I want to immediately free myself from the jacket, Anna, and the park. Not to mention the women on the other side of the fountain whose obliviousness to my presence is either genuine or a ruse. Good German spies would behave the same way.

I count the passing seconds of one minute to give my cover some validity. Turning slightly away from Anna, I watch the street beyond the fence, acting as though I've come to the park to meet someone who hasn't yet arrived. One minute becomes two. Why isn't Anna slipping away with the jacket? Something is wrong.

Then, like a cuff across the head, the answer hits me. I didn't give her the code word. Not only that, I can't for the life of me *remember* the code word.

Anna closes the book, gathers up her handbag and umbrella, and then she's gone.

The rendezvous has been called off. Anna couldn't take any chances. Without the password, I came across as a phony agent sent by the Germans to catch her.

I fold the jacket across my lap. Boy, I've made some bone-headed mistakes, but this outdoes them all. My first rendezvous could have gone worse only if I were captured.

I scour my memory for the code word, which is about as helpful as flipping open a dictionary and hoping for the best. *Gamble, gravel, gabble, rabble, amandine* . . .

In no time flat, Anna crosses to the far side of the park, using her umbrella for a walking stick.

I squeeze the wool jacket, woozy with panic. How frustrating to sense the word on the tip of my tongue. Word upon word leads me to *Aberdeen*, and that finally does the trick. Jogged from memory, the code word blares through my mind like a victorious bugle call. *Gabardine!* It wasn't at the tip of my tongue after all, but at the tips of my fingers.

I return to the entranceway, humiliated by my terrible first impression. I messed up, but I'm not incompetent. I tried my best to be professional. I can't let her get away, doubting me. What if she thinks my age prevents me from doing this job well?

I walk a parallel course to Anna, keeping her umbrella in my sights. Somehow, we must meet in a new location far away enough to elude witnesses of our original contact.

Evenly spaced shade trees border the park. I stay behind them to break up my movements and become less noticeable. Better yet, the trees along the back of the park aren't well tended at all. I'll run to the other side, relatively out of sight, and cut Anna off before she leaves. When I reach the corner post, I set off through thick weeds and vines, shoving branches out of my face. The anxiety of not knowing Anna's whereabouts pushes me to run faster. After several minutes, I slide through a slick patch of grass and tumble into open air in a secluded clearing by a stone archway.

Too preoccupied with catching my breath to explain, I thrust the jacket out when Anna comes into view. I expect her to bolt, but she walks straight over.

"Madame, you forgot your *gabardine* jacket at the park."

"I can see that." She raises her eyebrows at me. "And you followed me from there?"

"Yes."

"Well, that's a surprise." She takes the jacket from my hand. "Thank you for returning this. It would have been a shame to leave without it. However . . . I don't expect something like that could happen again. Do you?"

"No," I assure her, as she exits through the archway. "It definitely will not."

FIFTEEN

I may have mucked up my first rendezvous with Anna, but in the five days since, our meetings have gone by the book. I'm finally getting some real work accomplished.

What a different week it's been, compared to my first days in Paris. I'm surprised by how comfortable I am in the city now. I have a nice place to stay and friends to spend time with. It's made all the difference. I don't feel like such an outsider. I have a daily routine that I'm quickly growing to love.

But it's the routine of someone living a double life.

Inside Estelle's apartment, I'm a regular girl. In the morning, I eat my bread, vitamin biscuit, and coffee with Marie. We wash up and tend to the radishes and lettuce growing in her window boxes. We read books and magazines. We knit. We talk about movies. We laugh. A lot.

When I leave the apartment, I am Adele the spy. I meet with Anna to exchange passwords. We hand over encoded messages, or radio parts hidden beneath the false bottom of shopping bags, or huge sums of francs stuffed into jacket linings. I receive orders from Cammerts and deliver messages to his "letter-box," an older gentleman who runs a garage on the outskirts of the city. I courier messages bound for London to Denise, so she can transmit them to headquarters. I hatch a plan to spy on and sabotage the factory. I take food, toiletries, fresh clothes, and playing cards to the pilot I've promised to protect.

This afternoon, Anna and I have a prearranged meeting in a park to swap encoded messages. We're two contacts in a long chain of couriers. We don't know the entire route the messages travel or what information is contained in them. It's safer that way for both of us. All we have to do is hand them over and leave.

At the park, Anna is nowhere to be seen, which is unusual. I normally spot her on the fringes of our meeting places, chatting with women in the market stalls or pretending to window shop. I sit on the park bench to wait.

When three minutes pass and Anna still hasn't arrived, I try not to panic. Two Gestapo officers stroll past my bench and stop within three yards of me. My fingers grip dry wood. A splinter eases into the flesh of my palm. With my feet set in an imaginary starter's block, I wait for something to happen. The soldiers light cigarettes and continue on their way, paying me no attention.

I promise Anna one more minute. When every minute counts, sixty seconds seems like plenty of time for the Germans or French police to question what I'm up to.

In the heat, the stiff fabric of my pale-gray dress sticks to me like glue. I scratch an itch on my neck and glance at my watch as I lower my arm. By now it must be glaringly obvious that I'm waiting for someone. I have no choice but to call off the rendezvous.

Before I can move, a figure steps into my peripheral vision. Dark trousers, black overcoat, the brim of a hat pulled low over his eyes. Clearing his throat, he sits next to me. I put space between us on the bench. He ventures into it.

My heart thumps wildly. This is it. I'm about to get nabbed. I have to leave in a way that doesn't arouse suspicion. I can't appear to be fleeing the scene, when that's exactly what I have to do.

Somewhere between a walk and a sprint, I blaze a path toward the safety of the Metro. If the man in the trench coat follows, I'll jump on a train and quickly leave it before it pulls away.

And follow he does. Heavy breathing and disorderly footsteps hunt me.

"*Mademoiselle, attends!*"

Wait for him? So he can escort me to 84 Avenue Foch, Gestapo headquarters, at gunpoint? I will do no such thing.

I speed up when the first Metro sign comes into view, putting greater distance between us. Soon, I no longer hear his footsteps and wheezing breaths. I skip down the stairs, bobbing and weaving, and board the train without incident.

Then suddenly, he appears at the bottom of the stairs. I lean across an unoccupied seat to get a better look at him. Seeming to be midway through an asthmatic attack of some sort, he clutches at his chest. His red cheeks puff out.

I almost feel sorry for him, gasping away as he is, like a fish out of water. Nothing about him sets off my intuitive alarm. And the Gestapo and French police usually travel in pairs or groups. The man following me is alone.

He recovers quickly and runs straight for the train. Not anticipating this, as I should have been, my next move is delayed. I leap to the platform. My timing's bad. I leave the train while he stands within a crowd of last-minute passengers. Spotting me immediately, he comes at me from behind when I turn to run. He seizes me by the arm.

Even unarmed, I can get myself out of this. Fingers gouged in his eyes or a swift chop to his windpipe, and he'll drop from the pain. Certain blows or kicks to vulnerable spots have the power to kill. My instructor's words during training were, "This is *war*, not sport. Your aim is to kill as quickly as possible." I will be finished with this man before preoccupied crowds have time to form an accurate picture of me in their minds. It's him or me. If I don't react, it will be me losing this fight. So why am I getting cold feet? I practiced this same scenario over and over until it felt routine. But this is no training session and the man gripping my arm is no straw-stuffed training dummy. He's a real, living, breathing person. How can I be responsible for taking away his last breath?

His fingers relax and fall away. "Excuse me, miss. I apologize if I hurt you."

Sweat trickles from his forehead, down the bridge of his mountainous nose to the tip, where it pools before plummeting off the peak.

"You were at the fountain the other day—" He reaches inside his overcoat. I take a step backward; the first of the all-important fifteen-stride lead needed to effectively escape an enemy. "I saw you drop this."

He pulls out a white flag of surrender. I do a double-take. No, it's a handkerchief. My embroidered handkerchief.

"You appear to be in a hurry to get somewhere; I'm sorry to bother you," he says. Pudgy hands twist my handkerchief into a taut coil. "I wondered if you might like to get a drink. When it is more convenient for you, of course. My name is Georges."

Oh, Georges, I think. *If only you knew what a close call you had just now.*

"I'm afraid I can't." I coax out a smile. "I have a boyfriend. Thank you for the offer, though."

The handkerchief unravels limply. "I see. It never hurts to ask." He stands aside. "I'll let you get back on your way."

I take the warm, slightly damp handkerchief from him, not about to use it near my face ever again.

Back above ground, squealing children chase each other through the park, couples stroll hand in hand, friends meet for coffee. Regular life. It still goes on around me.

While a kind man was working up the nerve to ask me on a date, I was working up the nerve to kill him with my bare hands.

Sixteen

On the long walk to Estelle's, I drop by Cammerts's apartment to let him know my rendezvous didn't take place. I doubt he's in, and I'm right. But if he ran into trouble he would have placed a matchbox on the window ledge outside the apartment door. The sill is empty, so I figure he wasn't captured. Still, the elevator ride to the foyer seems to take forever, and the whole way down I prepare to be pounced on by German guards the moment the door opens.

I think about visiting Denise next, since she spends so much time by herself, hidden away. The SOE can't afford to lose a skilled transmitter like Denise, or her precious radio. Although, knowing Denise, she won't stay behind the scenes much longer since she's made it pretty clear she hates being stuck indoors.

When I spot a confectioner's shop, I change my mind about visiting Denise. A certain boy is hidden away too, and I have a gut feeling he's in need of some company.

Robbie was sent to a safe house owned by a woman who runs an escape route for downed airmen. She, along with a trusted group of assistants, smuggles the men through France, over the Pyrenees Mountains, and into neutral Spain. From there, they're returned by boat to Britain.

I learned from Marie that ration cards aren't required at the confectioner's shop, so I pick up candy for Robbie. I imagine him huddled alone in a dank cellar, craving fresh air and sunlight and someone to talk to. Something sweet might lift his spirits.

As I prepare to leave, a German soldier marches swiftly to the door from the opposite side. I freeze in place, clutching the bag of candy. Did he see me leave Cammerts's apartment? Did he follow me here? There are no other ways to exit the shop. I'm trapped.

He opens the door, stepping aside to let me pass. "*Après vous, mademoiselle.*"

"*Merci,*" I say as I hurry outside.

The soldier enters the shop. The door swings shut behind him.

I take a good look around, marveling at the number of German soldiers using the street. How, in two weeks' time, have I become so used to them that they're a normal part of the scenery?

When I arrive at Robbie's safe house, the woman who runs the escape line is just leaving through the front door. I meet up with her at the sidewalk.

"Hello, Adele," she says. "Are you here for the parcel?"

It seems strange to call Robbie a parcel, as if he's a gift waiting to be shipped away, but in a way it makes sense.

"Yes, is that all right?"

"Certainly. I'm off to pick up food for boxed lunches. The

amount some people eat, it's astounding. They don't fare well at all with the rationing restrictions."

She means American airmen like Robbie, who are taller and broader than the average Frenchman. He's probably willing to trade his right arm for a slab of roast beef and mashed potatoes right about now.

"Okay, thank you," I say, tacking on a quick good-bye as I jog down the pebbly path that leads to the cellar door.

At the far end of the cellar, an enormous wine rack conceals a room not much larger than a closet. Enough light filters through the window's lacework of cobwebs to let Robbie read, play cards, and stay relatively sane.

I find him seated cross-legged on his neatly made cot, hunched over what's probably his umpteenth game of solitaire. I tiptoe behind him and say, "Hi!"

The sudden jerk of his arm sends a whole row of neatly laid-out cards flying.

"Geez, Robbie, you're jumpier than a long-tailed cat in a room full of rocking chairs."

Shifting sideways to look at me, he says, "Oh, hi, Adele. Don't think you spooked me, because you didn't." The bright red blush climbing above the collar of his shirt and into his cheeks tells a different story. He pats the end of the cot. "Wanna play rummy?"

"Sure." After I'm comfortably cross-legged, I hand him the bag of candy. "I brought you a treat."

"You did?" he cries, with all the excitement of a little boy at Christmastime. He frees one candy from its cellophane wrapper and pops it in his mouth. "Mmm, sour balls," he says, his words garbled by the brightly colored ball of sugar. "Thanks, Adele. How'd you know they're my favorite?"

Laughing, I say, "I got them because they're my favorite."

Robbie passes me a sour ball. I slowly unwrap the candy while watching him deal cards. He really is cute. His fair hair looks so soft. And the single dimple that pops up in his right cheek when he grins always makes me smile. He's the sort of boy I would have had a schoolgirl crush on, back when I lived in Connecticut. I pick up my cards before he can catch me staring.

"Did they give you forged papers yet?" I ask.

"I'm getting them soon, I think. Since I can't speak French, my papers will say I'm deaf and dumb."

"When you get your papers we'll go for a walk. I've seen other girls walking downed airmen around the city. They must be airmen because they stick out like sore thumbs. I don't know how they don't get caught. None of their clothing fits them properly. They look nervous. They walk too slowly. They squint at their subway and train tickets as if they have no clue what's written on them. Because they don't! But we won't be like them." With a nod, I resolve to get him outside for some fresh air. "Don't worry. I'll be a lot more careful than those other guides."

"I'll bet."

The musty, depressing cellar already has me craving sunshine. What sort of mood must Robbie be in by now? The sooner he gets his papers, the better.

"It must be awful, stuck down here all day," I say.

"It's a lot better now." He glances away from his cards to give me a quick smile. "I'm glad you came to see me again. After being surrounded by my sisters, and then the fellas in my squadron, I thought it'd be nice to spend some time alone, away from it all, but I've never been so bored in my whole life. Now that you're here, I can finally have a conversation. Sometimes I sing, just to hear words I can actually understand."

"What do you sing?"

"Ah, nothin'."

He can't take back that spilled confession with a nonchalant shrug. I won't let him. "Sing something for me."

I lean forward. My unblinking stare commands him to do my bidding. Within seconds he cracks under the pressure and laughs.

"Don't make me sing, Adele."

"Just one song, that's all, then I'll never ask you to sing again."

He groans. "All right, fine. But don't look at me while I'm singing."

"I won't. Promise." I turn right around backward. "Look, I'm facing the wall. How's that for not looking?"

Behind me, he clears his throat. He inhales a deep breath. The soulful lyrics of "You Are My Sunshine" wrap around me like a hug I want to settle into and never leave. Robbie's voice is shy but strong, and the melodic sentiment of his singing brings tears to my eyes. After the echo of the final note fades, I keep my back to him until I'm confident my voice won't break when I tell him how great he was.

"You're not laughing at me"—he clears his throat again—"are you?"

Pretending to scratch an itch, I pat my eyes dry. I face him and cross my legs again. "No, that was good. Really good."

His shoulders droop with relief. "Ah, thanks."

He reaches out to pick up his first card from the stack, beaming his sweet, boyish grin with such happiness. All because I came to visit him.

Seventeen

In hindsight, I shouldn't have offered to help Pierre and his men by spying on the factory. What will I get in return? More work and more time on my bike, that's what.

The bright morning sky I woke up to in Paris has dulled to a lifeless steel gray, threatening rain. With my luck a rain shower will drench my notes. I'll be left with nothing to show Pierre, and no proof that I went through with it.

The area is new to me, and traffic here has been hit or miss all morning. When the roads aren't bustling with wagons, bicycles, and assorted German vehicles, they're startlingly empty. Intent on reaching the factory, I whizz past everything in my path, avoiding eye contact that might invite attention or conversation. If the Germans want me to stop, they can take the time to ask me to stop. Otherwise, I'm not braking for anything.

A few kilometers south of the village Pierre showed me on the map, the German presence picks up. I ride on, speeding past a truck hauling young soldiers. When they hoot crass innuendos at me, I don't even flinch. I pedal faster.

My confidence doesn't waver until I crest a steep incline and get my first look at the factory. I slog through the motions of pedaling, gradually slowing to a stop.

Nothing in real life ever plays out the way it does in my imagination. The factory is a multistoried behemoth of a building, bordered by extensive grounds that offer no cover. Two German guards patrol the perimeter fencing and one oversees the locked entrance gate. What's the sense in riding all this way to spy? Sabotaging this factory looks to be practically impossible.

On a sloping field of wildflowers a few hundred meters west of the wire fence, I lay down my bicycle and sit next to it beneath an old oak.

The lid of my bicycle basket flips open. The apple Estelle insisted I take with me to keep my energy up tumbles onto the grass, followed by the compact Tenax camera I bought from Marie for a few francs more than it's worth. She already used ten of the exposures. That leaves twenty-six for me. Twenty-six chances to capture the factory's exterior, and the surrounding area, on film. Estelle and the neighborhood photo developer are longtime friends, which gives me the freedom to photograph images that might otherwise raise alarm bells.

I study the expansive concrete wall and barred windows visible from my perch on the hillside. Photos from this angle won't do much to help Pierre and his men. To give them the complete picture, I'll have to move, shooting photographs from all sides. The guards will catch on to my plan immediately. If they haven't already.

I seriously underestimated the extent of this job. It can't possibly be wrapped up in one morning. And I was reluctant to come here in the first place. Now I'll have to come back another day to gather more evidence? No thank you. Even if I manage to collect photos of the exterior, the interior will remain a complete mystery.

I draw my legs up and wrap my arms around them, discouraged by the futility of traveling all this way. I should ride straight back to Paris without giving this mission another thought, as if I hadn't agreed to spy on it in the first place. What's to stop me? I'm not obligated to follow this through to the end. I never have to see Pierre again.

Kneading my temples with my fingertips, I sigh. Pierre expects me to quit. He knew I'd ride away, never to be heard from again. He warned his men that I'm just a girl. And a small one at that.

That does it. I am not just a girl. Somehow, some way, I will get inside the factory.

A mass of leafy ferns sways this way and that, revealing the whereabouts of a creature hidden there. Out hops a plump brown rabbit. He leisurely lops into the open to snack on grass, unaware that his enemy sits only ten feet away.

My hand slips inside my jacket. With the stealth of a hunter, I remove my notebook and pencil. What a challenge it would be to draw him before he catches wind of my scent and bolts. Just as I'm adding the final pencil strokes to his ears, he stands alert, nose twitching. Like a shot, off he goes, darting up the hillside and into the forest, to flee the girl who spared his life.

I tuck the notebook in my jacket and pick up the camera. I snap five shots of the landscape, capturing the factory and the grounds in the distance. Those five shots aren't enough, but the film can't be wasted on nearly identical images. I set the camera at my feet. I methodically tear a plucked blade of grass into thin strips while watching two exit doors for activity.

Outside the front gate, the guard paces, his hands stuffed into his pockets. Unlike other German soldiers I've seen, he has a relaxed way of moving, without the typical wind-up toy soldier rigidness. Is he bored? Does he wish for a job with more action? How would he react if a naive girl approached him and struck up a conversation?

An idea hits me. It might very well be a horrible idea, but before second thoughts can set in I stroll to the road, taking in the sights like a curious tourist. I capture five more shots of the factory. I pretend to photograph clouds and the pasture across the road. I kneel to take aim at a daisy. I pop the flower from its stem and tuck it in my hair the way innocent girls do in movies. Every chance I get to keep tabs on the guard through the view-finder, I take it. A German shepherd dog sits as still as a statue by his side.

"You, there! Mademoiselle!" he calls. "Come here please."

I jerk to attention, unable to help myself. Boy, I've really done it this time. I've gotten too confident for my own good. I force a smile as fear pulls my cheek muscles taut. If there's any hope of getting away with this tourist act, I have to give it my all.

With a spritely spring in my step, I march to him, saying, "Good morning, sir. How are you?"

"I am well, thank you." He stands more at attention now than he did the whole time I spied on him. "I would like to see your papers, please."

My fingertips try to discern the size and shape of my identifi-cation inside the bulging interior pocket of my jacket.

"Here is my *carte d'identité*," I say, still smiling as though I have nothing to fear.

My trembling hand pulls the correct identification paper from my jacket. The handoff seems to happen in slowed time. The guard reaches toward me. He secures the card. I could swear that he does. Believing he has it in his grasp, I release mine.

The card twirls to the ground.

"I'm sorry," I say, bending down to retrieve it. "Clumsy me."

My fingers wrap around the card. Everything will be fine, but only if I focus. If I stay calm. I'm on top of the situation. There's no need to be nervous.

As I rise to hand over my identification, I watch, too shocked to react, as the notebook supplied to me by the SOE slips from my pocket. Flapping open, it falls through the air, the pages rustling as if to taunt me. And then it lands, right on the guard's boots.

EIGHTEEN

He picks up the notebook and examines the nondescript cover from every angle.

I took all necessary precautions, I'm sure of it. Any and all pages that shouldn't fall into enemy hands were removed and burned.

He flips the cover open to the first page.

I wrack my brain for its contents. Is he looking at my doodle of the ducklings? Or the coordinates for the factory?

After memorizing this location, did I tear that sheet from the book? I must have. But within a matter of seconds I convince myself that the page is still there and it's about to give me away.

"What a beautiful dog," I blurt. "May I pet him, or will he bite?"

I gauge the guard's expression as he closes the book and returns it to me. My heart still beats with life and my hands aren't cuffed, so I guess he didn't find incriminating evidence. I quickly return the notebook to my pocket along with my identity card.

"She will bite you if I tell her to," he says.

My eyes widen with fear. He's about to sic a vicious Nazi hound on me.

His smile helps me breathe a little easier. Even though I don't doubt for a second that the dog will tear me to shreds if commanded to do so, the guard is just toying with me.

"Yes, you may pet her. Let her sniff your hand first." Addressing the dog, he says, "Zucker. *Hier!*" The dog obediently stands and takes her place next to the guard's leg. "Zucker. *Setz!*" he says, and she sits at attention.

I hold my palm to her nose, leery of her fangs. "Hello, Sugar." With a quick pat to her head, I say, "You're a good dog."

"Zucker does not speak French. She speaks only German."

I laugh. "Oh, I see."

"Do you speak German?" the guard asks. "You translated the dog's name."

"I speak only a little German." My mind spins, grasping at details and memories, no matter how small, to rework my cover story. "My name is Adele Blanchard, but my grandmother's maiden name was Ackerman."

He excitedly points to his chest. "Ackerman is my family name!"

"Is it really?" I say, cringing inside. "What a funny coincidence."

"Where in Germany is your grandmother from?"

One of my teachers at boarding school was a proud German woman named Olga Ackerman. Whenever students asked her for personal stories, she always gave the same reply: "Germans are a formal people. We do not make idle chitchat," and her mystique grew. We took it upon ourselves to create a thrilling life story for her that was sure to become legend.

"She grew up in Heidelberg," I say.

"I am from Speyer!"

I smile along with him, as if I understand the significance of that.

"Perhaps we are related," he says. "You said your name is Adele?" He extends his hand to shake mine. "My name is Gerhard. Pleased to meet you."

"Pleased to meet you, Gerhard."

We met only moments ago, and already Gerhard and I are chatting like friends. He doesn't behave like a German soldier. And he doesn't look like one, either. His dark hair, sleepy, almond-shaped eyes the color of army fatigues, and strong, handsome nose give him character, but in a regular-British-bloke kind of way. If he traded his uniform for civilian clothes, he'd fit right in at the London pub where I worked. Maybe not all German soldiers are mindless zombies with no will of their own, performing their duties without question. I almost wish he were a typical soldier. At least then I'd know what to expect from him.

"What brings you to this area?" Gerhard asks.

"I'm visiting friends. I don't travel often, so before I return to Paris I want to sightsee as much as possible. I stopped here because I was curious about the factory. I didn't expect to find such an impressive building in the middle of the countryside."

"It is even more impressive on the inside. Would you like me to take you on a tour?"

"A tour?" A warm bead of sweat rolls from my temple and joins the many others drenching my hairline. "But there are guards. Am I allowed inside the factory?"

"Ordinarily, no one is permitted inside without a pass," he says, "However, they make an exception for schoolchildren like you, for field trips."

Schoolchildren? How old does the guard think I am? My identity card clearly states an age of twenty-two. I think back to our meeting. The notebook drew his attention away from the ID check. He didn't actually look at my identification.

"I've never been inside a factory before." Excitement threatens to burst out of me like scorching rays of sunshine. "A tour would be very nice, thank you."

"Okay. Can you come back in three days? The same time you arrived today?"

"Yes, I think so." I wave. "Good-bye, Gerhard, I will see you then."

"Good-bye, and have a good afternoon."

I begin walking down the road toward my bicycle, when suddenly Gerhard calls out, "Adele, one moment please!"

The excitement drains out of me. How did I stupidly fall for his story? A field trip to a German-operated factory? Oh, I could just kick myself for being so gullible.

I spin around on my heels. "Yes?"

"I saw your drawings. In your notebook. They are quite good," he says. "If it is not too much trouble, could you please draw a picture of Zucker? In exchange for the tour? She is a good dog, more intelligent and obedient than some people, and so much like the dog my sister and I had as children. I believe you could capture that. The drawing would make a lovely gift for my family back home."

"Yes, I would be happy to draw her," I say. I run back, raising my camera. "I will take her photo, so I have an image to work from."

Gerhard and the dog stand side by side, at attention, and I position them within the viewfinder. Only Gerhard smiles.

I snap the photo of my canine subject, set against a backdrop of the factory's front entrance. The best shot of the day.

"I am finished," I say. "I will see you in three days."

We say good-bye once again. I hold back a smile all the way to my bike. As I ride away, the exhilaration building in my chest, like soda pop under pressure, bubbles out in a fit of uncontrollable giggling.

I did it. *Take that, Pierre! I'll be the best spy you ever saw!*

That pledge brings a hard lump to my throat. A memory unexpectedly rushes back to me. My tenth birthday. The day I said those same words to my brother.

That afternoon, my mother called me to the kitchen to bake a mystery cake. The kind of cake Nancy Drew would love. It didn't surprise me that she clipped the recipe from our local newspaper. She wanted to fit in with all the other American mothers. She'd even dropped her accent. Sometimes I begged to hear the voice of the girl she used to be.

Behind me, the back door rattled open. My brother rushed through the kitchen to set an armload of books and boxes on the table. Rocking on his heels, he grinned at me like he was up to something.

"Whatcha got there?" I asked, edging closer to the pile. My mother frowned down at me, a reminder that slang words belonged outside. "I mean, what do you have there?"

He wiggled the lid of the box free. Inside was a metal device with gadgets and a small light bulb on it. A plaque below the bulb displayed puzzling patterns of dots and dashes.

I leaned forward on my elbows, too excited to remember my manners. "What is that?"

"It's a Fleron telegraph signaler. Nick and I saw an ad for it in

Boys' Life. We've been saving nickels since February. That's why I couldn't go to the movies with you."

So that was the reason. I was worried Tom didn't want me around anymore.

I leaned closer. "What's it do?"

Tom flipped to the magazine advertisement and read it to me. "Thomas Edison and many a great man started his career as a telegraph operator. Every boy that expects to get to first base in scouting or in life should know the Morse code." He turned the page sideways. "See, right here it says this signaler is the latest and easiest way to learn the code, and no Scout can afford to be without one."

"Wow." I held my finger over the signal lever. "Can I try it?"

Tom pulled the device away, even though an understanding of Morse code was one of the most important skills a person could have to get through life! What would I do if he wouldn't let me practice on his signaler?

"Can I read the instruction booklet?" I asked, begging with sad eyes.

"I guess so," he said. "Don't bend the pages."

Mother picked up a book. The cover was filled with bold purple words. "*Secret Messages*: *How to Read and Write Them.* Written for boys and girls who like to exercise their minds." She set the book on the table. "That certainly sounds like you, Tom."

"And like me too," I said.

Her flour-dusted fingers patted my hand. "And like you too, Betty."

Within Tom's belongings, I saw his prized Boy Scout code wheel our aunt Libby had sent him all the way from Great Britain. I knew for sure he was up to something big.

"Are you playing cops and robbers?" I asked. "Jailbreak?"

"Nah, a bunch of us are playing capture the flag with Morse code clues."

"Wow, can I be on your team?"

"I dunno, Betty. You're too small. You'll get hurt."

"But I'm fast! Nobody will catch me. Can I play? Please?"

I squeezed my eyes shut and clasped hands to my chest, wishing with all my might.

"All right, listen. You're fast and sneaky, so I'll let you be our spy. Do you want to?"

"Do I!" I hollered, and Mother turned with a warning finger held to her lips.

With the smell of mystery cake hanging in the air and rainbows from the glass drawer knobs dancing about the linoleum at our feet, I gave Tom a tight hug that he didn't even try to wriggle out of.

"I'll be the best spy you ever saw!"

We never played that game of capture the flag. On my most memorable birthday we happily celebrated together, unaware that my mother and brother had only days to live.

Nineteen

Today's the day Robbie finally gets fresh air and exercise. My legs are still sore from yesterday's ride to the factory and they really need a rest. But I know how much Robbie is looking forward to our walk. I'd hate to disappoint him.

I knock on the side of the wine rack, saying, "It's me, are you in there?"

"Yeah, I'm here," he says.

I enter his hidden room. He's cross-legged on the cot, hunched over his playing cards.

"Are you ready to go?" I ask.

I walk to the end of the cot when he doesn't lift his bowed head. He's not looking at his cards, like I thought, but a letter and a postcard.

I sit opposite him. "Hey, what's up?"

He hands me the postcard. It looks like a miniature, hand-written newspaper, complete with articles, and a word jumble, and even a comic strip.

"*The Randolph News*," I say, reading the headline. I skim the articles and smile. "Is this a newspaper from your family?"

"Isn't it great? My sister Sarah makes them up herself. She keeps me up-to-date on all sorts of stuff. That's the last card I received before I"—he shrugs, giving me a half grin—"well, before I crashed here."

"I love her drawings," I say. "And her comic's really funny."

He picks up the letter. "When I left for my first flight, I brought along the last letter and newspaper I got from her. I guess I thought they'd bring me good luck."

I'm so curious to know what's in the letter. His sister Sarah is a fan of Deanna Durbin, just like I am. Are we alike in other ways? I'd love to know more about the rest of his family too.

"Want me to read you the letter?" Robbie asks, and I realize I'm leaning so far forward I'm practically already reading it.

I sit back, laughing. "Okay."

" 'Dear Robbie,' " he says. " 'I received your latest letter. I hope you received mine. Sorry if I seemed a bit moody. I had an awful cold then, and Mama said it made me downright miserable to be around. Well! I don't know about that.

" 'We had Uncle Earl and Aunt Mae to dinner on Sunday. We had chicken and all the fixings. And cupcakes for dessert. Your favorites. Am I making you hungry? Sorry if I am. You probably don't get to eat that well over there. Am I right? Uncle Earl said to tell you his golf game has suffered since you left. He and Aunt Mae think about you all the time. And they're not the only ones. See that wet spot on the paper (I circled it with fountain pen)? That's where Donna Sue's tear fell. I told her to quit the mush, you're not *her* brother! But she and Marlene pray for you daily. They're just sick with worry. My friends are such saps!' "

I frown, wondering about these girls, Donna Sue and Marlene.

They can rest easy. Robbie is in good hands, thank you very much.

Robbie pulls his knees to his chest and rests his head on them. Passing the letter to me, he says, "Can you finish reading it?"

"Sure." Holding the letter at arm's reach to catch light from the window, I say, " 'Liza had the baby. Mama says he's the sweetest, most good-natured baby around, just like you were. I don't know about that. You, good-natured? Only teasing! How does it feel to be an uncle? Do you feel older? I don't feel any different now that I'm an aunt.

" 'Mama can't write to you today, she's helping Liza tend to baby William. But she'll write again tomorrow. She wants me to remind you to be a good boy and above all be a gentleman.' " I read the next lines to myself first, otherwise I won't be able to keep my voice steady when I read them aloud. I take a breath and say, " 'Keep your head high. We miss you like the dickens. Stick it to the Germans and come home safe, Bub! Lovingly, Sarah.' "

I set the paper on his blanket.

"What a nice letter," I say, but Robbie's head doesn't rise from his kneecaps.

I don't know what else to say. It's heartbreaking to see him this unhappy. I scoot down the cot until we're side by side, put my arm around him, and lay my head on his shoulder. No matter how long it takes, I'll sit right here with him until he feels better.

After a few minutes, his hand squeezes mine.

"You're lucky to have a family that cares about you so much," I tell him. "You'll see them again."

Nodding, Robbie folds the letter over the card and tucks them under his pillow.

"My oldest sister, Liza, had a baby," he says. "I should have been there. I should be at home, helping out, and I'm not."

"I'm sure they understand. You left to do something really important. And really brave. They're pulling for you back home."

He nods again and says, "Thanks, Adele," but he doesn't seem convinced. "I think I just have too much time to think down here."

This dreary cellar has become a prison cell. Robbie is bright and sweet by nature, and being trapped down here all day is sending him to dark places.

"I can fix that," I say, pulling him up from the cot when I stand. "Let's get out of here. Do you have your identification?"

He pats his shirt pocket.

I lead him by the hand from his hidden room. At the cellar door, I say, "You'll have to follow my rules. No talking. If somebody asks you an offhand question like 'Have the time?' don't toss back an answer. I'll do all the talking. Don't gawk around like a tourist. Look at me. Don't dawdle. Walk as if we have a destination in mind. Got all that?"

"I think so." Robbie shields his eyes against the onslaught of sunlight. "I feel like a bat leaving its cave in the middle of the day."

"You're evolving into a creature of the night," I say in a spooky voice. "Now, *shush*."

Near the end of the laneway, he says, "Adele?"

He managed to string out my name into four syllables and a three-note vocal range. I smile at the pronunciation and say, "Yes?"

His Adam's apple bobs in his throat. "I, um—"

I lower his hand from his eyes.

"I don't know how to say this."

"But we're outside now," I say, glancing up and down the street. "Tell me later."

His mouth opens to say something else, even though I warned him not to.

"Robbie, you know the rules. Is what you want to tell me important enough to get shot and killed over?" He considers this for a few seconds, but since I already know the answer I say, "Didn't think so."

Arm in arm, we walk briskly to the Seine, never slowing to take in the sights or linger in one place long enough to attract more than a passing glance. Whenever we find ourselves in the presence of German soldiers, I lay my head on Robbie's arm. We stroll past like a lovesick couple with eyes only for each other.

I direct Robbie with a tug on his arm. We cross the avenue, dodging a steady stream of bicycle traffic, to connect with a cobblestone lane. We pass a handful of shops and a bistro before the road lets out onto a quiet residential street. Within the bustle of background din behind us, I pick out the faint clatter of a chair scraping against the rutted bistro patio. The noise might have been innocent, but the hastiness of it—as if the patron leapt up— triggers my suspicion.

I pull Robbie by the arm, upping the pace. We're walking targets, parading about in plain sight, in danger at all times.

A bristly feeling, like the static that makes my hair stand on end in winter, creeps up the back of my neck. I look behind us. A lone man is walking against the flow of the pedestrians, who are traveling in the direction of the shops. As he weaves through the crowds, I catch only glimpses of his clothing.

"I think we're being followed," I whisper.

I tug on him to change direction toward the livelier heart of the district in search of a crowd large enough to get lost in. We cross paths with a cyclist who gives us a cordial nod. An elderly woman sweeping her steps ambles into our path, and we jostle her in passing. Robbie wisely keeps his mouth shut and lets me do the apologizing. We're leaving witnesses behind like a trail of breadcrumbs.

Robbie glances over his shoulder.

I pull him frontward. "Don't look."

"But Adele, there's no one there. We're not being followed."

"We are."

He drops back to get a better look. "There's a young fella, but he's not giving us the time of day. He's entering a shop."

I put some real muscle into getting him moving again.

"Trust me. And be quiet."

The active hub of the district appears at the end of the street. Pedestrians are as likely to be German soldiers as anyone else. By walking into a crowd, we're giving the enemy on our tail the advantage of numbers. One shout and Robbie and I might find ourselves surrounded with no hope for escape.

My impetuous decision to dash for the alley across the street brings Robbie flailing down on one knee. The only pair of men's shoes available was a size too large. Like a puppy, his big feet are disproportionate to the rest of him. They are not making for a fleet-footed getaway.

"Oh, the misery," Robbie groans, rubbing his knee as he stands.

Once we reach the cover of the alley, I break into a run. Robbie flaps along next to me. We come out in a shaded courtyard, bound by buildings on all sides but one. There will be no getting at us without first funneling down the alley.

I release Robbie's arm and take a running leap at the low, crumbling stone wall that fences us in. I vault over the top and land feet together on the other side. Robbie straddles the wall. Wings of fabric flutter open on his pant leg to show a nasty scrape on his knee.

I wave him down. "Anyone coming?"

With a shake of his head, he drops to the ground.

I do a quick visual search for a hiding place. A nearby church will have to do. I loop my arm through Robbie's. We stroll crosswise through the street to the church.

The alcove behind the decoratively carved archway gives us a shadowed lookout. We nestle into it, jockeying for space. The tight squeeze forces our bodies to intertwine in a hug. Robbie's heartbeat pulses like a frightened rabbit's against my shoulder. The warmth of his hand radiates through my blouse. Goose bumps spring up on my bare flesh.

Our eyes meet. He leans toward me, tilting his head.

My breath catches. Robbie has chosen me for his first kiss? What do I do? Do I want to kiss him back?

Without giving it another thought, I stand taller to meet his lips halfway.

But Robbie's lips carry on past my mouth to my ear where he whispers, "Do you still believe we were followed?"

My cheeks burn. Robbie didn't want to kiss me after all. And I'd been prepared, excited even, to kiss him back. I could almost cry with disappointment. Dropping to flat feet, I press my back against the wall.

"Didn't you feel the sensation of being watched?" I say. "His stare was like a rope lassoed about my waist. You didn't feel that?"

"No, Adele. And if somebody was chasing us, he sure did a lousy job of it, don't you think? We didn't hear or see a thing."

I rest my forehead against the smooth stone wall.

"Hold on," Robbie says. "He's climbing over the wall."

I stretch on my tiptoes. "I can't see."

"It's the fella I saw going into the shop."

"What is he doing?"

"He's at the street. He's bending down, pretending to be preoccupied by something on his shoe. He's looking for us." Robbie flattens against the wall. "He's getting into a bicycle taxi. Here, quick, switch places with me."

We do a rigid circuitous dance, careful to remain hidden.

I move into position as the taxi rolls away. A cold sweat comes over me.

"Did you get a look at him?" Robbie asks.

"A young man in civilian clothes with a thin build and neatly combed brown hair?"

"Yes, that's him all right. What do you make of that?"

I honestly don't know what to make of it. We were followed by Shepherd.

Twenty

I drop Robbie off in front of his safe house.

"I can't come in. I have to talk to Denise right away," I say, turning to leave.

His sad droop can't sway me, this is too important.

"I'll visit tomorrow. Promise!"

Denise found housing in a charming stone home owned by a widower, Stefan, whose Jewish wife, a French-born citizen, was handed over by her own sister-in-law and sent to the German work camp on the outskirts of the city. She hasn't been heard from since.

Stefan often travels to the country for days at a stretch, to smuggle much needed meat and vegetables into Paris for his friends and extended family. This suits Denise just fine. She prefers to go through her day without relative strangers "hanging about and watching her every move," even if they are sympathetic to the cause.

I run the entire distance to Denise's until my throbbing shins feel ready to splinter.

Our coded knock—the first four notes of Beethoven's Fifth Symphony—allows us to identify each other without opening the door. The beats also represent Morse code for the letter *V*—dot, dot, dot, dash. As part of the V for Victory campaign, the BBC began playing the opening bars of Beethoven's Fifth to introduce its foreign broadcasts.

Against the weathered wood of the courtyard door around the back of the house, I follow three clipped taps with a heavier final knock. Denise lets me inside, and we sit across from each other at the kitchen table.

"Robbie and I were just followed by Shepherd," I say, catching my breath.

Her head jerks back in surprise. "The same Shepherd who got himself captured the night we dropped?"

"One and the same. We ran and hid, hoping to draw him out into the open. Robbie saw a man entering a shop behind us, and that same man showed up minutes later. I only got a peek at him, but I know it was Shepherd."

"Well, if it was him, there must be a logical explanation. He escaped or he was freed after questioning."

"But why was he following me?"

"Why wouldn't he follow you, Adele? Maybe he needed help from a fellow agent. Maybe he wanted to talk but couldn't approach because you weren't alone. He doesn't know Robbie. Seeing you with a strange man, he may have thought you were in danger."

Denise's reasoning confronts me with possibilities I didn't consider.

"He didn't run after us or follow too closely, though. He kept his distance. Why pretend to enter a shop? He wanted to watch us without being seen."

"I'll bet he was only curious. Or jealous."

I don't know what to think anymore. Did I totally misread the situation?

"Enough with that fretful face," Denise says. "Don't worry, if he needed help he would have found a way to get your attention." She drums her fingernails on the tabletop. "I know just the thing to take your mind off Shepherd."

I need her to take my mind off the other situation I read wrong, the near-kiss with Robbie. The closeness we shared in the alcove is something I didn't even know I wanted until it happened.

"Let's spend an hour at the Neptune Pool!" Denise cheers, as if that's a brilliant idea. "We'll relax, get some fresh air." My disapproving scowl forces her to add, "I know what you're going to say. You think it's a bad idea. I wholeheartedly disagree."

"I don't swim," I say.

"Please, Adele, I need some sunshine. I'm withering away in here. We're supposed to be playing regular French girls. And where are regular French girls on such a beautiful day? That's right, they're at the pool."

"It's not a good idea," I say. "And you can't wear me down, so don't even try."

Everywhere I look around the crowded pool deck I see scantily clad French girls and handsome blond men wearing skimpy shorts. Even Denise wears a two-piece bathing suit she bought off the black market. It covers her navel, of course, but just barely. I know what every man and woman at the pool probably looks like in their underwear now. And that's a whole lot more than I want to know about them.

A girl runs toward me, squealing, with a soldier hot on her trail. But we're surrounded by Germans. There's not much I can do to lend her a hand.

"I have you," the soldier says, scooping her up.

She bats his chest, putting on quite a show, as if being chased down and conquered by a German soldier behaving like a caveman is something to celebrate.

Denise taps my right shoulder. "Look. Twelve o'clock."

A soldier picks his way toward us, consulting a small book in his hands.

"Hello, girls. My name is Ludwig. It is sun and beautiful afternoon, I believe, and you?" he says. A nervous smile appears on his face, a rickety whitewashed picket fence of teeth. He searches the book. "Some time you would like a drink?"

"That would be nice, my friend and I would like that," Denise says, not slowing her clipped pace to help Ludwig understand.

"Fantastic. The Commodore Bar. Do you know it?"

Denise stretches her long legs in front of her to flick the water with her toes. "We do. We will meet you there at nine o'clock. My name is Lise. This is my friend Anise."

Yet another name to keep track of and answer to. When the war ends, will I remember how to go back to being plain Betty?

"Lise." Ludwig takes Denise's wrist. His lips brush the back of her hand. Switching to his native tongue, as though that might impress her, he says, "You are the loveliest woman I have seen in all of Paris." He turns to me, outstretched hand shaking, and tacks on a compulsory-sounding "Good day, Anise, it was my pleasure to be meeting you."

I cross my arms over the front of my blouse.

Denise's eyes narrow at the back of Ludwig's head as he saunters away. She rubs the back of her hand on her skirt.

"What's the big idea, dragging me into this?" I say. "I have a fifty-kilometer ride to a dead drop ahead of me tomorrow. You can't seriously be thinking of meeting him."

"You know what they say. Keep your friends close and your enemies closer."

———————

Denise calls on me at Estelle's at seven o'clock. With her last transmission for the day completed she hid her radio and eagerly raced out for a night on the town.

Transmitting radio messages from within the city carries enormous risks. The Gestapo combs the streets in vans equipped to detect radio signals. Whenever I see those vans coming, I wonder if some poor radio operator's goose is about to be cooked. Another detection method involves shutting down electricity. Like dominoes falling, the power goes out from house to house, apartment to apartment, to narrow the search. If the transmissions stop, a swarm of men in trench coats descend on the area with precision, leaving little chance for escape.

Limiting transmissions to five minutes is nearly impossible, even for Denise, a skilled and quiet transmitter. She pushes her luck to the brink. The way she sees it, the longer she goes without getting caught, the less likely it is to happen, which is the opposite of how I see it. Eventually, she might start believing capture isn't even a possibility for her anymore and get sloppy.

"Denise, you're done up like the dog's dinner," I say, borrowing one of my aunt's favorite phrases. It doesn't sound all that complimentary to me. I learned not to question those things while in Britain.

"Thank you." Denise holds up a handbag, wincing as if she expects me to hit her. "I had to have it. It's a wee little thing. And it didn't cost much. Do you like it?"

"Everything I know about handbags wouldn't fill that little handbag."

She gives my simple black skirt and blouse the once-over. "And yet, there would still be room in it for everything you know about fashion. Never heard of an iron?"

She unclasps the purse, reaches inside, and launches a surprise attack, wielding a tube of lipstick.

"Please don't make me look like a circus clown."

"Then you'd better stop fussing." She presses the makeup onto my bottom lip with feathered strokes. "You have nice lips. You should wear lipstick more often."

"I've never worn lipstick a day in my life."

Denise recoils in horror. "Sincerely? I will not leave this country without rectifying that." She licks her lips, mashes them together, and pops them apart. "Do that."

I try to follow her instructions, but my lips won't cooperate. And the lipstick is messy. I scrub my teeth clean with my finger.

"When I was a girl, I loved watching my mother apply her makeup. Putting on her face, she called it." Denise chuckles. "She's a character, my mum. I hope she's doing well back home. I'm sure she is. She's a tough old bird." She returns the metal tube to her handbag. "Are you going to do something with that mop you call hair?"

"I did. Thank you." There is nothing moplike about my best feature.

Denise takes it upon herself to make me more presentable, combing and tugging and molding my hair with pins until I feel like smacking her. Hair isn't worth as much effort as she's putting into it, especially when that hair belongs to *my* head.

"What about that pretty bracelet of yours?" Denise says. "Why aren't you wearing it for our special night out?"

"I don't wear jewelry."

"You'd rather it rot in your pocket?"

I had a hunch her curiosity would get the better of her, and she'd bring up my bracelet sooner or later. I draw it from the pocket of my skirt.

"After boarding school, I lived with my aunt and uncle in London. When I left for this mission, literally as I walked out the door, my aunt gave me this bracelet." I go through the tiny charms one by one. "This hedgehog represents my cousin Paul. He collects ceramic hedgehogs and has a pet one named Roly-Poly. The Yorkie dog is my cousin Philip. He and his dog, Biscuit, are inseparable. For reasons you can probably guess, the beer stein is my uncle Edward. Also for obvious reasons, my aunt Lib is the teapot."

I drop the bracelet into my pocket.

"What a thoughtful gift to remember them by." Denise runs through a cordoned-off section of my hair several times with her comb. "You're from the United States. Rather than return home, you went to live with your aunt?"

"My father remarried after my mother passed away. He was going to send for me when I left school, but the war changed his plans. And besides, he and his wife have a new baby. A little boy.

It ended up being for the best that I moved to London. I would have just gotten in the way."

After some hesitation, Denise says, "Oh, I see." She switches to her brush to tug out a tangle. "Robbie wasn't too pleased that you're going to the Commodore this evening."

My head jerks to glance over my shoulder. The large chunk of hair clutched within Denise's hand stays put.

I rub the sore spot on my head. "You talked to Robbie? What did he say?"

"It wasn't so much what he said. His mood took an abrupt downturn, even though I'd brought him some beans and canned fish from the black market." Denise wheedles a pin into my upswept hairdo. "You know, he likes you, Adele. Have you not noticed the lovesick goo-goo eyes he's given you since that day we rescued him?"

"We're just friends." My heart pounds as if I've been cornered with nowhere to run. "We're supposed to take care of him until he's sent back to Britain. That's what we signed up for." Through the window next to the sofa, I watch a pigeon waddle along the stone ledge. "I don't want him to be lonely while he's here, that's all. We owe it to his family to keep him safe."

"That's admirable. But he isn't like me, and he's not like you. He's soft, like a turtle without a shell. There's a war going on. War is dangerous. It's terrifying. Protect him too much and he might not last a minute out there. He has to reach England a man. Not a boy."

I rest my chin on the back of the sofa to hide the tears welling up in my eyes.

"Where is Marie?" Denise asks. "She should join us."

In the evenings, Marie sings her tone-deaf heart out in the

hallway to drown out the radio. Only one neighbor complained. She should be thankful for Marie's singing and use it to muffle the sounds of her own radio. Madame Richelieu, a sourpuss with a mean clenched mouth, is a neighbor to keep an eye on.

"Where will I be joining you?" Marie asks, entering the apartment.

"Speak of the devil," Denise says. "Were you eavesdropping outside the door by any chance, Marie?"

"If I say yes, will you be angry?"

"No, of course not."

"Then yes."

Like a butterfly setting down on a flower petal, she takes up the sofa opposite me and wraps her coltish legs within her skirt.

"We are going to the Commodore Bar tonight, Marie. Would you like to come?"

"What Denise means to say is we're going to a bar to fraternize with the enemy."

Skirt twirling, she runs to the door undeterred. "Oh, thank you, thank you, thank you! I will get ready. You won't tell Grand-mère, will you?"

"No, we won't," Denise says. "Right, Adele?"

I shrug. As if I have any say in the matter.

"I don't think this is a good idea," I say, after Marie skips home on cloud nine.

"You look divine. And that lipstick is hard to come by. Don't let it go to waste. We'll get tipsy on free champagne and laugh as men fall all over themselves to talk to us."

I bite my lip, seriously contemplating coming clean about my age. Denise is my closest friend. She'll understand. I've never gone out for a night on the town. My work shifts at the London pub ended in time for supper. The Commodore is a place for social butterflies, not caterpillars like me. I'll be the only inexperienced, socially inept person there.

"Marie's too young," I say.

"She will be fine."

Denise can't go to the bar without me, and I know it. Either we both go or neither of us does. I have an obligation to headquarters to keep us alive and out of trouble. They can't risk losing their link with France now, with the Allied attack possibly right around the corner, all over some free champagne.

"Just tell me this," I say, "why did you accept Ludwig's invitation?"

"Adele, the Germans don't have to play by the same rules." She grins. "And I am desperate for a cigarette."

Twenty-One

Piano music and cigarette smoke invite me inside the Commodore, where gorgeous women hang on the every word of officers attired in smart white dinner jackets, caps, and gloves. The distinguished atmosphere explains why Ludwig and his three friends greeted us in their finest uniforms.

Denise, smoking already and we haven't even found a table, taps me on the shoulder. I turn face-first into a swirling current of smoke.

"Your eyes are giving you away—you're thankful to be wearing lipstick, aren't you?" she says in her mile-a-minute French. "Can you imagine if we had left your hair down? Whatever would you do without me? Frump around like a man, that's what."

I crack a nervous smile. "You couldn't pay me to doll myself up like these women."

"Too late, my dolled-up friend."

Ludwig watches us with bewildered amusement. Why, the

evening promises to be a downright gabfest, what with everyone unable to understand one another. I, for one, can scarcely contain my excitement.

"Remember, we're here for the free champagne," I say to Denise, out of the corner of my mouth. "After a few drinks, we're leaving."

The last train of the day departs at eleven o'clock. Taking travel time into account, we need to leave the bar at ten thirty. And, really, how much mischief could Denise and I possibly get into in only an hour and a half?

I had too much to drink only once in my life, the night of my aunt's last Christmas party. I smashed two tiles in the parlor's Art Deco fireplace, nearly set a curtain ablaze after a brief reintroduction to cigarettes, and let a sweet Canadian soldier, who showed up on my aunt's doorstep wistful for Christmas, kiss my cheek beneath the mistletoe. But none of that bad behavior was my fault. My aunt's neighbor thought spiking my eggnog was a clever way to liven up the party. He changed his mind about that when I got sick on his shoes. I haven't touched a drop of alcohol since.

The waiter sets a glass of champagne in front of each of us.

Marie lifts her glass to peer through it. "I like the bubbles. They look so pretty."

"And expensive," Denise says.

Ludwig's friend, a blond boy named Karl, raises his glass. The other boys do the same. "*Zum Wohl!*" they cheer.

We join them in the toast, and I have a sip. Before I know it, my glass is empty. And then, before I know it again, another glass of champagne magically materializes on the table in front of me.

It's not long before my attention drifts away from intimidating surroundings to be swept up in the witty stories of charismatic Karl. When he offers me a third glass of champagne, I say yes. Just to be polite.

Denise leans into me from her neighboring chair. "For a girl who doesn't smoke, you look awfully cozy with that cigarette."

Smoke rakes burned nails down the back of my throat. A rasping cough all but shatters my Kate Hepburn–like air of sophistication. "I don't smoke. *Anise* does."

I giggle along with Denise, but then clarity splits my champagne haze. For a few seconds of fun over a private joke, I spilled a truth about my identity in a none-too-private place. No one appears to have heard me, but the time has come and gone to shape up. What's happening to me? My sense of duty has shriveled like a grape in the sun.

When I close my eyes, the room rocks this way and that, tipping and swirling like a carnival ride. Opening them, I visually grab hold of objects to steady myself. The night is turning into my aunt's party all over again. If I don't get off this wild ride, I might end up kissing Karl in the coat-check room.

"Denise, I think it's time for us to leave."

She gulps her champagne. Taps the bottom of her glass to catch every last drop.

"*Pourquoi?*" She checks her watch. "We have more than twenty minutes. Do you know how many glasses of champagne I can drink in twenty minutes?"

Across the sea of heads and caps, I notice a couple entering the bar. The woman, draped in a fur stole, wears a smile that can be seen clear across the room. And that's why I don't recognize her at first.

An officer seated at a table near the piano raises his arm to attract their attention. Recognition comes into their faces, and Dr. Devereux's wife, whose hand-me-down clothes I'm wearing at this very moment, gives him a friendly wave in return.

She hangs off the arm of her officer, beaming with pride, as if he's a trophy she won. When the soldiers in the bar salute him she gazes at his face in adoration.

I watch their every gesture as they join the party at the table. So, too, did the *Blitzweiben*, or "little gray mice," as they're called; the women of the German Auxiliary. They scowl their disapproval, but if François's wife notices, she doesn't let on. She is having a marvelously scandalous time and she doesn't care who knows it.

The lover of a German officer would have no qualms about informing. I'm willing to bet she visits the Avenue Foch whenever she can, chomping at the bit to give up neighbors she's known for years. What would stop her from turning in a mangy young stranger who showed up on her doorstep, an obvious outsider looking for help?

In Denise's ear, I say, "Honestly, we should go."

"Yes, you said that a moment ago. We are not leaving until that champagne flute of yours is empty."

I pick up my glass, swirling the pretty, expensive bubbles, and try to relax. I guess a few more minutes of fun can't hurt. Besides, I'm sitting quietly on the opposite side of the crowded bar, not dancing on tables and singing "The Star-Spangled Banner." Madame Devereux will never recognize me from the back of my head.

At the next table, the officer seated behind me begins to complain rather loudly. Paris doesn't have quite the spark he anticipated. I eavesdrop for a while, snickering over his blundering use of the French language.

"Where is the life?" he asks. "The joie de vivre I heard so much about? I ask you, where is the party?"

That final question, enunciated for dramatic effect, receives a big laugh from his tablemates. How clever of him to expect a party in a country squashed beneath Germany's thumb. How funny to demand joy from people living without fuel and light and heat and hot water. Everyone I've met since coming to France has friends and loved ones who were taken away or killed.

"Where is the party?" My fingers clench into aching fists. "You should have come before you were here."

Marie coughs a mouthful of champagne back into her glass. She covers her gaping mouth with her hand, looking at me with complete shock.

Denise grabs my forearm so tightly it's sure to bruise. She sends a seductive grin over her chair's headrest. "Please forgive my naughty friend, she's only teasing. Champagne makes her ever so cheeky."

The hint of depravity in the officer's laugh makes my skin crawl.

Denise presses against me. "That wasn't funny. We're lucky that soldier is intoxicated enough to overlook such a comment."

"I'm sorry," I whisper. "I didn't mean to say that."

Things are steamrolling out of control. I never should have come to the bar. Denise seems at home in a place like this, but I've waded into territory I'm not cut out for yet. I'm floundering and about to take Denise and Marie down with me.

In that same moment, I become aware of anti-British jokes darting around on the other side of me.

"Denise, we've been here an hour and a half. We really should go now."

"Yes, we'd better leave. You're two sheets to the wind."

It becomes clear to me that we aren't meant to get out of this bar without a fight, when one of Ludwig's friends, an ugly duckling whose name I didn't bother to remember, stands at the head of our table, his hand raised to mimic holding a cup of tea, pinkie out. In a near-perfect, effeminate British accent he says, "I'm off to fight for my king and country." On any other day the impersonation alone would be enough to send Denise flying over the table. Not content to leave it at that, he follows up with a slur against homosexuals and wraps it all up with this little bow, "We Brits love to have our arses handed to us on silver platters."

I sit tight as a coiled spring, waiting to intercept Denise before she can tear the ugly duckling to unidentifiable shreds. Feathers are about to fly.

Denise stares at her empty champagne glass. She doesn't budge.

Like a pious figurine, Marie presses her delicate porcelain-white hands together on her lap and stays perfectly still, her stunned gaze locked on Denise and me. I promise to be eternally grateful if the prayer coursing through her mind receives a swift response.

Things go on that way for the three of us for a heart-stopping minute, while the festive mood outside our little bubble doesn't take so much as a hit.

During our SOE training at the manor, our ability to handle anti-British sentiment was put to the test. It's a surefire bet agents will encounter it in the field, not only from the Germans, but from the French. Anti-Allied propaganda posters and leaflets litter Paris. Some trainees, unable to take the mock bashing lightly, cracked and started shooting their mouths off.

Denise must have held up well enough during those tests, but it's one thing to deal with fake insults in a training session led by a fellow Brit and quite another when the insults come from the mouth of a soldier whose maniacal leader has partially destroyed your hometown and continues to bomb it on an almost daily basis.

A murmur whistles out from between Denise's clenched teeth. "Get me out of here before I do something I'll regret."

I stagger to my feet. "Thank you for the lovely evening. We have to be going."

Karl, the only boy in the group who speaks French well, comes around to pull my chair out for me. "Must you leave so soon? Stay and talk some more with me. I can see you home after curfew."

"No," I insist. "I enjoyed talking to you, but we need to catch the train."

He gives me a peck on the cheek. "It was nice to meet you, Anise. See you another time, I hope."

"My pleasure to meet you all."

I grab Denise's arm. Marie scrambles up to grab the other one. For a slim girl, Denise certainly is hefty. I stuff her new handbag into her hands.

One step at a time we inch closer to the exit and Mrs. Devereux's table, with Denise wedged in the middle of our slow, tipsy procession. I untie the silk scarf from my neck and fasten it around my head to shield my profile, then pretend to study the artwork on the walls. As I pass the wife's chair, her distinctively catty voice can be overheard.

"Dieter is taking me to the coast for a romantic holiday," she says. "My husband believes I've arranged a visit with my sister. Gullible old fool." In a whisper that isn't much of a whisper at all, she adds, "That woman's scarf is gorgeous. I own one similar to it, but hers is an obvious fake."

Sure and steady, we keep moving. Just when I feel confident we're in the clear, Denise growls, "This place would be great if it weren't for all the damn Germans!"

I drag her from the bar without looking back, until cool fresh air brushes my cheeks.

"Denise, what were you thinking?"

She sucks in an indignant breath. "You heard that son of a bitch. I should have killed him when I had the chance!"

Despite the impending curfew, the streets are deserted. Right about this time the theaters are dropping their curtains. The commissionaires will be shouting to the crowds in the cloak-rooms to hurry up. The bars, too, are about to empty.

"You're making a scene, Denise. Stop, please, before somebody hears us."

Her finger wags beneath my chin. "Do not tell me what to do. Those men, those evil men, are drinking champagne. They are having a party in a city that does not belong to them. With not a care in the world. What will they do tomorrow, and the next day, and the next? Kill wonderful, loving British sons and brothers, and—" Her fists shake at her sides. "Those men in the bar are alive! That is not fair!"

"What does fairness have to do with it? This was *your* idea."

"You have some nerve, don't you, Adele? All high and mighty, acting innocent after the fact. I didn't see anyone twisting your arm; you're here same as me. What was wrong with you in there? Three glasses of champagne and you become a babbling idiot?"

I glare at her, unable to come back with the truth. How was I to know? Those were the first three glasses of champagne I ever had!

Marie dabs her eyes. "Please don't fight. Let's go home for a nightcap."

"Yes, let's go, Marie," Denise says, taking her by the arm.

She volleys unsure glances between Denise and me.

"It's all right, Marie. You two go ahead."

I watch them until they've traded one moonlit street for the next, Marie's attentive hand at Denise's elbow.

In the middle of the street, I stand trembling and alone, trapped within a river of emotions.

So much damage can be done unintentionally, in the blink of an eye.

When I turn to leave, I catch sight of a shadowed figure creeping out from the nearest alley. He pauses. We consider each other. He marches straight for me.

We did lengthy cross-country runs at Wanborough Manor, and mountain treks through the rugged Scottish highlands. At the best of times, stone sober, I can barely walk in the heeled shoes I borrowed from Marie, much less run to save my life, as I've been trained. The man giving chase will be on top of me in seconds.

"*Adele, c'est moi.*"

I skitter to a stop. "Robbie?"

"*Oui.*"

The voice matches Robbie, the language does not. The darkened shape steps into a sliver of moonlight cascading between two trees. Even with so little to go on, I recognize him. He runs to me.

When he's close enough to switch to English, he says, "Why did Denise leave you by yourself out here in the middle of the street?" He draws closer to my face. "Adele, what's the matter? Are you crying?"

"Denise and I had an argument. I'm okay," I say, even though I don't feel or sound the least bit okay.

Robbie's arm slides around my back. He slowly pulls me into a loose hug. I throw my arms around him with such intensity it knocks him off balance. Hugging tighter, I press my bleary eyes against his chest.

"Don't worry, it will all work out," Robbie says in my ear. His hand strokes my hair. "Denise is your friend."

We gradually part from the hug.

"Feel a bit better now?" he asks.

"I do." It happened so quickly, but I do feel a little better. "You shouldn't be here. It's too dangerous. Let's get you back to the cellar."

"Adele, I'm leaving." He takes my hand. "Tomorrow. I came to say good-bye."

I knew Robbie would leave, of course, but it never fully sank in that one day he wouldn't be here anymore.

My time with the boy who literally crashed into my life has come to an end. There will be no more shared jokes and stories. No more card games. He has run out of chances to beat me at rummy. If only I knew this morning that our walk in the sunshine would be our last happy time together.

Emotions well up in my chest all at once and come out of my mouth a half-stifled sob.

"I'll miss you, Adele. I'm falling in love with you."

Why is Robbie telling me this now, when he's about to leave

forever? Even if I feel the same way, I can't tell him so, and it's tearing my heart in two. I can't tell him how much he means to me. I can't tell him about the utter panic I'm feeling now, as I imagine myself walking away from him tonight. I can't say anything that might sway him to stay here with me. If he stays here any longer, he will be captured or killed. How could I do that to him? How could I ever do that to his family? I pull my hand away.

"Robbie, you don't love me. In two weeks' time you'll be back with your squadron, where you belong. I'll be just a fading memory. Someone you knew during your adventure in France."

"No, Adele." He takes my hand again and holds it firmly in his. "My feelings for you are real. I won't forget you. Not when I get back to my squadron. Not ever. And when all this is over, I'll do whatever it takes to find you again."

His hand cradles my chin. He tilts my head back. My eyes slip shut as he leans in. I stand on tiptoe to meet him halfway.

The kiss is shy, and sweet, and perfect.

"Robbie, you have to go now. Please don't think about me anymore."

"But Adele—"

"I mean it. Concentrate on getting home to your family," I said, falling to pieces inside. "Stay safe."

"I will. I guess this is good-bye, then."

We stand in the middle of the street, staring into each other's eyes. The last good-bye has to be mine. I hold it back as long as possible.

Finally I whisper, "Good-bye."

I run past the bar to a parked horse-drawn hansom carriage with tears streaming down my face. I give the driver Estelle's address as he helps me onto to the seat. He takes his place at the rear, on his raised platform, and shakes the reins.

Champagne sloshes in my stomach, threatening to come back up. Clearing tears from my cheeks, I concentrate on the clomping of the horse's hooves.

I hope I did the right thing in breaking our hearts.

Twenty-Two

Twenty-five kilometers into my ride the pounding headache I woke with shows no sign of letting up. I vow to never, ever drink champagne again.

I turn onto a dirt path that disappears into the bush and appears too narrow for even one vehicle to safely travel. When I find an overturned rusted birdcage at the side of the path, I climb off my bicycle and wheel it the length of fifteen strides. Right away, I spot the Queen Anne's lace wildflowers at the base of a massive oak, marking the location of the dead drop where a top-secret message and hard to come by crystals for Denise's radio are hopefully hidden.

When I first learned that wireless radio frequency is tuned by crystals, I imagined they were glittering gemstones. But they're actually a sliver of quartz encased in a black plastic box that plugs into two sockets on the top of the set.

The crystals might not look like treasure, but they are

valuable. Without them, Denise's suitcase radio—our lifeline with London—is useless.

I lean my bicycle against the tree and sit on a woody seat of thick, exposed roots.

One log among the sticks and branches littered about the forest floor stands out. I'm confident I wasn't followed, but I don't want to rush straight to the dead drop and give away its location. Keeping my eyes and ears open, I rest only long enough to catch my breath. If my muscles cool, they'll tighten and protest all the way back to Paris. And if I sit still too long I'm bound to obsess about last night's final good-bye with Robbie.

The lichen-covered log looks real enough until I touch it. It isn't wood at all, but carved plaster, carefully painted to resemble the oak. I wiggle the end of the log free of the base. Inside the hidden compartment is a small silk bag. Loosening the drawstring, I check the contents. The contact came through. The coded message and the radio crystals are present and accounted for.

It's now my job to guard them on the next leg of their journey.

I cap the plaster log and hide the silk bag in the hollow handlebars of my bicycle for safekeeping. If the bag is discovered during a search, I face instant arrest.

I leave the secluded spot in the woods and set off down the road. For an hour I ride through the countryside, cheeks baking stiff in the sun. Wind whistles through my hair. A river of sweat trickles the length of my back.

The longer I ride, the more time I have to think about last night. I ruined what should have been a fun evening. I imagine Denise is in no mood to see me, but I have no choice but to visit her when I return to Paris. What if I messed up badly enough to ruin our friendship?

I don't have to think too deeply to remember how Robbie's lips felt on mine when we shared our first kisses ever with each other, how good it felt to be in his arms after my argument with Denise. And I'll never be able to forget the pain and confusion in his eyes in our final moment, as if everything was happening too quickly. As if our good-bye didn't go the way he hoped it would.

I shake myself free of these thoughts as I descend into the valley, welcoming the cooler air.

As I round a sharp bend, a wall of dense fog greets me, having already erased the landscape as if it were merely a pencil drawing. Tendrils swirl across the ground, beckoning. Braking hard, I swerve but keep the bike upright. The tire kicks up a spray of dirt and gravel.

I ease forward on the bike, slower now. I glide through a surreal white dream, with no more than ten feet of road visible to keep me on course, past the occasional eerie shadow of a tree at the road's edge or the metal carcass of an abandoned car, left where it ran out of petrol to decay or become target practice for fighter planes.

The minutes languidly tick by. Peace fills me. I can't remember the last time I felt this free, soaring alone, like a bird through a heavenly cloud. Within the shroud of fog, the war doesn't exist. I might be anywhere I want to be outside of France. I don't have a high-risk job to do. I'm a girl on a bicycle, out for a ride. For these all-too-brief moments I savor the break from reality.

At last, the fog thins to reveal the crushing truth.

I roll to a stop. In my mind, a rational voice issues a flurry of commands, but my suddenly sluggish reaction time stalls what should be a swift getaway.

Roughly three hundred meters ahead, a German roadblock is

set up on the same bridge that was clear on my first pass earlier in the day. Ten armed men wander the area, talking and casually observing the river. If even a single soldier had been facing this direction as I came cheerfully rolling out from the fog that would have been the end of the road for me, in more than one sense of the word.

Hunkered low, I wheel the bike backward, watching the bridge for signs that I've been spotted. I have no idea who they intend to snag at the roadblock. I haven't seen anyone on this road for miles.

That bridge is the only way to access the road on the opposite side of the river. Rerouting will add half a day to my timeline. And Denise will be forced to postpone her scheduled transmission of messages to those relying on her at London headquarters.

I can't turn back and I can't go forward.

At the river's edge, smooth stones are visible below the surface. Beyond the span of a few strides, murkiness hides the depth. I snap a reed and toss it into the water. The rushing current carries it away in no time flat.

Warm foamy water swirls around my shoes. I drag the bike across the rocky riverbed. Knee-deep, I stop, shaking with fear. I can't do this. If only I could stay put, right where I am, I wouldn't have to worry about drowning or the ten Nazi soldiers.

I think of Denise waiting for the messages and the parts she needs to operate her radio. I force my feet to shuffle forward. The river climbs steadily to my waist. I hoist my bicycle above the surface. The message, written on rice paper to make it edible in an emergency, and the fragile radio crystals won't hold up to water. My arms sag under the awkward weight, muscles aching from the constant counterbalance.

At the center of the stream, intense panic settles heavily in my chest. My legs fight the current. I rest the bicycle on my head, secure a firmer hold on the frame. With a grunt, I hoist it higher, huffing shallow breaths, as cold water corsets my ribcage.

Faster and faster I push through the receding river. When the water level drops to my knees I lower the bike, shuddering inside and out. Able to run at last, I storm the bank on trembling legs. With everything I have left in me, I haul the bike up the steep muddy slope. At the top, I honestly don't know whether to let loose a triumphant scream or collapse into a blubbering heap.

"You there!"

A German soldier steps out from behind a bramble of wild roses. He gives me a curious stare, not quite sure what to make of the sopping wet girl frozen with fear like a snared rabbit. He must be suspicious of me. People with nothing to hide don't wade across a river fully clothed while carrying a bicycle. They cross the bridge.

We stare at each other. He's young, like me. Is he also frantically thinking through training lessons, unsure of the correct next move? If he knew what to do in this situation he would have already done it.

To escape, I have to get the upper hand before he pulls a weapon or calls for help. I throw one drenched leg over my bicycle and settle onto the seat. I eye him up through damp, windblown curls.

In German, I say, "I have grenades. Come near me and I won't hesitate to blow us both sky high."

He looks over his shoulder in the direction of the others, and then back to me. After a brief hesitation, he begins a cautious retreat.

"Pretend you never saw me," I say, pushing off.

Pedaling like mad, I blaze across the field on a course that eventually intersects with the road. Many kilometers later, I pull over to the side of the road to catch my breath. I may not be able to put stars in an enemy's eyes the way Denise can, but now I know which trick works to get me out of a mess.

I'm a very good liar.

TWENTY-THREE

As I ride up to Stefan's to meet with Denise, I check the surroundings for soldiers hanging about suspiciously close to the
house. When the house and courtyard get the all clear, I hop off
my bike. I spin it to face the direction of the road, in case I need to
make a quick getaway, before leaning it against the vine-covered
wall.

Denise opens the door. Her smiling face flinches at the sight
of me.

"What happened to you? You look like a drowned rat!"

"It's a long story," I say, even though it really isn't. "Can I
come in?"

"Yes, yes, of course." She steps back from the doorway, waving me inside. "Stefan is away until the end of the week. We have
the house all to ourselves."

Patting sweat from my brow, I say, "Nothing like a fifty-
kilometer bicycle trip to make you regret a champagne binge."

"I felt rather under the weather this morning as well."

I walk toward the stairs, eager to lie down and put my swollen feet up, when Denise grabs me by the arm.

"Adele, last night was not my finest hour. I behaved very unprofessionally. I don't know what to say, really. I feel as if no amount of apology can make it better."

"It's okay." I'm glad to have the unspoken tension between us broken, no matter how much it embarrasses me to rehash my behavior.

"Please forgive me, so we can go back to being friends."

"I forgive you. And I'm really sorry too, Denise. Do you forgive me?"

"Of course I do. From here on out we fly right, no more mucking up. Let's never allow anything to come between us again!" Denise holds her head with both hands. "Lord, I need to quiet down a wee bit."

We make our way to the attic, which is empty apart from a large, velvet-covered divan, a tattered rug, and Denise's small stash of belongings.

I remove my notepad from my breast pocket and carefully tear out two sheets.

"Here are my notes from today's ride: the locations of German troops and garrisons between Paris and Taverny," I say. "And you don't need to tell me, I know my penmanship looks like chicken scratch. If you need help reading it, just ask."

"Fantastic. Headquarters seems to really appreciate your inside information, Adele. They want you to keep up the good work."

Taken aback by the compliment, I say, "Then I guess I'll keep taking notes."

"You really should. D-day is coming soon, I'm sure of it."

"What makes you think that?" I say, and my thoughts automatically jump to Robbie. If the invasion arrives soon, he could get caught in the crossfire on his way to Spain.

"Things are picking up. In the past few days, Cammerts has sent three couriers to me with info for headquarters. My fingers are worked to the bone," she says. "I need to change my radio frequency. Did you get my crystals?"

I hand the silk bag over to Denise, relieved to be passing it on.

"Thanks, Adele. You're a peach."

My exhausted smile does the talking for me. I shove some scattered fashion magazines off the rug and stretch out, regardless of the dust, as Denise sets to work deciphering the coded message from the silk bag.

When the scratching of pencil against paper stops, I say, "One of my contacts, the doctor I told you about who drove me to Paris, he's married to a Nazi sympathizer. She was at the Commodore last night. Wearing a German officer."

"She'll get what's coming to her."

"Do you think so?"

Denise leans back on the sofa with her hands clasped behind her head. Her legs dangle over the armrest. "Haven't you heard of karma?"

"Should I tell him? The husband?"

"My money says he knows already."

Eyes closed, I enjoy a few minutes of quiet.

"Do you still intend to spy on that factory tomorrow?" Denise asks.

"Yes."

"Cammerts and Bishop know nothing of your plan. You don't

have to go through with it if you don't want to. It's not as if you were given an order."

"I know."

Denise chuckles to herself. "Pierre really gets under your skin, doesn't he?"

I quietly laugh, surprised she picked up on that. I don't understand why I feel the need to prove myself to Pierre. His lack of confidence in our skills irritates me, but plenty of other men probably feel the same way. Why do I care what *he* thinks?

My body, finally at rest after nonstop motion, begs me to give in to the head-to-toe exhaustion I've been too busy to notice. Just when I become one with the floor, Denise's feet touch down next to my face.

"Please don't tell me it's time," I mutter.

"It's time."

I sit up. "I need you to update headquarters about my contact, Anna. I'm worried she's been captured, but I don't have proof."

"I'll let them know she's gone missing so they can ask around about her. Other agents may know her situation or whereabouts."

"Thanks, Denise. I hope she turns up safe and sound. I hate being in the dark all the time, don't you? For all we know, the Germans are picking us off faster than headquarters can replace us."

"Replace us? Adele, you make it sound as if they're dropping in machinery parts and not flesh-and-blood people." Her freckled nose scrunches up. "Do you think headquarters is going with quantity rather than quality?"

"I don't know. I guess they'd want the advantage of numbers

at a time like this. But I'd hate to think they're sending a bunch of girls here knowing it would be a death sentence for most or all of us. We're not disposable. We're not just numbers."

Denise shakes her head. "I'm sure they want every one of us to get out of here alive. They're realistic, that's all."

She sets out her transmitter, and we take our places at small windows on opposite ends of the room. Through mine, I watch the street below. Through hers, she places the end of the transmitter's aerial. At her radio, she turns the Send/Receive and Aerial Matching switches and the Anode Tuning knob to the positions required to transmit on a certain frequency. Head bent in concentration, she taps out her Morse code transmission while I keep watch. I'd prefer to stand by a second-floor window close to our emergency exit, but Denise wants me to keep her company, surrounded by four walls and perched at the very top of the house with nowhere to go but down.

When I'm settled into my familiar place at the window, I zero in on a face unfamiliar to the neighborhood. A man in a trench coat strolls down the sidewalk, glancing at the nearly empty storefront displays. He drifts to a stop directly across from Stefan's house.

Even though I can't expect her to perform her job any quicker without making mistakes, I say, "Get cracking, Denise. I think the man across the street is either Gestapo or French militia."

"Bloody hell." *Tap, tap, tap.* "How certain are you?"

"His collar is turned up. It looks like he's concealing a set of earphones. You tell me."

Her fingers fly. "Watch him like a hawk. At the very least, I need six more minutes."

Six minutes. She may as well ask for a steak dinner with all the fixings.

The man in the long coat tugs his collar higher and moves on.

"I've lost him, Denise."

"I'm doing my best. Get my pistol."

I leave my post to retrieve her gun from beneath a floorboard in the corner of the room. After intense SOE training I'm able to handle and fire Sten guns, Bren guns, bazookas, what have you, but the pistol is my personal favorite.

I lick my finger to spit shine the window glass. "Wait, he's back."

A neighbor rushes past him, tugging two children, with a baguette of dark bread tucked under her arm. I catch her backward glance as she too recognizes a stranger in our midst.

Again he stops directly in front of Stefan's home. He leans against a lamppost, doing absolutely nothing—nothing that I can see from my vantage point anyway—for several minutes. My intuitive alarm clangs.

Cheek flattened against the glass, I have only a smudged view of his head and torso.

"If he moves even a hair, I'll lose him. I can be at a downstairs window in seconds. If you hear the signal, you know what to do."

I bolt from the attic, pistol at my side. At the second floor I stand next to one of the slender bedroom windows, careful not to send a flutter through the drapes.

The man is nowhere to be seen.

I sidle around a chest of drawers and peer out the other window.

I've lost him. If the Gestapo doesn't kill me, Denise will give it a go.

Slipping into the hall, I listen for the sounds of an impending arrest. Shadows will gather outside the front door. They'll lurk at the back to nab us. I imagine an arrest must be loud—cracking wood, throaty commands, the beat of boots giving chase.

Instead, there's nothing but silence.

"What do you mean, he's gone?"

"I searched everywhere, Denise. He left."

"He wasn't Gestapo then. Not French milice either, or we'd be having this conversation in a van on our way to Avenue Foch. Your imagination got carried away."

"You didn't see him, Denise. We were under surveillance, I'd bet my life on it. Think they're keeping tabs on us?"

"No." Denise's thumb taps her fingernails. "No, they'd have arrested us."

"But what if their goal isn't to arrest us right away? What if they're observing what we do, where we go—"

"Who we meet and talk to."

I feel duped; outwitted at my own game. "It makes sense that they'd take their time, doesn't it? Spy on us to collect information and lull us into a false sense of security? You should tell Cammerts you need to find a new safe house. Maybe there's work for us in the country. Madame LaRoche told us we're welcome to go back to the farm. We'll relay a message to Bishop. If you're right, and D-day is near, it's more important than ever that you don't get caught."

"The farm is too far from Paris." Denise's head bobs toward her transmitter. "And you know what a rigmarole it is to move all this without being spotted by a prying neighbor looking to get in the Gestapo's good graces. People aren't exactly lining up to take in girls like us. You've seen the posters. They all know what will happen to them if they harbor a spy. I was lucky Martin found me this place."

Denise is right, but I feel as though she's stubbornly digging in her heels to get her own way.

"I'm tired." I return the pistol to its hiding place. The gray mood I woke up with is making a comeback and dragging another headache with it. "I'm heading to Estelle's. I'll see you tonight during the radio broadcast."

In the courtyard, I climb aboard my bicycle and begin to pedal away.

"Adele, wait."

I turn my head and the bike follows, curving in a slow circle back to the door being held open by Denise.

"I'll find a new place," she apologizes with a smile. "Soon as I can."

I give her a weary last-minute wave.

At this very moment, I'd give anything to pedal out from behind Stefan's house and find myself transported to my aunt's street in England. But no matter how hard I wish, no Victorian terraced houses appear before my eyes. My aunt's street remains hundreds of miles away.

I think of my small, square bedroom there: a postage stamp of a room, tucked into the back corner of the house. Without a heater, it was cold as an icebox all winter, but my aunt piled my white metal-framed bed high with blankets. The rag rug she taught me to make with scraps of material became a landing pad on the chilly floor between the door and the bed. My photo of Tom, tucked within the pages of *The Adventures of Tom Sawyer*, his favorite book, is inside the bottom drawer of my chest of drawers. I intended to look at it again. Someday.

An envelope atop that same chest of drawers contains the pub wages I managed to save. *To Aunt Libby*, I wrote on the envelope. Nothing more. I didn't even take a second to scribble a short note of thanks before I left for good. I hope my aunt's pride didn't keep her from accepting the envelope. If I know her, she sees it as one more thing to dust.

Did she keep my room the way I left it?

I press hard against the pedals of my bicycle. Only after I speed off do I realize I forgot to tell Denise that our trio of misfits has dwindled to two.

As I cycle past Estelle's favorite neighborhood sidewalk café, a craving for lemonade hits me like a bolt from above. The draw of freshly squeezed *citron pressé* pulls me back.

I prefer this quiet café. The customers tend to be older, but enough are girls and young mothers that I don't stand out. And no matter the time of day I can always find a shaded table at the back of the outdoor terrace near the bicycle stands.

Lemonade in hand, I take a seat at the table nearest my bicycle. Sun-weathered and parched, I smile at the glass as it rises to my lips. But before I get the chance to quench my thirst, a woman collides with my bent arm. Droplets of lemonade splash onto my skirt.

I whip around at the waist to give her a piece of my mind. My eyes widen. The clumsy woman is Anna, my contact who went missing.

"Mademoiselle, I apologize," she says. She bends to swipe lemonade from my clothing with a handkerchief and slips a cylindrical object into my hand. "I'm sorry."

I slide the object into the deep pocket of my skirt.

"No harm done," I say.

Anna continues on her way. It's murder to keep still and not track her.

I deliberate my next move in the time it takes to down the lemonade. The object in my pocket feels like a wine cork. There's nothing valuable about a cork. That means it hides something that is. My uneasy glance skims the street.

From my chair, I can see the twin chimneys of Estelle's apartment building. Without knowing if I'll be chased it's the last place I can go. I jump on my bicycle and ride for Denise's. Only another cyclist could keep up with me to the end of my chaotic route, and if someone was crazy enough to follow my shortcut through the clothing factory on a bike, I definitely would have noticed.

Immediately after I knock the beats of our code on the door, it swings open. Denise pulls me inside.

"What's happened?" she asks, visibly antsy. "Should I get my things?"

"You can relax. It's not a matter of life and death."

"Tell that to my heart. When I heard your knock I got all set to skedaddle."

"Denise, I have something to show you."

I set the cork on the table.

"That's not an ordinary cork, is it," she says. "Where did you find it?"

"I stopped for lemonade at the café near Estelle's, and Anna bumped into me. She gave me the cork, and then she was gone."

"Intriguing. What could be inside? Microfilm?"

I locate the panel along the side of the cork and slide it. "It's a tiny roll of paper." I unfurl the tube. After studying it front and back, I say, "That's strange. It's blank."

Denise plucks the slip of paper from my fingers to check for herself. "You're right. It's blank."

We look at each other in surprise as I say, "Invisible ink."

"Must be, but what kind?"

Denise stretches to retrieve a box of matches from the stovetop. Lighting the misshapen candle at the center of the table, she says, "One that develops with heat, I bet."

I shimmy my chair closer to Denise's, and we watch faint lines of minuscule script appear on the paper as if by magic.

Safe houses compromised. Being followed. Cover irreparably blown. Suspected leak within circuit. Watch your back. Trust no one.

"Watch your back. Trust no one," Denise says. "Those are the deluded ramblings of a paranoid agent, if you ask me."

"I don't know. When I met with Anna, she seemed no-nonsense and tough minded. I think we should take her warning seriously."

"A double agent within our circuit." Denise arcs an eyebrow at me. "That casts a long shadow over agents we're supposed to trust with our lives."

"What about Shepherd? Think this has something to do with him?"

"I'm not convinced he has the bollocks to pull something like this off. He's intelligent, but I got the impression he lacks street smarts."

I think back to the night we parachuted in. Shepherd was captured right off the bat, while marching down the center of the road, a move that definitely bordered on soft-headedness.

"We'll have to tell Cammerts about this," Denise says.

"Should we? Anna warned me to trust no one. But she trusted me enough to pass along the note, right? Did she tell Cammerts about the leak herself? If not, then why?" Rubbing my temples, I groan, "Why can't anything be straightforward for once?"

"That would be nice, wouldn't it?" Denise stands. "You'll probably see Cammerts today, won't you, after your walk with Robbie? You can tell him then."

"Denise, Robbie left. He's on his way back to Britain."

She picks up the kettle from the stovetop and sets it right down again. "Is he? I'm sorry, Adele."

"Don't be sorry. He had to go back to his squadron. Taking care of him was part of my duties. I should be glad he's out of my hair."

Denise grins at me over her shoulder. "Methinks the twitchy-faced lady doth protest too much."

My heart aches just thinking about my last moments with Robbie. An image of him happily playing cards with me in the cellar comes to mind. There's that cute grin of his. A grin I'll never see again. I will myself to stay strong.

Taking a deep breath, I roll Anna's note into a tight tube. I return it to the cork's compartment.

"Getting back to the note," Denise says, "there is one person you can trust completely. You do know that, don't you?"

"Yes." The answer takes me by surprise. I must have already made up my mind on the matter without realizing it.

"The same goes for me. We may not be able to trust anyone else, but at least we have each other. One for all, and all for one."

"Friends till the end?"

"Absolutely," she says, smiling. "Friends till the end."

TWENTY-FOUR

The factory appears over the hillcrest. Try as I might, I can't breathe away the nervous fluttering in my stomach. For three days I've played out the sabotage of the factory in my mind, again and again, fine-tuning my plan. Taking in too much information on the tour could be as overwhelming as taking in none, so every detail has to be worked out before I set foot in the building. I know exactly what to look for and what questions to ask.

As I push my bicycle toward the gatehouse, I overhear Gerhard say, "Zucker, here is Adele."

"Hello, Gerhard," I say, waving. "I've brought the drawings."

"Wonderful. I cannot wait to see them."

"May I first say hello to Zucker?" I ask.

Zucker obeys Gerhard's command to sit, and I let her sniff my hand.

I mimic the mispronunciation of boarding school students reciting German for the first time to say, "Hello, Zucker. You are a very good and intelligent dog."

The praise is part of my act, but I really mean it. Compared to Zucker, my cousins' dog Biscuit is an unruly little halfwit.

"Did you learn that phrase so you could speak to Zucker?" Gerhard asks.

"I did," I say, laughing. "Do I need more practice?"

With a polite smile he says, "Yes."

I rest the bike against the fence. My basket is empty apart from the drawings of Zucker. The photos and notes I gathered for Pierre on the first visit are safely hidden within a thick laurel hedge at the bottom of the hill.

"What do you think of the pictures?" I ask Gerhard when I give him the charcoal drawing on paper. Impatient with anticipation, I hand him the watercolor before he can give me his thoughts. "Do you like them?"

"Adele, I thank you and commend you on a job well done. These are the works of a truly talented artist. You captured the intelligence in her eyes, as I knew you would. My sister will love this." He props the pictures on a ledge inside the guard station. "And now, once my replacement arrives to man my post, we can begin the tour. Are you ready?"

For a few fleeting seconds, I feel downright awful for tricking Gerhard. He only wants to do something nice for me.

But I didn't come to this factory to make friends with German soldiers.

I look Gerhard in the eyes and smile. "Yes, I'm ready."

Propping myself up against my bicycle at the side of the road, I watch the wagon I hitched a ride in drive away, bound for a village north of the LaRoche farm.

When the area is clear, I cycle directly to the secret entrance of the Maquis camp as quickly as my worn-out legs can pedal.

At the tangle of branches, I continuously shove my hand through in search of the latch. Pierre opened the gate and transported a horse and wagon inside the forest in less time than it's taking me figure out the door's secret. At last, my fingers brush cool metal among the leaves. I fiddle with the mechanism until the gate swings open to reveal the storybook tunnel of trees.

I close the gate and set off. Thinking it might not be such a good idea to ride straight in on the men unannounced, I call out, "Hello? Is anyone there?" when the brightly lit clearing comes into view.

I climb down and wheel my bike into the camp. The men must not have heard my call. Three pistols that were aggressively protruding from trouser waistbands are suddenly aimed straight at me.

"You know me!" I call. I frantically search the camp for a familiar face.

Marcus appears in the doorway of a hut. "Wait, wait, wait!" As he runs to me, he tamps the air with his hands, telling the men to stand down. "You are that girl!"

"I am," I say, my voice ragged with nerves. Lightheaded, I lean my bike and my exhausted body against a tree. "Is Pierre here?"

"What's going on?"

When Pierre speaks, there is no mistaking him for anyone else. He leaves a canvas tent, pulling a woolen sweater over his head. Ruffling a hand through his hair, he gives me a long, drowsy stare.

"It's that girl," Marcus calls to him. "She has come back."

Squinting, Pierre steps closer. "Adele?"

"Yes, it's me, Pierre. I've come back after spying on the factory."

His eyes widen with shock. He shakes his head, exhaling a loud sigh. "All right, come here."

I take the photographs from my bicycle basket and hold them in the air for Pierre to see.

"The factory is producing gun carriers and turrets for German Panzer tanks," I say.

Marcus rushes ahead of me to the table. "Panzers! Pierre, did you hear that?"

"Yes, I heard her. How do you know this?"

"I toured the factory this morning."

Pierre's head tilts questioningly. "You toured the factory?"

"Yes."

"And how did you manage that?"

"They mistook me for a student."

"They mistook you for a child and then showed you around? I don't believe it."

"It's true. I guess, when you think about it, what do they have to fear from schoolchildren? They're next in line to enter the labor draft and may one day end up working at that very factory. It's just a building, after all, and hardly a secret. The Germans *do* have to worry about the Resistance and the RAF, of course, but you said so yourself, I don't look like I belong to either of those groups."

Marcus pats me on the back. "Bravo, Adele."

I spread the photos across the tabletop. "I took these the first time I visited the area. They show the grounds and the building's access points. I know the location of the assembly areas, the metal presses, the transformer hall, and even the night watchman's room. I wasn't able to take notes during the tour. That would have looked too suspicious, but I have it all up here." I tap my temple. "I'll write up notes before I return to Paris this afternoon. And I'll draw you a map to use with the photos."

Pierre picks up one photo after the next, studying them closely.

"What do you think?" Marcus says. "Can we do it? Can we destroy the factory?"

Pierre's satisfied nod fills me with pride.

"Yes, Marcus, we can do this." Gathering the photos into a pile, Pierre says, "Adele, this will require heavy explosives. Are you still in contact with a wireless operator? She can transmit our list of requirements to headquarters?"

"Yes, I can give the list to the girl I dropped in with. Her name is Denise."

Pierre closes our conversation with a sharp nod and he strides away from the table.

I bite my lip, wondering what to do next, rapidly deflating over his lack of enthusiasm for my hard work. I put my neck on the line to get him that information.

Midway to the tent, Pierre spins around. With a shake of his head, as if he's coming to his senses, he says, "Great work, Adele."

"Thanks."

Outside the tent's canvas flaps, he spins around once again.

"New men have recently joined us. They desperately need

training. The weapons that come in with the drops are unassem-
bled, and if they are not cleaned and put together properly"—he
smirks—"well, you know what could happen."

"Yes, the person standing behind the weapon is in greater
danger than the person standing in front of it."

"That's right. These men are more liable to shoot each other
than the enemy. Would you mind giving them some instruction?"

Pierre wants me to train the new men. Did I hear him correctly?

"I don't mind at all," I say, grinning over my hard-won pro-
motion. "I'd be happy to train them."

———————

A group of fifteen men have assembled in the large field within
walking distance of the camp. They huddle into a tighter bunch
when I begin the lesson, giving me their rapt attention as I show
them the proper way to clean and assemble a Sten gun.

As I disassemble it for a second time, I say, "You see, because
it is such a light, simple-machined weapon it can be stripped down
like this and easily concealed."

One of the Maquis, who refused to take part in the training
when I introduced myself as their instructor, lets out an audible
harrumph. "Go back to your kitchen where you belong, woman."

Ignoring him is difficult, but I bite my tongue and move on.

On a fully assembled Sten, I display the cross-bolt button near
the trigger. "With this control you can select your firepower—
single shots as well as automatic fire. In a close-combat fight the
key is to have great speed and accuracy, so it's best to fire single
shots. You'll have more control that way. Because it's so light and
simple, the Sten can be raised and fired quickly. It can be an
excellent weapon, but you must keep it clean. I can't stress that

enough. It has a long opening, which can allow foreign objects to enter."

I don't expect the man in back to have a sudden change of heart, but his rude howl of laughter sends a jolt of anger buzzing through me, like an electrical charge. If he doesn't want my help, why doesn't he just leave?

"As I was saying, this can be a good close-range weapon." I struggle to keep my voice even. "But if it's dropped while cocked it can go off on its own."

Clutching his ample midsection, laughter nearly fells my tormentor to his knees.

My cheeks flare hotter. My lips press tight.

A burly man who introduced himself as Big Edgar peers down at me, his eyes sympathetic.

"And as I mentioned it can be prone to blockages, so keep those drawbacks in mind. Should the gun jam you may be able to clear it by tilting it this way to clear the rounds"—I exhibit the motion—"and recocking."

I pass out a Sten gun to each of the men. Almost in unison, they raise the weapons—without first checking to see if they're loaded—and take aim.

During my training in London, the first time I held a weapon in my hands I made every mistake in the book. The moment I set foot in the long practice corridor, the target—a life-sized figure in a trench coat—popped out and sped at me. I brought my gun up to assume the position I'd seen in films. In my ear, the instructor didn't offer the glowing words of praise I was expecting. He burst my confidence with a sharp, "Right, then. You're dead."

I go through the group, showing each man how to properly hold the Sten at his shoulder, in line with his eyes the same way my instructor did. These men will require quite a lot more training if they expect to survive firefights with German soldiers who lie in wait and kill with precision. But I can't give up on them now that I've stepped up to train them. My instructor made sure no one left our class a bad shot, because every student's life depends on how well he or she has been taught. If one of these men dies because I failed him in training, I would never forgive myself.

"The gun is like an extension of your body. Feel the trajectory, as you would your pointing finger. You don't need to look at your feet to know where they're headed; you can envision it in your mind. If you practice enough, firing your weapon this way will become automatic."

Only Big Edgar watches me without skepticism.

"After you fire one round, immediately fire off a second. Both rounds should strike within one to two inches of each other to be most effective."

The man who refused to take part leans against a tree, one hand on the trunk and the other at his waist, giving me an arrogant once-over. "Impossible!"

To the men, I say, "Accuracy might be more difficult with a submachine gun than with a pistol, that is true."

I exchange the Sten for a pistol and take aim at a circular knothole in the center of the tree trunk. At this distance, there's no chance I'll miss. But the jackass propped against the tree doesn't know that.

I fire off two rounds before he has time to react. The bullets hit the knot exactly where I wanted them to, within millimeters of each other. I watch the man slowly come around to what just happened, his body leaping to action one flabby bit at a time in a comic, erratic dance.

"You crazy woman!" he hollers, red with rage. "You could have killed me!"

I finally turn to address him. "No, I'll leave that deed to the Germans."

He points a threatening finger at me and storms off into the woods.

Picking up where I left off, I say, "But with practice either weapon will get the job done with speed and accuracy. That is called the double tap."

At the end of our hour-long training and target practice, Edgar gives me a sheepish grin as he hands over his weapon. "You were good."

"Thank you, Edgar. That means a lot to me."

"Will you train us again?"

"That's up to Pierre, I suppose."

His eyes go wide as he notices a change in scenery over my right shoulder.

Without turning to look, I know Pierre is on his way. He's probably been made aware of my unconventional teaching methods. I prepare myself for a humiliating lecture. Looks like I won't be training Big Edgar again, after all.

"Adele did a good job!" Edgar calls out in my defense, before rushing off.

Pierre comes up beside me. "I spoke with Charles. You shot at him?"

"Pierre, I didn't. He insulted me, so I shot the tree to scare him. He wasn't in danger."

"Okay."

"What do you mean? Do you believe me?"

"Yes, I believe you. I told him he should have followed your instructions. I chose you to train the men. By disregarding your training, he also disregarded me."

"Thank you, Pierre."

He extends his hand. "Apparently you did a good job. You're welcome to come back." The corners of his lips tweak into a smile as he says, "Next time you can teach the proper use and handling of explosives, so the men don't blow each other to bits."

It isn't an outright apology for his "flimsy little girls" remark, but it's much better than nothing. From Pierre, it's probably as good as I'm going to get.

I press my sweaty palm to my skirt before taking his hand. "I'll come back," I say, as we shake on it. "You can count on that."

Twenty-five

Twice in the next week, Cammerts met with Denise and me for drinks at Le Colisée, in the middle of the afternoon. A dangerous move, I thought, to lump several agents together in the open like that where we could be watched, followed, or nabbed all at once. Both times, I patiently waited for the perfect opportunity to speak up about this security risk, but it never arrived, and before I knew it we were shaking hands good-bye.

"He's not alone today," I tell Denise while we park our bicycles next to the terrace. "Looks like he's brought new agents to meet us."

Denise grumbles, "Rookies."

Cammerts and a lithe young man with elfin ears stand when we join them at the table. The woman, whose perfume I smell from yards away, remains seated.

"Adele and Denise, this is Agnes Purdon and Benjamin Baker."

Denise and I say hello to the new agents as Cammerts excuses himself to order lemonade inside the café.

Agnes has a kind smile that shows a lot of teeth. She's probably a nice enough person, but when her wide smile parts, English words come out her mouth.

"It's a thrill to meet you," she says, smack-dab in the middle of the crowded bistro. It stuns me like a slap.

It won't be such a thrill to meet Denise and me if we clobber her.

"How are you finding Paris?" Benjamin asks. He speaks French, at least, but not well. No dialect like his exists in any region of France, or anyplace else for that matter.

"It's a beautiful city."

Generic answers are all he'll get from me. I sure hope he takes the hint and doesn't try to carry on a full conversation. Whatever draws attention to him draws attention to me. And to Denise.

Agnes slips her long dark hair behind one ear. "You must be forever on the go. You've been to the Louvre? The Eiffel Tower was splendid." Again she speaks in her native tongue.

Flabbergasted, I stare at her. It's a good thing Denise isn't too dumbstruck to put Agnes in her place.

"Speak to us in French," she whispers. "Your carelessness is not appreciated."

Agnes blushes. "*Je m'excuse.*"

Cammerts returns with our drinks. Along with my lemonade, I receive an envelope, which he slides across the table. "Adele, this letter came for you."

A personal letter. I look to Denise, and she looks back with a hint of a grin.

"Thank you." I set it on my lap, unopened.

Like bumps on a log, Denise and I drink our lemonade, without adding a single thing to the conversation. Benjamin's god-awful French accent grates against my ears. The odd English word pops up here and there.

Was I naive to assume that agents are taking matters of security as seriously as Denise and I are? That only the cream of the crop passed training and agents who muck up will be dealt with? Agnes and Benjamin are a rude, almost frightening, awakening. Are Denise and I kidding ourselves, buying into a promise of covert professionalism that doesn't even exist?

"Adele, I can't have Benjamin and Agnes residing in the same house," Cammerts says. "Agnes will spend a portion of her time with you."

My head snaps up. The agent who spoke English in a public place is going to stay with me? I wouldn't dream of putting Estelle and her family's lives at risk. Not for anyone or anything, but especially not for this careless woman I just met. She is not my problem and not my responsibility. I have to draw the line.

"No," I tell him.

"Pardon me, Adele?"

"I won't do it. Everyone makes mistakes, but I don't think Agnes will learn from hers. I can't take a chance on someone who's not cut out for this."

Agnes's rouged cheeks tremble as she fights back tears. I don't want to hurt her feelings, I really don't, but it's the truth.

My words warble as I force them out. "She can find her own way. As we have." I bend the envelope in half and tuck it in my brassiere for safekeeping. "C'mon, Denise. We're done here."

Denise appears lost in thought with her lemonade. For a split second, I wonder if she's about to jump ship and leave me.

"Good day to you all," she says. Handshakes go round the table. "We'll keep in touch, I'm sure."

At our bikes, I give my head a shake. "What did I just do?"

"Should I start calling you Boss?"

I climb aboard my bicycle. "It'll wind up being the right decision."

"No argument here. As I see it, Agnes is behind bars within the week, and if Benjamin lasts even that long with that pathetic accent of his, then I'm a monkey's uncle." She belts me a good one on the arm. "With those freakishly long toes of yours, you'll make a splendid monkey's aunt."

I laugh and stick my tongue out at her.

Pedaling away, she says, "What kind of mad world are we living in, where you and I are the experienced ones?"

"I'm as baffled as you are, believe me."

We ride side by side through the sunny streets.

Too many shops display signs that they have no merchandise to sell. A sign in a restaurant window proclaims the establishment off-limits to dogs and Jews. Makeshift street signs in German point the way to Denise's district. A cluster of women lower their heads and skitter away down an empty alleyway, illegally dragging bulky tree limbs behind them, fuel for their cooking fires.

"Who do you suppose the letter's from?" Denise asks when we turn the corner onto her street. "Do you think it's from him?"

"I don't know."

The letter could have only come from one person. My aunt, the other choice, doesn't know my whereabouts; another one of those security measures that are supposedly vital to follow.

"Aren't you curious to read it?"

"Not really."

Without giving me even a sideward glance, she says, "Liar. Your face is twitching."

"I'm too good to let anything—"

"Twitch," she says, when I don't elaborate. "Yes, yes, I've heard it all before."

My hands, clammy with sweat, slip against the handlebars. I regain my grip. "Denise, a radio van. It crept past the end of your street. Did you see it?"

"I saw it."

We push our bikes around back to Stefan's tiny courtyard.

"You thought I transmitted lightning quick before. Wait until you see me today."

"You're not honestly thinking of transmitting," I say, though I'm not actually too surprised. "They're in your neighborhood at this very moment."

"That's good, isn't it? I'm not transmitting at this very moment. By the time I am, they will be long gone."

Once in the attic, Denise falls like a sack of flour onto the divan. I take up my usual pose, flat on my back on the floor. The envelope within my brassiere digs into my skin, a reminder that it exists and has yet to be acknowledged.

I hold out as long as I can, then casually get to my feet. "If you need me, I'll be in the loo.'"

I leave the attic, feeling Denise's stare on my back.

Inside the bathroom, I lock the door and take a seat, not on the toilet but on the rounded rim of the bathtub. I'm reminded of my cousin Philip who was assigned the role of fuel warden in his family. We were permitted one five-inch bath per week back in Britain, and he took his job seriously enough to paint a line five inches from the bottom of the tub.

The small brown envelope feels crisp and new in my hands, as if it hasn't made a perilous journey. I turn it over, licking sweat from my upper lip.

Finally, I open it and let Robbie speak to me again.

Dearest Adele,

How are you? Well, I hope. And Denise? I'm all right, in fine health and good spirits. There have been a few close calls, but my escort is sharp as a tack. He's a real capable fella. You'd like him.

Tonight we toasted my birthday with the elderly couple accommodating us. The effects of the champagne are making me nostalgic. I couldn't sleep without passing along sincerest thanks for everything you did for me. I'll never forget you or your kindness. I think of your smile often. You haven't seen the last of me, Adele. That's a promise. Good night, until we meet again.

I reread the letter twice, lingering over the bit about him being in fine health. I return the folded letter to the envelope. Why did he make an empty promise to see me? It only raises my hopes so they can be dashed even more painfully when we never meet again.

Overhead, footsteps rush about.

"Aaadeeele!"

I spring from the side of the tub, forcibly stuffing the rigid envelope back into my undergarments. I burst from the bathroom and sprint, heart pounding, to the attic. The first thing I notice is Denise's pallor. Always a pale girl, her freckles now stand out against her ashen complexion.

"What's going on?" I run to help her pack the suitcase.

"I happened to glance out the window," she says, breathless, "and there was the van. It drove away at first, but now it's parked down the street. The noose is tightening."

With Denise's all-important radio and belongings packed, we make for the second-floor emergency exit.

At the window, Denise grips her suitcase and throws one leg into the open air. When it's my turn, I follow her. The height of this window is startling. The possibility of a violent fall seems all too real, so unlike the height from an airplane that is almost too enormous to take in. We shimmy down the gutter to the court-yard, and thankfully the first part of me to touch the ground is my foot, not my head.

Denise fumbles as she attaches the suitcase to her bicycle.

"Hurry, hurry," I say.

She finally secures it, and then we're off, cycling toward some safe place that only exists in our hopes.

The screech of brakes fills the air, a terrible sound that means only one thing. A black Citroën Avant, a menacing-looking auto-mobile if I ever saw one, roars to the side of the road. The doors simultaneously fly open. Four uniformed men exit the car, shout-ing in German. They swiftly close in on us and block our escape route, pistols pointed at our heads. Grabbing hold of our bicy-cles, they nip our brief flight in the bud.

We are captured.

Twenty-Six

Denise and I wheel our bicycles down the sidewalk, sandwiched between the two plainclothes secret police officers tasked with taking us in for questioning.

"I don't trust these two," one of them says. "Puncture their tires."

I push on, willing him to change his mind.

The soldier minding Denise shakes his head. "The tires alone will fetch us a good price on the black market."

I know Paris well enough to know we're being led to German headquarters. For weeks I've lived among German soldiers, but under their radar. They go about their business. I go about mine. At headquarters, all that will change. The Germans will have complete control, and I will have none. To know I'm only minutes from being at their mercy terrifies me. I don't want the Gestapo to hurt me. I don't want them to hurt Denise. I dread being separated from her when we arrive. Apart, neither of us will know what is happening to the other. And they will use those worries against us.

The training lectures on interrogation gave me such a splitting headache I had to lie down afterward. The SOE hammered home the brutality of the Gestapo, who will do whatever it takes to get a confession. No rules. Nothing barred.

A dire warning from one of our instructors comes rushing back to me. *The Gestapo is above the law! Its activities cannot be challenged or investigated!*

The SOE also made sure we learned the Gestapo's tricks of questioning. When a student seated next to me said, "We won't be fooled by the Krauts now," I agreed with him, so confident I wouldn't get caught in the first place. As I walk toward a real interrogation alongside Denise, the embarrassment of being wrong brings me to tears.

Denise isn't a stranger, or even just a fellow agent. She's my best friend. I might not fall for "confessions" supposedly signed by her, but what if the Gestapo threatens to hurt her unless I talk? Can I stay silent as they describe her torture to me, knowing I have the power to end her suffering? What if I break down to protect her and put the lives of hundreds, including Estelle's family and the LaRoches, at risk?

Out of the corner of my eye, I watch Denise. She stares straight ahead, her teeth methodically tugging on her bottom lip. I want to be stoic like her, but the more I think about what we're passively walking into, the more I want to bolt. We have to at least try to escape. The only time to do that is now, before we reach headquarters.

Our lucky break shows up at the exact moment I set my mind to running.

The soldier beside me points to a café down the street. "There's another one!'"

He darts off, abandoning his comrade who is now outnumbered.

I glance at the remaining soldier and Denise's suitcase, still strapped to her bicycle.

I try to relay a message to her with my eyes. *I'll distract. You go. I'll catch up.*

No. Her lips press together, resolute. *I won't leave you.*

I mouth the word "Estelle's."

She gives me a slight nod of agreement. Holding her hands to her mouth like a megaphone, she screams toward the café, "Jacques! Run, they are coming for you!"

The other soldier immediately stumbles into the street, frantically glancing between the café and Denise. In the seconds before he can get his wits about him and realize he is being tricked, Denise throws her leg over her bicycle. She rides away in the opposite direction as if blasted from a cannon.

I lift my bicycle, empowered by every ounce of backbone I have in me, and heave it at the soldier before he can fire his raised weapon at Denise. The bike knocks him off his feet. Whether or not he falls to the ground is anybody's guess. I don't stick around to watch.

I run for my life down a side street. Fear churns a landslide of thoughts through my mind. I desperately cling to those that are helpful.

Get a fifteen-stride lead.

Objects whiz past me and ricochet off the street, sidewalks, buildings. Bullets.

At the sounds of shots being fired, the street clears. I stand out like a lone tin can on a wooden fence, just begging to be shot at.

Become a moving target! Dodge and weave!

I leave the road. Shortly after entering the scrub behind the neighboring buildings I find a concrete-encased opening in the ground. An entranceway to the sewers. I can't remember Robbie's exact words. Something about a labyrinth of enormous proportions. To Istanbul, he said. Above ground, I'm as good as dead. The putrid depths offer hope; a chance for survival.

I climb down metal rungs until safely able to fall the rest of the way and land without breaking an ankle. The smell is bearable enough; a shock, considering that a broad river of human filth and excrement flows beyond my feet. A stale blanket of humidity instantly smothers all fresh air in my vicinity.

The tunnel, celestially lit from above by the circular manholes, extends for some way forward and backward before branching off. All I can do is run and hope for the best possible end.

The clink of boots against metal interjects the sharp staccato of my footfalls. Without missing a beat the soldier pounces onto my trail. At the first intersection, I turn left. The decision costs me a second.

A rat, easily as large as any cat I've seen, squeaks my location to the enemy and then scurries into a black crevice, narrowly escaping the beating to his skull my unstoppable wooden-soled shoes would have delivered. No sewer rat rivals the size or tenacity of the rat tracking me down.

I send my bulky shoes to a watery grave. At the next crossroads, I build upon my forward momentum, edging closer to the brink of exhaustion. The carved stone slices my feet, shredding the black-market stockings Denise bought for me. Aside from the burning ache of my lungs as they strain against my ribs, I barely feel any pain.

Seconds too late for me to change course, I realize the way forward is blocked by a grated arch. Losing my lead, I spin around. The soldier's grim face meets my gritted determination. We sprint toward each other on a collision course.

I make the turn onto the land-locked passageway before him. A chest-high pile of rubble cuts my getaway short.

"It seems your luck has run out." The soldier blocks my only exit. The glass within his wire frames has fogged. Sneering with the conceit of a supposed hands-down victory, he wipes the glasses on his sleeve.

Mustering the last of my strength, I barrel into him, shoulder thrust out. My weight sends him tumbling backward. Glasses spin end over end through the air and land with a splintering crack as he struggles to regain his balance. I deliver one final push to knock him over the edge. Not willing to go down without taking me with him, his hand shoots out. Fingertips graze my blouse.

The impact of his extended body smacking the water erupts noxious fumes into the air. A wave crashes into the platform. The splash soaks my torn stockings to my knees and splatters the rest of me. The soldier bobs to the surface and holds himself afloat. In time he'll climb out, sodden and putrid, and too humiliated to continue the chase. But by then my trail will have grown cold.

The clock begins to tick, chipping away at my head start. I double back to retrieve my shoes, which float near the edge like little boats.

A gurgled scream echoes through the tunnel. *"Helfen Sie mir!"*

Help me!

I sense his agony in my chest as if it were my own. I turn back.

He thrashes about like a helpless child who's been plunged into a deep swimming pool. What have I done? The man clearly can't swim. He sinks like a stone in his boots and overcoat, battering the water to raise himself to the surface.

I race back. At the water's edge, my legs stiffen with fear, forcing me back a few ungainly steps. Taking rapid breaths, I lie facedown and creep forward on my belly until my head and arms dangle over the water.

"Come to me!"

Near the center of the stream, he gasps and takes in a mouthful. His face, a bruised shade of red, bulges beneath a slick sheen of refuse. His arms wheel through the air, but he goes nowhere.

He cries out to me with his eyes and slips under. The dank waters calm.

A tremor shoots straight through me as I stand. I stagger into a run.

At my shoes, I kneel. Lean forward. A terrifying image of the dead soldier's hand bursting up to yank me into his watery grave flashes before my eyes. I snatch up the shoes and make for daylight.

———————

When I enter Estelle's, Denise and Marie look up at me from the couch. Marie's face shines in the candlelight, wet with tears. Denise isn't crying, but she appears to be on the brink.

"Adele, is it really you?" Marie squeaks from behind her slender fingers.

I close the door. All I want to do is lie down, alone in my room.

Denise rises from the couch. "What did I tell you, Marie? Our Adele wouldn't get herself nabbed." She takes a good look at me. "What happened?"

"He followed me into the sewers," I say. "He's dead."

Marie bursts into a round of fresh tears for the fallen German.

"He doesn't deserve your sympathy, Marie," Denise says quietly. She steps toward me. "Did anyone see you do it?"

"No one," I say, though that changes nothing.

We've been sniffed out. We have to leave the city as soon as possible.

Twenty-Seven

Saying good-bye to Marie was easier said than done. Tired of school and eager to prove herself she begged to come with us. "I am a skilled eavesdropper. Please take me with you!"

I felt torn over letting her come with us, because I didn't see the harm in it. I understand her desire to get involved. And she's so much fun. Part of me selfishly wanted her to be around longer. In the end, though, I went along with Denise's answer, a resounding no, which set off more tears than I've seen any girl shed in one sitting. It's a shame we had to leave. Estelle, her daughter, Cecile, and Marie treated us like family. I really will miss them.

Martin Cammerts, still peeved with me for breaking ties with him in front of new recruits yesterday, nearly blew a gasket when he heard I'd handed another bicycle to the Germans. Denise was quick to point out that at least I held on to that one for more than a week. He was reluctant to give me another bicycle, to say the least, but he did. It's a bit beat up and not as spiffy as the last one I lost. Cammerts also telephoned Bishop's contact in town to let him know Denise and I were headed back to him, but he did so grudgingly, not keen to do us any more favors.

Once again, Denise and I are on the road. German troops, vehicles, and supplies are all over France's major roadways, scurrying north to reinforce the Nazi-held front along the shores of the English Channel. Denise and I mapped out a different route to Madame LaRoche's farmhouse than the one we used to reach Paris.

"Bloody hell!" Denise smacks the handlebars hard enough to crack her fingers. "I left my good blouse on Marie's wash line."

"We're not going back to get it, if that's what you're thinking."

"I know it. Onward not backward, that's my motto today. You won't find me adding extra kilometers to this blasted ride."

Over the course of a month, without realizing it, I've become an expert cyclist. I'm flying on the trip back to Madame LaRoche's, as if I sprouted wings. Denise is matching my pace, but thanks to the close friendship she developed with the comfortable divan in the attic while hidden away with her radio, the ride is taking a toll on her. We hope to reach the farm by nightfall without stopping like we did last time, but the stiff upper lip Denise wore throughout the day is setting as rapidly as the sun into the valley.

"Listen to that," she says.

Not wanting to be outdone by her doglike sense of hearing, I coast on my bicycle, listening. "I don't hear a thing."

"I know. Isn't it wonderful? Absolute silence for the first time in weeks. I could soak it up like a sponge."

"I thought I had tuned out the air-raid sirens," I say. "But now that they're gone, I guess I must have been aware of them after all."

"Sometimes the sirens and screaming of planes overhead

reminds me of the Blitz all over again. The bombings went on for months, but remember the terror of the first day?"

"Of course," I say, thinking back. "It's been almost four years, but I remember as if it were yesterday. It was a sunny day like this when it began."

That September 7, we planned to celebrate Aunt Lib's birthday at the home of her best childhood friend, Emma Berkshire. My uncle wasn't fond of Emma's tendency to gossip, and my cousin Paul swooshed a hand behind his backside, saying, "She has too much wind. You may wish to hold your nose, Betty."

As we turned down Emma's street, my aunt said, "Not a cloud in the sky. I couldn't ask for a more peaceful and beautiful day than this."

At that, the air-raid sirens began to wail.

"Oh now, look what I've done," she said.

Uncle Edward calmly said, "It's likely nothing. Another military target only."

"Daddy, I hear aeroplanes," Philip said. "A lot of aeroplanes."

My heart slowed, along with my plodding feet. "I hear planes too."

Our small motionless group watching the sky steadily grew as the drone of planes became unmistakable.

"Mum, look!" Philip's eyes went wide with wonder. "Here they come, up the Thames."

"My God," Uncle Edward said. "There must be a thousand of the buggers."

Across the sky, three formations of German warplanes made their approach, shearing a calculated path toward us like a plague of roaring metal locusts. They blotted out the sun, shrouding the city in a shadow of impending catastrophe.

From the planes, bombs began to drop.

Chaos erupted in the street. Small children watching the sky with innocent curiosity began to scream, as their mothers lost all composure above them.

Uncle Edward gripped his wife by the shoulders. "Take the children to the public shelter. Stay there until I come for you."

We lost him to the frenzy. And we ran. Aunt Lib dragged her terrified sons behind her. I followed, keeping an eye on the bobbing royal-blue hat she wore on special occasions.

Inside the shelter, I sat next to my aunt and cousins. I drew my knees to my chest to fill as little space as possible. All around me, children screamed.

"I want Daddy," Philip whined when the ground beneath us began to rumble.

The squalling inside the shelter and the explosions within the city reached a shared crescendo. I wrapped my arms tighter about my legs, held on for dear life, and willed myself to stay strong for my much-younger cousins.

As soon as the quaking ebbed, I got to my feet. "I'm going to find Uncle Edward."

"Betty, no, we have yet to be given the all clear."

I ran from the safety of the shelter, directly into a hellish nightmare.

Thick smoke had poisoned the cloudless sky. Fire bells clanged throughout the city. Ash and smoldering bits of the barrage balloons fell through a wispy plaster-dust haze. Some homes had withstood the bombardment with only blown windows and doors to show for it. Others had been reduced to ruin. Rubble of all sorts littered the road.

A tenement building on the corner was sheared apart, the cleaved apartments open to the street as if half of a giant dollhouse. Pretty blue curtains dressed a kitchen window in one demolished apartment. An upright piano had survived in another.

From a nearby destroyed home my uncle strode through the debris. Over his shoulder lay a wilted woman, her torn dress exposing a shocking combination of blood, bare flesh, and undergarments. Her body swayed. I couldn't tell if she was dead or alive.

For a moment, the mayhem surrounding my uncle faded. The din became muffled to my ears. I stood rooted in the middle of the street, too awestruck to move, only able to focus on the measured rise and fall of his broad chest, his swift, regimented movements, and the bravery of a true hero. On that day, the horror of the war became a reality for me.

"It was as if the world turned upside-down," I say. "Nothing was the same after that."

Denise rides alongside my bike, nodding. "The peace and quiet is about to be turned on its end again. Can you imagine what must be happening in Britain? Ships in the Channel, planes set to go, thousands of men at the ready. It gives me chills thinking about it."

I think about Robbie. How far has he traveled on the evasion line? At least when he was under our protection I knew his exact whereabouts. Who's looking out for him now? I wish I could pop in on his journey, just for a moment, to see with my own eyes that he's all right. There's no way of even knowing whether he's alive or dead. It's the uncertainty that eats away at me the most.

We reach the farm by half past ten, a stunning achievement that has me beaming with pride and Denise wobbling weak-kneed to the bushes outside the gate to vomit.

"I disliked every second of that ride." She staggers back into the swath of moonlight illuminating the road. "I should check you for rivets. Look at you, hardly out of breath, for Pete's sake."

We push our bikes up the darkened lane. Being outside after curfew no longer seems frightening or defiant the way it did before. We've done worse.

Just as she did that first night we met, Madame LaRoche throws her arms around each of us in turn. I return the hug, happy to see her again.

"Girls, thank God you've arrived safely. Come inside. You must be famished."

"And crippled," Denise says.

The kitchen appears smaller, less imposingly grand than before. Her home has lost some of its mystery. In a way, that saddens me.

"A drop is taking place," Madame LaRoche says. "The men are there now."

She shoos us from the kitchen to wait in the parlor. We're immediately drawn to the two matching side chairs.

Denise settles onto the padding. "I'm not sure this is such a good idea," she groans. "I fear I may never be able to leave this chair. Also, please tell me your arse hurts as much as mine does or I may never be able to speak to you again."

"It sure does," I say. That is no lie.

From behind the glass door of Madame LaRoche's walnut curio cabinet, the young boy with tousled hair and wiry arms and legs smiles at me from a framed photograph. I give a groggy smile to little Pierre, before admiring her other treasures once more.

Next thing I know, Bishop is in my face, rousing me from sleep.

"Adele and Denise, it's wonderful to see you. Wake up. Come join us for a drink."

At the sound of his voice, Denise is on her feet, drowsily mumbling, "Drink, you say? Who's sleeping?" She rubs the sleep from her eyes with reckless abandon.

We shuffle behind him to the kitchen table. The first person I set eyes on is Pierre. Dressed in denim trousers and a black sweater, with a hint of stubble and his hair wavy with the sweat of dangerous work, he looks more handsome than ever. My cheeks burn and I have to look away.

"Hello, Adele." He places a wineglass at my place setting and moves on.

I fumble for words and the glass. "Hello."

A slender, dark-haired woman and a balding man with a prominent mole on his chin, both in jump overalls, sit across from Pierre and his mother, joined by Marcus and Gus.

I know how those new agents feel, surrounded by new people in a stranger's home. I wish Denise and I could go back and experience the exhilaration, and even the fright, of parachuting into France all over again. For us, that first night is nothing more than a fond memory.

TWENTY-EIGHT

I sit on a log near the creek, my face tilted skyward, impatiently waiting for billowy clouds to reveal the midafternoon sun. I'm happy to be away from the bustle of the city and back at the farm, but throughout the night I dreamed of the dead soldier's face as he drowned in front of me, his eyes pleading with me to help him. I woke up in a rotten mood that I can't seem to shake.

Pierre comes up behind me through the woods. He stands on the end of log, balancing sure-footedly; an indistinct but decidedly masculine form in my peripheral vision.

I saw him watching me from the barn. Each time he came and went, he tossed a glance my way. The man is tireless with stamina to spare, I have to give him that. I don't know when or if he makes time for sleep.

"Mind if I sit?"

"No, go ahead," I say.

He settles on the log and leans forward to sort through river rocks scattered at his feet. I set my chin in my hands, watching the brook—dehydrated to a muddy shadow of its former self— swirl around a mossy rock.

"You've been here a while." Pierre tosses a pebble. It sails in a slow arc. Circular ripples spread out across the water like tiny dartboard rings. "Keeping busy, I see."

There's plenty I should be doing. Madame LaRoche asked me to pick strawberries, my bike tires need air, and if I want to freshen up I'll have to pump water from the well. All I want to do is sit in the forest, me and the songbirds, with nobody around to put me to work.

Pierre pulls a worn notebook, curved to the perfect imprint of his shape, from his back pocket.

"We received word that two code phrases will be relayed to the Resistance during broadcasts of the *messages personnel*. The first phrase will signal the D-day attack on France's shores within the week. The second will let us know the attack is set to occur within forty-eight hours."

"What are the phrases?" I ask.

"They sounded familiar, but I couldn't recall when I'd heard them before. Then I remembered this book of poetry. It belonged to my father." Fiddling with a damaged corner of the cover, he says, "Everyone who met my father respected and liked him. He had an almost magical knack for machinery. He loved to work with his hands, but he also appreciated art, cinema, and litera-ture. He could talk circles around most people, but in a way that never made anyone feel inferior."

"He reminds me of my brother. One minute he'd be building a car for the soapbox derby, the next he'd be working out a com-plex arithmetic problem." My cheeks tremble, and I worry I might not be able to hold myself together. For weeks, I've thought about my brother more than usual. "He was destined for great things."

Pierre opens the book to a page marked by a blade of grass. He reads the first stanza of *"Chanson d'Automne,"* a poem by Paul Verlaine.

"Les sanglots longs des violons de l'automne. Blessent mon cœur d'une langueur monotone."

"The first phrase is, *the long sobs of the violins of autumn.* And the second is, *wound my heart with a monotonous languor,*" I say. "Did I translate that correctly?"

Pierre's English, which I haven't heard him speak until now, is weighted down with a heavy French accent. "I prefer, *the long sobs of autumn's violins.* A slightly different arrangement with the same meaning." Switching back to French, he adds, "My father was a physical laborer with a sharp mind. The Resistance's call to violence and sabotage is lovely and poetic. I think that irony would amuse him."

"Isn't it incredible? *We* will have advance notice of the Allied invasion. My ear will be glued to the radio, listening for those lines of poetry."

"The end is in sight." Pierre tucks the notebook into his pocket. "I will do whatever it takes to help the Allies free my country and the people of France."

Only a brave and honorable person would make that pledge and mean it.

For the first time, I put shyness aside to really look at Pierre. A fading white scar carves a swath through his stubble, from the corner of his mouth to below his jawline. His eyes appear tired, creased with fine wrinkles near his temples.

"I'll do whatever it takes too," I say.

He stares at the brook, lost in thought, then after a moment his slow nod seems to change everything between us. We trust and believe in each other.

Pierre holds his hand out. "Adele, come with me."

After some hesitation, I let him pull me up to standing. "Where are we going?"

"You'll see."

The secrecy is making me nervous. Something fishy is going on. At the barn, he leads me through the double doors. We stop next to the grimy canvas sheet draped over the unusually big bicycle. The canvas sheet he accused me of touching when we first met.

He yanks the sheet away, like a magician unveiling a trick.

"It's a motorcycle!" I cry, although I've never seen any motorcycle quite like this one, with its sleek all-black frame, shiny chrome, and golden detail on the gas tank. "It looks like a machine from the future."

"It does, doesn't it," he says, "It's a Saroléa, from Belgium. It was my father's."

"I bet it can go really fast."

"It can," he says, and I didn't think it was even possible for him to smile this broadly. "I doubt it will start, but if it does, do you want to go for a ride?"

"Oh, I don't know," I say. All the two-wheeled vehicles I've ever ridden travel only as fast as I can pedal them.

Pierre straddles the seat and slams the kick-starter with his foot. The motorcycle roars to life, sputtering and rumbling, but starting on the first try.

"Well, I guess this means we're destined to go for a ride," he shouts over the motor. "Climb on behind me and hold tight."

I look at the seat, the impossibly small space I'm supposed to fit myself onto. I climb on behind Pierre and mold my body around his. Squeezing tightly to his ribcage, I press my face against his back as the motorcycle rolls through the double doors. His sweater smells of gun grease, and the farm, and campfire smoke.

At the road, Pierre calls out over his shoulder, "Are you ready?"

I raise my head to say, "I guess so."

As if it's been let loose from a slingshot, the motorcycle shoots across the countryside, ripping through the solitude. I open my eyes briefly to watch the landscape whiz past at exhilarating and frightening speeds. Wind whips my hair against my cheeks. Squealing from the thrill of it all, I squeeze Pierre so hard I think his ribs might crack.

Pierre lays his hand over mine, pressing it against his chest to keep me safe. His strong heart pounds beneath my palm. Gripping each other tightly, we speed away.

With the motorcycle beneath us, no one is a match for Pierre and me. Not the Germans. Not anyone.

Twenty-Nine

Madame LaRoche's radio, a black box about the size of a bread-box, sits on the kitchen table. Denise, Pierre, Bishop, and I hover around it like moths to a flame, elbows rudely resting on the tabletop. If we accidently get too close in our excitement and bump the radio, the signal crackles to incoherent fuzz. Denise is a real stickler about keeping our distance. Pierre has ignored most of her warnings tonight, and I swear she'd slug him if Bishop weren't watching.

Madame LaRoche, the only one of us who seems able to eat throughout the nine o'clock news, brings spoonfuls of creamed soup to her mouth and sips her wine.

"London calling with messages for our friends," the radio announces. We take a collective breath, as if to ensure none of us further muffles the already static-filled broadcast. *"Et voici quelques messages personnel."*

Personal messages to other circuits of the Resistance fill the kitchen: "John has a long mustache." "The sap runs in spring-time." "Over the mountains, there is a comfy inn." "The nurse has found the cure for Michael."

What we hear next sends our breaths out in a collective gasp.

"The long sobs of the violins of autumn."

"*Mon Dieu!*" Madame LaRoche says. Soup dribbles back into her bowl.

Pierre shushes her.

"*Je répète*," says the announcer. "The long sobs of the violins of autumn."

The messages continue, but I don't think any of us are able to pay attention.

"Did you all hear that?" Bishop says, as if needing confirmation that what he heard was real. "This is the word we've been waiting for. Our Allied boys are preparing to storm the beaches. The next week is imperative. It is our time to shine."

Pierre's foot anxiously thumps the floor in spite of the hand he laid on his knee to keep the leg still.

Bishop places his hands on the table. "German reinforcements of fifteen thousand men each are at the ready in the south. Those troops are about to reroute to the landing beaches. Our goal is to make that process a confusing, muddled mess. With their phone lines down, they will have a right devil of a time trying to coordinate. We will make life absolute hell as the troops advance north. We will make life absolute hell as they retreat. We will do everything in our power to help the Allies drive them back to Germany. This is what we are here for, folks. We are about to make history."

Hot and shaky, almost drunkenly overcome with pride and anticipation, I fan my face with my hand.

Bishop turns to face Pierre and then me. "Tonight, the two of you are to blast phone lines to the local German garrison. Pierre, you know which lines I'm speaking of?"

"Yes, of course," he says, smiling to me when I catch his eye. "Consider it done."

———

Driving during the day is suspect. Driving at night well after curfew, as we are, is lunacy. Only members of the Resistance run the risk, and if they're caught, the Germans don't bother to ask questions.

Pierre parks within a forest clearing secluded from the road. "From here, we walk."

We hoist our supplies onto our backs.

"The telephone lines are two kilometers away," he says.

I figure we will reach our target in half an hour. All things considered, we should be back at the farm in less than three hours.

Pierre marches ahead, forcing me to keep up. Riding a bike and running are two surprisingly different things, and I'm definitely better at one than the other. There's no chance I'll confess to the pain in my ribcage. There's even less chance I'll ask Pierre to slow down for me. I will match his speed or collapse trying.

At the main road, we come to the phone lines we're expected to sabotage. We go about rigging the explosives, one pole to the next. The moldable plastic explosive smells of almonds as I smooth it into shape with my hands.

Pierre rigs the chain of explosives to the detonator and we take our places in the ditch next to the road.

"Ready?" he asks with his hand on the plunger.

I sit back at least another foot to press my body farther into the curve of the gully.

He takes that as my answer, when really I'm about to suggest we're too close, and cranks the plunger to set off the explosives.

The first blast hits me full-on: an ear-bursting, body-rattling surprise. The wooden pole shears apart at its base and falls across the ditch. The next powerful explosion sends another pole crashing. Spellbound, I watch the poles go down like mighty trees at the hands of Paul Bunyan.

Pierre's arm snaps around my waist. He lifts me into the air and scrambles backward. The final explosion, a wave of thundering sound, hits me. Everything goes silent except for a slight hum in my ears. I collapse onto my back. My head bounces off the hard ground. Pierre's body protectively envelops me.

We stay locked in each other's arms for a moment, cheek to cheek, chest to chest, hearts hammering.

Stubble skims my cheek. His warm breath, so very close to my lips, sends a shiver through me.

I run my hands over powerful arms and shoulders that see work from sun up to sun down. With the weight of Pierre's body pressed against mine, I feel so protected and cared for. I don't want the feeling to end.

I want Pierre to kiss me. I want him to *want* to kiss me.

I close my eyes.

Pierre tucks my hair behind my ear. His fingers trail down my neck. He kisses me, softly. I kiss him back. His kisses grow more and more passionate until I have to lay my hands against his shoulders and pull away.

Pierre rolls onto his side. Cold air rushes to fill the spaces where his heat had been. He watches me, his face partially masked by darkness. A silver thread of moonlight twines through his hair.

If only we could ignore curfew. If only the demolition we caused wouldn't bring the Germans running. If only the world could go back to normal for a few moments.

If only.

In the dim light, I read Pierre's moving lips as he speaks too quietly for me to hear.

"Adele, you are the most . . ."

"Pierre, I can't—" I begin to whisper. My heart pounds frantically. The buzzing in my ears intensifies.

At my shocked whimper, Pierre's face lowers closer to mine, his lips moving rapidly. But I can't hear him, because I also can't hear myself.

The final explosion left me completely deaf.

THIRTY

Pierre refuses to let go of my hand as we walk back to the truck. We can't risk becoming separated in the dark.

I slide onto the truck seat. Pierre closes the door for me. The sore spot on my head thumps a pain wave through my skull with every beat of my heart. I close my eyes and apply pressure with my hand, although that does nothing to dull the ache.

Pierre starts the truck. A few kilometers down the road, he brakes within a pale patch of moonlight. I read his lips as he says, "Are you all right?"

I nod, desperate to get back to the safety of the farm, and he drives on.

I've proven myself to Pierre. I don't want to mess that up. The work he believes to be too dangerous for girls isn't too dangerous for me. If I complain or appear weak, he might change his mind about taking me along on the next sabotage mission. But the loss of my hearing is worrying. I rest my head against the back of the seat, staring at the darkness outside my window. Will the silence last only minutes or hours? What if the damage is permanent? I can't possibly work for the SOE then. What good is a deaf spy? On the next moonlit night they'll send in a Lysander and fly me straight back to Britain.

As the drive wears on, my ears come back to life gradually, picking up the truck's low rumble, and the air streamlining us, and the mellow tune Pierre sometimes hums when he's lost in thought. By the time we reach the farm, my hearing seems to have returned completely. The real test will come when one of us speaks, but since I hope to avoid an awkward conversation with Pierre about what went on between us, I keep quiet. Things made a lot more sense in the heat of the moment. Now I'm left with horrible, stomach-clenching guilt that I've somehow betrayed Robbie.

Pierre parks in a thatched garage next to the barn. "Adele, I hope your hearing has come back." I'm the first out of the truck, saying, "Yes, it has. Thank you. Good night, Pierre." I can't run to the farmhouse fast enough, glad my hearing is back but wishing I hadn't heard Pierre end our exciting night on an awkwardly formal note.

Denise wakes up the instant I try to slip into my bed without disturbing her.

"How did it go?" she mumbles.

"About as well as could be expected, I guess. I was deaf for a bit, but I'm okay now." I lay my arms, prickly with heat and sweat, on the outside of the sheet to catch the cooling breeze coming in through the open window. "And he kissed me."

That erases all traces of sleep from Denise's voice. "Who kissed you?"

I calculate how few hours remain until daylight. If I conk out within the next minute, I can squeeze in the bare minimum of sleep required to stay on my toes tomorrow. "Let's pretend I didn't say that and get some sleep."

"Not bloody likely. Spill the beans. Pierre? Pierre kissed you?"

"Yes."

Turning onto her side, she says, "I bet he's a good kisser. Those strong silent types usually are."

"Was he ever." I sigh.

"On a scale from one to ten, how did he rate? Ten being he made your toes curl and one being he made you retch."

"He was a solid nine."

"You don't say," Denise says, clearly impressed.

"It was strange. When he kissed me, you know what my first thought was?"

"Am I wearing clean knickers?"

"No." I laugh quietly, wanting to toss something at her. "I remembered Rhett Butler telling Scarlett that she should be kissed often and by someone who knows how. Did you see *Gone with the Wind*, Denise?"

"Several times."

I close my eyes and smile as the film plays across my dark lids. "Don't you love the part when Rhett is about to go to war? And he wants to take the memory of Scarlett's kisses with him, so he can die with a beautiful memory. Isn't that romantic?"

Dressed only in her nightgown, Denise streaks across the room, barely able to sob out the words, "I'm going to get some air."

In a jiffy, my cheerful soar plummets into a perplexed tailspin.

"Now, Denise? It must be half past four. I'll stop talking if you like, so you can sleep."

She's gone before I finish speaking. I can't help but feel as if I've been a terrible friend. While I desperately want to drop into a deep sleep to recuperate from explosions and deafness and my first real passionate kiss, I fold back the sheet and get out of bed.

I pick out sounds of her movements, down the stairs, through the kitchen, and out the front door, and even though I doubt she wants to be followed, I go after her. Barefoot and dressed for bed, I catch up with her at the woodpile around the side of the house. She sits on the old stump Pierre uses for chopping.

It doesn't take long for dew to find us. Denise's teeth chatter and mine clatter an echoed reply.

"You needn't have come after me," she says.

"I know I didn't need to."

The farm's sleek calico cat slinks out from around the woodpile, a fresh catch still in her teeth. She dutifully carries the dead mouse to Denise and drops it at her feet.

"Bring me a present, Moxie?" She scratches the cat's head. "You're a sweet girl."

Denise bestowed names on all the cats. She says that every cat, even a barn cat, needs a good and proper name of its own.

"Moxie's a brilliant huntress," she says to me, but she won't look up to my face.

"Denise, do you want to be left alone?"

Moxie nudges the hand that's gone stationary behind her ears back into motion.

When I step toward the open doorway, Denise says, "Stay! That is . . . if you want to."

I roll a stout, uncut log onto its end; an impromptu and uncomfortable chair.

"*Gone with the Wind* was the last film I saw with Simon." The fingers on Denise's left hand, all bare, flick out on her lap. She reins them back. "My fiancé."

This news catches me by surprise. It seems like the sort of thing she would have told me about before now.

"You're engaged?" I can't even imagine myself with a fiancé at Denise's age.

"I was." Patting her eyes, she says, "Simon is dead."

The words almost take my breath away. I can't imagine how devastating it must have been for her to lose her fiancé. I've only known Robbie a short time, and it would truly break my heart to hear that he had died.

"I'm so sorry, Denise."

"I miss him every day."

We take a quiet moment to dry our eyes. Moxie decides she has better places to be, and we watch her scamper off to make the most of the last remaining hour of night.

"Simon and I were sweethearts since primary school. He was my first and only love. My mum and dad told us we were too young and foolish to be thinking about engagement and marriage. But we knew they were wrong. I knew I wanted to spend the rest of my life with him. I wanted us to be together forever. We were *meant* to be together." Denise lets out a weepy sigh. "Three and a half years ago, the sixteenth of September, his Spitfire was shot down. He never made it out."

I put my hand on Denise's.

"I didn't understand how a person as good as Simon could be taken away forever, while I was allowed to keep on living."

My throat tightens. "Yes."

"For a while, I wished my life had ended with his. It didn't. I kept going. That's just what you do, I guess. At first I sat around with a woe-is-me attitude, feeling sorry for myself. Then I realized that everyone I knew was also suffering. I could continue moping around or I could get out and do my part. And that led me to where I am now, sitting here with you. We all have our own reasons for coming to France. I wanted to get back at the people who took Simon away from me."

I raise my eyebrows at her. "That night at the Commodore, you wanted revenge?"

"I can't say it didn't cross my mind. Like I said, it wasn't my finest hour." Resting her chin on her hands, she says, "It made me realize one thing, though. My anger was getting the better of me. Driving me mad almost. Since I've come back to the LaRoches' I've had time to think. Somewhere in Germany, there's a girl mourning the love of her life. Perhaps my Simon shot him down. Perhaps if she and I met, we'd be friends. That really got under my skin, you know?"

I nod.

"What about you, Adele? Why are you here?"

"When asked if I like adventure, I said yes."

"But it can't be so straightforward, can it? Answering a simple question doesn't get you through four grueling months of training and propel you to jump from a plane into an enemy-occupied foreign land. Most people run away from danger. Not toward it, arms spread wide."

"Well, I guess so much about this war is so terribly wrong that eventually I felt like I had to do something," I say. "And I wanted to be brave, like my uncle. After rescuing nine people the first day of the Blitz, he didn't go home and wring his hands. As I sat seething in my bedroom that night, I overheard him saying to my aunt, 'They cannot get away with this. We mustn't let them.'

I knew he was right, but what could I do? I was only a young girl. I couldn't go off to war like he did."

Denise leans toward me. "And then you grew up."

"Three years later, I was invited to Baker Street. At first I didn't take the invitation seriously. The more I thought about it, though, the more I wondered why they'd asked me. I felt flattered. Maybe they saw something in me that I didn't? It wouldn't hurt to see what it was all about. Nothing had to come of it. But when I arrived one of the first things the captain said to me was, 'We must make it clear to Germany that Britain will never surrender. We will not bow to their tyranny!' All my anger came flooding back. Everything sort of lined up and clicked into place in my mind. They handed me that opportunity at the perfect time. I'd already burdened my aunt longer than I should have, but I wasn't sure where else to go."

"That's right. Your father had abandoned you."

I draw in a long breath and release it slowly, as I would before firing my weapon.

"So that's why I'm here," I say. "Who knows where I'll go after this. I guess when the time comes I'll think about it then."

After a moment of drowsy silence, Denise says, "Thank you, Adele."

"What for?"

"For telling your story. To me."

I smile, and we watch the first traces of light appear on the horizon, while the world still feels tranquil, a flat, calm sea before an approaching storm.

Thirty-One

It's going on half past ten when I return to the farm after cycling through the countryside all day on the lookout for more fields the SOE can use in their night drops of agents and supplies. After jotting notes, I score each one on a points system I made up. Two fields are perfect, I think, and with any luck Bishop will agree. Riding around on a bicycle and gazing into wide-open spaces doesn't sound like hard work, but the success or failure of a drop depends on the choices I make.

Feeling mentally exhausted and like a wet rag wrung out and hung to dry in the scorching sun, I enter the house with only food and sleep on my agenda. I plan to tick them off in short order.

Straight away I spot Shepherd, seated alone at the kitchen table, tearing a chunk of crusty bread into halves. My heart leaps in my chest.

"Hi there," I say.

"Hello, stranger, good to see you again."

My mind whirrs while I remove my shoes. As far as he knows, the last time we saw each other was on the plane. He doesn't know I watched his capture from the forest, or that Robbie and I saw him in Paris.

"Good to see you too," I say, stepping forward. "I heard you got captured."

"Luckily my captors were two sluggish gendarmes with their heads in the clouds. I would have been daft as a brush not to take advantage of the first opportunity to escape. I took off like my pants were afire. I've never run that bloody fast in my life."

"I'll bet," I say. "Did they get you to talk?"

He glances down at his bread. "No, of course not."

"Well, that's good."

"I'm just relieved to have finally found Bishop again," he says. He points over his shoulder. "Madame LaRoche asked me to tell you there's soup on the stove."

Weak steam escapes the pot when I lift the lid. I fill a bowl with tepid broth and vegetables, pull a chair out from the table, and sit my aching body down. Since nobody's around but Shepherd, I drink the liquid straight from the bowl.

Meticulously ripping his bread as if along a seam in the crust, he says, "So, you and Denise were sent to Paris. What did you think?"

"It was how I imagined it would be," I say with a shrug. "Did you get to spend any time there?"

"Unfortunately no, I've been busy in and around Caen."

"That's too bad."

I polish off every vegetable, including the lowly rutabaga. Still hungry, I lick the spoon clean.

Shepherd passes the bread plate to me. The sheen of his wrist-watch band reflects the glow of the table's candles. I lean forward to take a piece of bread to get a better look, and my heart just about stops. There are enough diamonds and gold in the thing to keep a small town fed for a month.

"Handsome watch," I say, sopping up broth at the bottom of my bowl.

He rolls the upturned cuff of his shirt sleeve over his wrist. "It's a fake, naturally."

"Of course." The bread hits the spot. I yawn, stretching my arms. "I'm off to bed. See you in the morning."

"Yes, good night to you."

I place my bowl in the sink and head upstairs to bed.

If Shepherd thinks he can fool me, he is sorely mistaken.

———————

When I wake, I roll over, careful not to flex my calf muscles the wrong way. The charley horses I get after long rides are excruciating.

I'm surprised to see Denise's neatly made bed is empty and she's already left the room. I usually can't sleep through her morning beauty routine. I dress hurriedly, shocked to have overslept. I have to catch Bishop and talk to him about Shepherd before he leaves for the day.

My reflection streaks across the washstand mirror like a disheveled hag from a Shakespearean play. One foot inside the room and one foot out, I hem and haw over the decision to give in to vanity when I'm in such a hurry. But what if I bump into Pierre? I splash some water on my face and drag a comb through my hair.

Luckily, Pierre isn't in the kitchen when I get there, but

neither is anybody else. Through the window I spot Madame
LaRoche pushing a wheelbarrow across the yard. I cram my bare
feet into my shoes and go outside.

"Good morning, Claire," I say, jogging to her. "Have you
seen Bishop, by any chance?"

"Good morning." She sets the wheelbarrow down. "Yes, he is
over there."

Behind me, Bishop is leaning against the side of the house,
smoking a pipe. I thank Madame LaRoche and run to him.

"Can we talk privately?" I ask. "I have something important
to tell you."

"Yes, of course. Let's take a seat on the bench in the flower
garden."

On the way to the bench, I say, "It's about Shepherd, sir."

Continuing to look straight ahead, Bishop says, "Tell me
more."

When we're seated, I tuck my hair behind my ears. As I fell
asleep last night, I put together everything I want to say. I get
straight to it while the words are still somewhat organized in my
mind.

"I think Shepherd is a double agent. That's a heavy accusation,
I know, but I was awake half the night thinking it through."

Bishop tilts his head, watching smoke curl from the pipe. "What
makes you think he has been turned, Adele?"

"Nothing about his arrest and escape make sense, Bishop.
After our jump, I watched him get captured by four gendarmes,
not two as he told me last night. And he assured me he didn't talk
under interrogation, but it didn't ring true."

With a slow nod, Bishop says, "Go on."

"Denise and I dodged capture in Paris a few times because

luck was on our side. Our first safe house was compromised, maybe by Shepherd, maybe not, but because of that we became separated for a while. He may have lost track of us. Then one afternoon he found me. He followed at distance, and he doesn't know I saw him. Soon after, on a ride, I had a close call with a German roadblock that had been set up in the middle of nowhere. It was as if they knew a courier would be traveling through. I think that net was meant to snag me."

Bishop's dignified features give infuriatingly little in the way of a reaction.

"Anything else you'd like to add?"

"My contact warned me that she was being followed. She even suspected a leak in our circuit. The most damning evidence against Shepherd came to me last night, though. That watch of his is worth a small fortune. And he lied right to my face about being in Paris."

"Is that all, Adele?"

"Yes, sir."

"Thank you," he says, rising. "I'll take that under advisement."

He strides off, leaving me alone on the bench. Doubt creeps over me. Should I have kept my nose out of it? I don't want to be a brown-nosing snitch. I only want to do the right thing. I stay at the bench a few minutes, mulling everything over, point by point.

I leave the spring garden of wilting daffodils and woebegone tulips, stripped by the wind of half their red and yellow petals, along a winding gravel path.

At the barn, I call through the open door. "Denise, are you in here?"

From deep inside the building, she hollers, "I'm in Daisy's stall."

I just saw Daisy, the farm's milking cow, grazing in the pasture with her playful calf, Clover. When I reach the back of the barn, I find Denise mucking the stall with a tall, handsome stranger.

"I thought you were never going to wake up." Denise wipes sweat from her forehead with the sleeve of the old work shirt protecting her clothes. "Adele, this is Frank. Frank, this is Adele."

Pokerfaced, he extends his hand. In a voice as bland as his handshake, he says, "Nice to meet you."

"He's a downed airman," Denise tells me. "You've been working hard, Frank. Why don't you get something to eat?"

He leans his pitchfork against the wall. "That is a good idea. I'm hungry."

Frank's mesmerizing pale-green eyes are almost too pretty for a man's face. Even they can't make up for his apparent lack of personality.

We watch his back—and a rather fine back it is—until he's out the door.

Denise lets loose a snippy "My word!"

"Geez, I've seen wood with more charisma."

"I have never in my life met anyone so boring. The ways he talks it's as if he's reading from a textbook. I asked about Connecticut, where he's from, and he said something about missing the rolling hills and the many horse farms. Who speaks that way? And the dull bugger has latched himself right on to me, following me around like a lost puppy."

"I thought you liked puppies."

Denise sticks her tongue out at me.

"He's from Connecticut? So am I."

"Don't tell that to Professor Frank. He may strike up a conversation about population density and average seasonal temperatures."

Laughing, I grab the pitchfork Frank used. "Want help with the chores?"

"Yes, thank you. I have yet to do the calf stall. Claire and I are collecting manure mixed with straw to add as compost to the gardens."

Denise and I work a good hour together, mucking and hauling and spreading fresh straw, before the hunger pangs wrenching at my gut force me to quit. Cycling long distances has given me a ferocious appetite. Circumstances being what they are, I'm never able to keep my stomach entirely happy.

At the house, I open the kitchen door and peer inside, hoping Frank is long gone.

The kitchen is empty. The adjoining parlor isn't.

"Hi, Pierre." On the table in front of him is a bottle of red wine. "It's a little early for wine, isn't it?"

He brings the bottle to his merlot-tinged lips. When I enter the room he offers it to me.

"You might want to drink this," he says.

"Why?" Something is very wrong. Pierre refuses to look me in the face. "What happened?"

He takes another long swig. "I killed Shepherd."

Thirty-Two

The strength seems to drain from my legs. I sit in the other side chair.

"You killed him?" I cry. "What do you mean?"

"I shot him. He's dead. There is no other meaning."

"I don't understand. Why did you have to shoot him?"

"What would you have had me do?"

"I thought he would be sent back to England. He's only twenty-three, Pierre! It wasn't necessary to kill him."

"You can take that up with Bishop. He left it in my hands. I have to do what is right for me. I will defend my family, my farm, and my men at all costs. Had others in the Maquis found out about Shepherd's dealings, his end would not have been so humane."

I stare at Claire's treasures in the cabinet, at a loss for words.

"But he was one of us," I stammer.

"One of us? By that do you mean one of the good guys? There

are good guys and bad guys on all sides of this war. He was not one of us."

"Oh my God," I say, shielding my eyes. I can't breathe. Can't gather my thoughts. "This is my fault."

"His greed is to blame, not you. Weeks ago, Bishop caught wind of suspicious behavior from an agent fitting his description. He was seen from here to Calais and as far south as Lyon, flaunting expensive jewelry and wads of crisp unused bills."

I lounge against the backrest of the chair. "The agent was Shepherd? Please tell me you know that without a single doubt."

"Yes, believe me." Pierre glances at me out of the corner of his eye, and I know exactly what the look implies. "I have no doubt it was him."

"Where did the money come from? Did he steal from the SOE?"

"The Germans were paying him for information. And he was selling them weapons and supplies from drops intended for the Resistance."

I draw in a sharp breath. "No!"

"Yes," Pierre says. "And he didn't escape. He cracked and they let him go. Were you and Denise captured in Paris?"

"Yes, once. A van detected Denise's radio transmissions."

"Shepherd knew next to nothing of your whereabouts, but he knew right where to find Denise. They watched her there for some time."

If Shepherd stood in front of me now, I wouldn't think twice about wringing his disloyal neck with my own hands. My fist slams the tabletop. A glass candy dish jumps as if to seek a safer location. The curse that follows the thumping has such resonance I bet Madame LaRoche is clear on the opposite end of the farm, covering her ears.

"The no-good weasel! We would have gone to prison!"

"He wasn't working alone, Adele. He had help."

I lay my hand over my pounding heart.

"Shepherd knew his accomplice only by the name Henri." Pierre sighs. "That man is still on the loose. Without knowing his identity there's nothing we can do to find and stop him."

It was shocking enough to uncover one traitor. I don't want to believe that Shepherd had an accomplice. That proves there are others like him out there. Men like Henri. People may end up imprisoned, tortured, or dead because of him.

"Just wait till I tell Denise."

"Please don't," he says. "Can we keep this between you, me, and Bishop?"

I don't know how I can possibly keep the news from Denise, but I agree.

"Did he honestly think he'd get away scot-free?" I ask. "What was he thinking, coming here? He must have been out of his mind."

"I don't think he knew the two of you were here. The moment he walked in the door he saw Denise. He got an odd look, like he was about to be ill. I didn't think much of it at the time." His head drifts back to rest against the wall. "The power and money went to his head. He seemed genuinely surprised that we caught on to him."

"I can't believe this. It's no wonder you knocked back a bottle of wine."

"I'm not upset because I killed him."

I straighten to look him in the face.

"I'm upset because I've become hardened to the things that should sicken me." He stares out the window. "My life was never perfect, but it was peaceful. It was good. Our family was happy.

I've seen more misery in the past four years than I did in the eighteen years before them. I don't know how I got from that time to this one, in which I'm willing to kill a man. What if when this part of my life is over, I'm unable to go back to the person I was? What if I'm damaged forever?"

His fingers intertwine with mine. I bring our palms together.

"I wonder about those same things," I say. "I guess we'll just have to trust that when this ends, we will be all right."

———

I speed up the lane to the farm on my bicycle with two minutes to spare before Denise and I are to meet at her hidden radio behind the barn.

Moxie slinks out from the bushes into my path. While I swerve to avoid her, she leaps several feet in the air and spins away, tail puffed and fur on end. My back tire slides out from under me. Down I go, crashing first to one knee, then to my hands. The bike adds insult to injury, falling straight on top of me with a pedal to the kidney and a handlebar to the back of the head.

I scramble up, righting the bike and glancing around to make sure no one witnessed my clumsy fall. Of course, there's Pierre, strolling out the barn door.

"Are you okay?" he asks.

"I'm fine." I sweep my throbbing skinned knee clean with my hand. Wheeling the bike toward him, I say, "Can you do me a favor and tell Denise I'm running a little late? I'll be around back in a few minutes."

"Denise isn't here."

I lean my bike against the barn. "I have a crucial and

time-sensitive message for her to transmit to London. She's waiting at her radio."

"No, I have been in and out of this barn all day, and Denise
isn't here."

"She must be with the cats then."

"Once again, she is not here."

"In the house?"

Pierre's huffy exhale borders on a growl.

"All right, all right. Wait right there." I cast my finger at his
feet like a wand, as if that might freeze them in place.

I run around the barn. A crescent-shaped row of bushes buf-
fers the fallen log from view. I round the first shrub. Our meeting
place is empty. I drop to my scraped hands and knees to check
the fallen log.

Both Denise and her transmitter are missing.

I race back to Pierre. Incredibly, he obeyed my command
to stay.

"She wasn't there."

"Sorry, I should have told you that."

"Pierre, something isn't right. Her transmitter is gone.
Where could she be?"

"The last time I saw her, she was going somewhere with that
downed pilot, Frank."

"Frank?" I cringe at the mention of him. "Where were they
going?"

"I have no idea. What Denise does is none of my concern."

"What did you see?"

"I have things to do, Adele."

"Please, Pierre. Denise wouldn't miss a transmission. Tell
me what you saw. Any detail that sticks out in your mind."

"They were going into the woods by the stream, looking rather friendly. Frank had his hand on Denise's back." Pierre's ordinarily beautiful lips take on a leering smile. "It can be easy to lose track of time."

"Get your mind out of the gutter. There is nothing romantic going on between them. She can hardly stand him."

"I don't blame her. He has only two things on his mind, automobiles and baseball. We could talk for hours about cars, if he weren't so strange, but what do I know about baseball and his beloved Boston Yankees? I've taken to avoiding him."

"I do know baseball," I say. "And believe me, he did not combine the words 'Boston' and 'Yankees' in the same sentence. The Sox sold Babe Ruth to the Yankees. He must have said either the Boston Red Sox or the New York Yankees."

Pierre shrugs his shoulders, as if I spoke gibberish. "He said the Boston Yankees. The mistake isn't mine. How could I jumble proper team names if I don't know any?"

"But that makes no sense at all. There isn't a self-respecting American boy or man alive who would make that mistake."

Our heads snap up in unison.

"It makes sense if Frank is pretending to be an American pilot."

"We have to find her!"

Pierre clutches my hand. I sprint alongside him.

"Did Shepherd bring him to the farm?" I cry.

"Yes, but Bishop questioned him about his squadron, air base, and personnel. He passed."

"Bishop's a Brit. He wouldn't know the sorts of questions that might trip him up. Frank wouldn't pass my test."

At the stream, Pierre's grip on my hand clamps down,

crushing my fingers, knuckle against knuckle. He pulls me to a stop. Pain shoots across my shoulder blade. Wrenching downward on my arm, he sends me earthbound like a sack of potatoes.

I had nearly burst straight into the clearing where Frank sits bent over Denise's radio.

Pierre taps my chin to the left. A few paces in front of us, Denise is gagged and bound with rope to the opposite side of a tree.

"You take care of Denise, I'll get Frank," Pierre whispers.

That's the extent of his plan. He leaps to his feet. All of a sudden, Frank and Pierre are entangled in a wrestling match on the ground.

I run to untie Denise.

Grunting through the torn fabric gag, she lifts her shoe. Eyes widening, foot swaying, she grunts louder, as if that might help me understand. Somehow it does.

"The dagger!"

Denise's eyes bulge. She screams incoherently through the gag.

I remove the blade from the shoe and hack at the rope. Denise strains against the bonds until the weakened cord frays to its breaking point. She rips the gag free.

Frank slugs his fist into Pierre's stomach hard enough to stagger him. His punches connect again, pummeling Pierre's ribcage. Pierre seems only seconds from collapse. Frank must think so too because he confidently drops his hands. Pierre pounces on the opening. His swinging fist plows into Frank's jaw with an audible crack.

Frank's entire body stiffens, hands clenched at his sides. Like a tree, he crashes to the ground, out for the count.

Denise doesn't give up the opportunity to kick him while he's down.

"That's for thinking you could steal my radio." Her foot deals his thigh another blow. "That's for boring me to tears!"

Denise still holds the rope that bound her to the tree. With it, Pierre lashes Frank's wrists behind his back.

"Adele, take Denise to the house."

"I will."

Denise seems perfectly fine until halfway to the farmhouse. Then between one glance and the next, her composure melts like hot candle wax.

"Want to take my arm?" I offer.

"No, no, I'll be all right."

I hold her arm to keep her on track.

"Denise, you're really pale now." Her hair, sopped with sweat, lays plastered to her cheeks. "We can rest. Do you want to sit a while?"

"No, no." Her feet shuffle to a stop. "Well, all right."

We take a break on the fallen log within our meeting place.

"I thought I was a goner. If it hadn't been for you and Pierre—" She slaps her knee. "What a bloody fool I am. He nearly got my radio. He intended to impersonate me to communicate with SOE headquarters in London."

Every radio operator has a personal style of hammering out the Morse code dots and dashes, called his or her "fist."

"You showed him how to use your radio?"

"He had a gun on me. I did everything I could think of to make the transmission suspect. I even dropped my security check at the beginning. I thought that would tip them off. Do you know what they transmitted back to me?"

"I'm not sure I really want to know."

"Their reply to my transmission under duress was, 'You forgot to include your security check, dear. Next time be more careful.' Can you believe that?"

"You're joking."

"If only," she says. "Of course, then Frank realized I wasn't being straight with him, which made him angry." She shakes her head in pained disbelief. "The spelling error I deliberately insert into messages is supposed to prove to headquarters that I'm operating the radio. Any change to that error signals that I'm in danger and the radio has fallen into enemy hands. That's *their* rule. And they not only completely ignored the rule, they told the enemy that our transmissions have a secret security check."

If Frank had done his job slightly better he would have tapped into the flow of classified communication between Denise's radio and SOE headquarters. And a mistake by headquarters would have helped him do just that.

To Frank, Denise was nothing more than a nuisance. Another meddling agent standing between him and a radio. Her life holds less value than an object. That she's a good and caring person— that she's my best friend—none of that matters.

Denise and I came into this mission as a duo. I can't fathom us not leaving together. Or not leaving at all.

Thirty-Three

Denise lowers a spoonful of her breakfast porridge, listening to the creaks and groans of the staircase as someone descends to the kitchen.

When Bishop enters the room, suitcase in hand, she says, "Bishop, I want to blow something up!"

"Denise, you are one of the few transmitters in all of France who hasn't been killed or imprisoned. We can't lose you. Now if you'll excuse me, I have a train to catch. With my rotten luck, they will blow the line to Caen before I even board. What will I do then?"

I munch on my bread, thinking, *Ride a bicycle, perhaps? Just a thought.*

Undeterred, Denise blocks his path. "It's been four days since we were put on standby for D-day. The second line of the poem will be read in tonight's messages. I feel it!"

Sidestepping her, he says, "You don't know when the Allied

invasion is coming any better than the rest of us. I have it on good authority the weather along the Channel has been abysmal; heavy rain and pea-soup fog. If anything, there will be a delay. Consider for a moment how vital you are. Be logical about it now. You are the link between SOE operations in France and headquarters in London. Without you, without your transmissions, headquarters would be running blind. Take a moment to think about that."

I don't see a great deal of thought going on behind Denise's stare.

"Now I ask you, have you given that some serious consideration? Do you understand how vital it is that you remain hidden and safe?"

"Yes, sir."

"Excellent!" He gives her a swift pat on the back. "I'm off. Cheerio, ladies."

With that, Bishop is out the door. Through the dusty windowpane, I watch him march to the vegetable garden where Madame LaRoche tends to her plants as if they're the small children she no longer has. She hastily calms her frazzled hair for his benefit before brushing her hands free of dirt.

Denise drops into the chair across the table from me. "I have been here a month without firing a single bullet. It's not fair."

"Bishop's right, though, Denise," I say. "After the close call you had, don't you think you should lie low?"

"I'm fine. And I'm not here to hide. I'm here to make hell for the Germans."

I try not to laugh at her exaggerated pout, but it's hopeless. A chunk of dry bread nearly lodges in my throat. "Bishop's gone. See what you can do."

I smack my chest to send the leftover crumbs down.

"Denise, I almost forgot to give this to you." From my breast pocket, I remove the rigid square of paper I feel beneath my hand.

She dutifully unfolds it, probably expecting boring notes or instructions.

"Oh, Adele," she cries. "I don't know what to say. It's beautiful."

The sketch of Moxie and the rest of her lazy barn cats snuggling together for a nap in the hay drifts to the table. Squealing, she gives me a bone-squashing hug.

And I hug her back.

———

Bishop should have taken Denise's gut feeling seriously. Tonight as we hovered around the radio listening to a waveband not jammed by the Germans, we heard the second code phrase.

"*Blessent mon coeur d'une langueur monotone.*"

Denise leaped out of her chair. "I knew it! Tonight is the night!" She mussed Marcus's hair with a brisk kiss. "That'll teach you to take a wager from an intuitive woman. Pay up, my boy."

With Bishop out of the picture, Denise ignored his order to stay put. She hopped right in the back of the truck with Gus, Marcus, and three men from the group I trained earlier.

Up front where Pierre and I sit, I keep a sharp lookout.

A full night of sabotage awaits not only us, but all Resistance members, no matter how separated and cut off we are from each other. A common goal will unite us for one long night.

"The fifth of June," Pierre says. "This is it, Adele. This is the beginning."

The world is about to change drastically, within hours, for better or worse. This is the beginning. But how will it end?

Once Pierre has parked the truck within some trees near the rail line, we unload our supplies and set off toward our targets.

Moments later, when the metal bridge becomes visible in the skyline, Pierre stops our group. With a beckoning wave, he chooses me as his demolition partner, and I follow him.

Under a muted aubergine sky, Pierre and I creep through grassy reeds as tall as my shoulders, our Sten guns slung across our backs. Denise and the Maquis men crouch in the forest out of sight, awaiting the all clear to plant charges along the bridge.

Rail sabotage creates short-term headaches for the Germans. Demolishing bridges throws a bigger monkey wrench into the works, since more men, equipment, and time are needed for the repair. Our plan is to blow the bridge we're approaching and derail a trainload of Nazi soldiers at the same time—as long as the explosives, timers, and detonators don't malfunction, and the train runs on time, and the line hasn't already been blown elsewhere, and luck remains on our side. That's not too much to ask, right?

The low bridge is an easily accessible target, but as Pierre and I discover on our patrol, it's guarded by two sentries.

We sneak back to Denise and the men.

"Two guards," Pierre whispers. "You see the helmet of one"—he points to the top of the slope where the bridge began— "the other is outside the gatehouse. Denise, take the bike and ride in from the opposite direction. Draw their attention to you, far down the rail. Gus and Marcus will be in position at that time to take care of them."

A short time later, Denise rides back. When the going gets rough she jumps down and pushes the bike the rest of the way.

"Gus and Marcus took care of the sentries," she says. "The others have begun work on the bridge. I can do a recce patrol of the area if you'd like."

"Reconnaissance. Good idea," Pierre says. "Don't be away long. Adele and I will be finished soon."

The sentry guards I saw only moments ago patrolling the tracks are no longer alive. Here one instant, gone the next; their deaths ticked off a checklist of tasks. But it's us or them. I can't afford to think too deeply about what we're doing.

Destruction brings Pierre and me together like a couple of cogs in a well-oiled machine. With the rail line explosives rigged, Pierre hides in the gulch with the detonator while I race back to our meeting place in the woods.

I crouch low between the trees, lay my gun across my lap, and wait. Before long the only light comes from the stars, the moon, and lamps hanging above the gatehouses.

Within one of the rotting logs that litter the forest floor, a deathwatch beetle bangs its head against the wood in search of a mate. Superstitious people like my aunt believe the noise, which sounds remarkably like the ticking of a watch, foretells an impending death.

I think bad omens are a load of hooey.

The rumbling of a train grows louder, drowning out the beetle. I fight the urge to stir up some action too soon.

Then, as if from a magical door in the forest, a uniformed German soldier appears on the field not ten feet from me. I hold my breath, watching him with curiosity and fear.

He considers a point in the distance. Noiselessly, I lean forward.

Spying between two trees, I catch sight of a dark form, a woman on a bicycle, gliding alongside the tracks.

The soldier kneels to one knee. He nestles the buttstock of his weapon into the crook of his shoulder.

My hands don't need light to see. They go to their places, as if the gun is an extension of my body. The silenced barrel of my Sten rises in front of me.

And I hit my target.

Thirty-four

I see the explosions take place through a gauzy veil of dreamlike shock. I stagger around the body of the dead soldier, aware enough to remember that if the gun's silencer touches my skin it will burn.

The first train car shoots off the tracks and lands overturned in the gully. In a chain reaction, the cars slam into the one next in line. The bridge collapses with great grinding and screaming of metal. Bursts of flame gobble up the darkness. In the new light, shadows materialize out of nowhere, dancing across the field and trees like evil spirits.

Denise has left the tracks to join Pierre. They emerge from the reeds and run to me.

"We have done it," Pierre says.

Terrified soldiers flee the burning train, leaping from windows and doors of the tilting, mangled cars.

Pierre grabs my hand. "Adele, are you well?"

"I—" I run my tongue along my lips. "I need a drink of water."

"I have a canteen in the truck. We must go." Pierre begins to pull me along, but then he finds the soldier in the grass. He shines a light in my face. "What happened here? Did he hurt you?"

I lower the blinding beam from my eyes. "No, I'm fine. He didn't even see me."

"Good." The tender pats to my back steadily grow more professional. "Good work."

Further explosions rock the train.

Pierre slings the German's machine gun over his shoulder. "Let's go. We're wasting time."

He holds my hand all the way back to the truck, not once letting go.

———

Pierre parks the truck around the side of the barn. The back doors slam shut.

There's a chipper rapping at my window.

"Tell Denise to go in the house without you."

My stomach flips, as if we're on the downward coast of a Ferris wheel.

I partially open the door. "Go on without me, I'll just be a minute."

"But why—" Denise peers back at me with saucer eyes. "Oh, I see."

As I shut the door, I hear her call to the men heading toward the barn, "All right, let's give these two some privacy."

I stare at the round moon through the windshield.

Pierre slides down the length of the seat. He stops short as our bodies are about to touch.

Our last kiss was spontaneous. There wasn't time to think, or overanalyze the situation, or work myself into a nervous tizzy: all things I'm doing this time around. Being this close to Pierre seems to knock the sense from my head. I can't think straight. My stomach knots. My palms sweat. But when I'm with Robbie, everything between us feels so natural. I can't look at him without smiling. I miss him when he's not around.

Now I'm hopelessly confused. I didn't expect to come here and fall for anyone, much less two different men who couldn't be more unalike. How can I have such strong feelings for both of them?

Pierre strokes my hair. "Your hair is very pretty."

"Do you think so?"

"It was the first thing I noticed about you. I like the way it shimmers in candlelight."

His finger trails my jawline.

"You have a scar here," he says. "Were you badly hurt?"

I keep the memory of that day buried deep inside me.

"Yes, I was badly hurt."

"I also have a scar." He brings my hand to his face. "It reminds me every day that I could not save the life of my father."

We look into each other's eyes with understanding. His hurt mirrors mine.

While we're huddled together in the quiet truck, apart from the rest of the world, I will let Pierre see the real me.

My heart pounds as I unclasp the top two buttons of my blouse. I lay his hand over the bony lump that will forever remain at the crook of my collarbone.

"I was in an automobile accident." I haven't said those words or replayed the worst moments of my life for years. "My brother and I were goofing around in the backseat on the way home from the barber. I teased him about his haircut. I hurt his feelings, but I didn't mean to. I remember the sky, changing color to a strange grayish green. A storm whipped up out of nowhere. A crack of thunder startled my mother, and my brother and I laughed. Sheets of rain streamed down the windows. I couldn't see anything but rain. Suddenly, the car seemed to float on air. My mother said, 'Oh.' That was her last word, calm as can be. I don't really know what happened after that, I only remember a man in a fedora carrying me from the car, through the downpour. Then I woke up in a hospital room. A nurse told me my mother and brother—" Tears flood my eyes. I cover my mouth, shaking. "They were dead."

Pierre wipes tears from my cheeks. He knows not to say anything at all. His strong arms wrap around my back. I lay my head against his chest. Caught somewhere between the sadness of our past and the uncertainty of the future, we can only hold on to each other.

THIRTY-FIVE

"Wake up, Adele." Denise's vehement shake to my shoulder jars me awake. "The BBC won't be silent much longer. You don't want to miss the announcement."

I fly out of bed fully clothed, clumsy and half-asleep.

"It's like Christmas morning," Denise says as we race downstairs to the kitchen. "I can't believe you were able to sleep."

Madame LaRoche stands in the middle of the kitchen, repeatedly sweeping the same patch of floor. I take the broom from her hands, alarmed by the dark circles beneath her eyes, and lead her to the table.

In the corner nearest the radio, Pierre reclines on a kitchen chair, snoring.

The radio flickers to life. In a flash, so do we.

"This is the BBC Home Service—and here is a special bulletin read by John Snagge.

"D-day has come. Early this morning the Allies began the

*assault on the northwestern face of Hitler's European fortress. The
first official news came just after half past nine, when Supreme
Headquarters of the Allied Expeditionary Force, usually called
SHAEF, from its initials, issued Communiqué Number One. This
said, 'Under the command of General Eisenhower, Allied naval
forces, supported by strong air forces, began landing Allied armies
this morning on the northern coast of France.'"*

The day we've all been waiting for, D-day, has finally arrived.
We scream with excitement, hugging and wiping happy tears
from our eyes. The energy in the room is astounding. All the pent-
up fear and anxiety we hold inside day after day exhales from us
like stale breath.

The Allies are coming. France will be free.

I stagger backward to the wall. A swell of emotion sends me
running from the kitchen. I hide in the larder, nauseated and
mortified by my reaction. My trembling legs go as rubbery as if
I had just completed a marathon bike ride. I sink to the cool
cement floor.

There's a quiet tap on the door, and Denise says, "May I
come in?"

"Uh-huh."

The door creaks open and shuts with a soft click.

"You're shaking like a leaf," Denise says. "This isn't like
you."

Every time my concentration slips, I see the same bloody,
wretched scenes playing over and over again in my mind like
horrific movies.

"Adele, I don't understand. This is a momentous day."

"We've been told so many times that the Allies would storm
the beaches. We've looked forward to this day. But I never stopped

to think about what that means. I know it's a time to celebrate, but what if thousands are dying as we speak?"

"Adele, we can't think about it that way. D-day is happening. There is no turning back. We need to stay positive and strong to help the Allies reach Germany. We are going to pull through our time here and come out the other side together, me and you. I can't have you folding like a house of cards now, or else I'm doomed."

Denise puts out her hand.

Staying positive won't wipe the terrible images from my mind. The boys and men storming the beaches aren't nameless, faceless soldiers. How many are people we know? Patrons from the pub, schoolmates, neighbors, the cute Canadian soldier from my aunt's Christmas party, or my brother's friends who dreamed of one day enlisting in the army? What if Robbie rejoined his squadron in time to help with this attack? The thought of him back here engaged in bloody battle nearly makes me sick to my stomach.

I stand without taking Denise's helping hand, feverishly hot and clammy with sweat.

"I just need some time alone," I say, hurrying past her. "I'll be upstairs."

Denise nudges the bedroom door open with her foot. A charcoal-gray kitten rests in her bent arm, peering at me with eyes as round and black as buttons.

"Smudge and I came to see if you are all right," she says.

"Yes, I'm okay now." I sit up in bed. "Is Smudge allowed in the house?"

"Nobody has to know." Denise sits cross-legged on her bed. Smudge wanders in circles on her lap, staggering round and round until sleepiness gets the better of her. She curls up in a ball and promptly falls asleep. "Claire thinks this litter is about six weeks old. Smudge is my favorite. She's the runt, which makes her even more darling. I wish I could take her home with me."

The kitten's contented purring crosses the divide between our two beds.

"I've never seen a cat that small before," I say, watching the rise and fall of a ribcage not much bigger than a walnut. "I like to draw animals, but I'm not good with them the way you are."

"I wasn't always this way." Denise's hand gently glides along the curve of Smudge's back. "As a child, I loved to hunt with my father."

The Denise I know wouldn't dream of harming an animal.

My legs swing over the side of my bed. "You hunted, Denise?"

"Yes, but when I was eleven I shot a bird. When I went to retrieve it, I saw the poor thing on the ground, still alive, petrified and suffering. Only moments earlier it had been soaring through the sky quite happily, not hurting a soul. I had to put it out of its misery, and it was just awful. I practiced so that could never happen again."

"Is that why you were the best shot out of us all?"

"That's why."

She lifts the sleeping kitten to her chest, cradling it in her hands—hands that could shoot a man in the heart from three hundred yards.

"Smudge and I had ulterior motives for coming to see you," Denise says, getting to her feet. "Pierre sent me. He's waiting for you in the barn."

"Why?"

"We're sabotaging the factory tonight."

I leave the bedroom with Denise. By the time we reach the kitchen I'm jittery with nervous excitement.

At the sound of the front door opening, Pierre's attention snaps away from the stack of photos he's carrying from the barn. Denise and I meet him in the middle of the yard.

"Adele, I just realized there is a dog in this photograph. How did we miss this? We didn't discuss a dog."

"I thought I mentioned the dog in my notes," I say.

Denise jumps in to say, "I'll return the kitten to her mother."

The expression she gives me as she sneaks away seems to wish me good luck.

"No, there is no mention of a guard dog. Now we have to do away with that dog before the rest of the plan can be put in motion."

My scalp tingles with adrenaline. "We are not killing that dog."

"What choice do we have? Its barking will bring the night watchman running. If you are too sentimental for this, I can take care of the animal before you get there."

"No!" I lay my hand on my tightening chest. "The SOE supplied us with a powerful sleeping draught. I'll soak a piece of stale bread and feed it to her."

"The people of France are starving and you expect me to throw food to a dog? We can easily solve this with a bullet."

"If you kill that dog, the Germans will know the explosions were an act of sabotage, not an accident. They could retaliate by killing innocent civilians." The stubborn resolve in Pierre's face begins to crumble, and I push forward. "Please, Pierre. My plan will work. I promise you. And if it doesn't, I will take care of the dog myself."

He hangs his head, giving in against his better judgment. "One bark, Adele. One bark will lead to our capture. Do you understand that?"

"Yes, I understand completely."

"The plan must come together without a hitch."

"It will."

The plan has to come off without a hitch. If it doesn't, I will have to kill Zucker. Without giving it a second thought.

THIRTY-SIX

The ride to the factory, down desolate country roads, gives me plenty of time to think. All the preparation I did for this moment is about to be put into action. I should be thrilled. Instead, I'm so wound up I can barely breathe. In one hand I hold a satchel containing the stale piece of bread. In the other I hold a silenced pistol. Of those two things, only one is a realistic solution.

What do I expect to happen when I reach the fence outside the dog's holding pen? Do I think I can walk right up, toss her the bread, and watch her fall fast asleep?

Pierre, Denise, and I sit sandwiched together in the truck cab. Pierre takes his eyes off the road for a split second to glance across the seat.

"Let's go over the plan one more time," he says. "Denise and I will meet up with Marcus and Gus after they arrive with the ladder. We will wait in the trees outside the northeast corner while Adele takes care of the dog."

My stomach clenches as I picture Zucker's black-and-tan face. Her clever eyes.

"Adele will join the team after the night watchman has passed and continued around the building. We will have approximately two minutes to get over the fence with the gear, pick the lock of the supply room door, and move inside. Adele and I will rig the transformers. Marcus and Gus will rig the assembly area. Denise will keep watch from the trees. At midnight, she will signal once with her flashlight to give us the all clear to exit the building. Two flashes signals danger. If we miss her signal, we are on our own. The explosives will be set with timers. We will have only minutes to get back over the fence and escape the area before it is swarming with SS soldiers."

Denise says, "What if we're wrong to assume the Germans are no longer wasting manpower on guards? What do we do if two sentries are making rounds tonight?"

"We will move twice as quickly."

Pierre drives the truck down a strip of land separating two pitch-black woods south of the village. He cuts the engine within deep shadows. I leave the warmth of the truck, drawing my hands into the sleeves of the soft sweater Pierre lent me to replace my bulky jacket. We remove our supplies, slow and steady, to prevent metal parts from grinding or banging out our position. At the last minute, Denise included her bicycle as backup transportation. That seems like a good idea, now that it's too late for me to do anything about it.

Pierre hoists a heavy rucksack onto his back, and we begin the trek to the factory. For a kilometer we keep a brisk pace, marching single file along the roadside, close enough to the forest that we can quickly dive for cover if we have to. Behind me,

Denise's bicycle rolls across the grassy ground so silently I forget she brought it, until the ping of a twig catching in the spokes reminds me.

A spotlight near the entrance casts a wide glow over the factory grounds. Hugging the tree line, we approach from an area sheltered from the moonlight, well beyond the spotlight's reach.

"Adele, we will wait here for your return," Pierre whispers. "Take your time getting down there. There is no need to rush. You will be more likely to panic and make mistakes if you do. Wait until you feel comfortable. Watch the guard from the shadows. Count the time it takes him to complete his circuit around the building."

I add my pistol to the satchel and wind the drawstring around my hand. "I'll see you in fifteen or twenty minutes."

Pierre and Denise sit on the grass. Within seconds of leaving them they've disappeared from my sight. I pick out a concealed spot behind the factory where I can observe the guard, and Zucker's fenced pen in the corner nearest the guardhouse.

Just as I hunker into position, the guard appears around a corner of the building. He patrols the length of the back wall, unaware of my presence. I wait for his return, counting the time in sixty-second increments. Five minutes later, there he goes again, marching by my location. His second rotation completes in five minutes, as does his third. Throughout those minutes, Zucker lays stretched out on the ground between a wooden shelter and the fence, occasionally raising her head from her paws to check the security of her surroundings.

I loosen the drawstring of the satchel. I choose the loaded pistol over the bread.

After the guard's fourth circuit, I jog to Zucker's fenced

enclosure. She rises to her feet, warning me to stay back with a low growl. Snarling, her head and shoulders aggressively lower as she prepares to bark an alarm to the guard.

"Zucker. *Pfui!*" Stop that!

She tilts her head, ears alert, listening to the sound of my voice.

I quickly pull the sleeping-draught-soaked bread from the bag and lob it over the fence. It lands at her feet.

"Zucker, it's me, Adele."

Crouching, I aim my pistol at her head, nauseated and shaking so badly I'm sure to miss her when I fire. One bark. That's all it will take. One bark and the beautiful dog I drew and painted will lie dead on the ground.

Zucker sniffs the crusty heel of bread. In one violent snap of her jaws, it vanishes. Teeth bared, she lunges at the fence. In a drugged stupor, she staggers backward, whining and incapable of alerting the guard. Lurching sideways, she tries once more to reach the fence. Her hind legs give out beneath her. She collapses into the shadow of her wooden shelter—which will hopefully protect her from the blast—before falling into a deep sleep.

I run back to my hiding spot. After all the stress and worry of the past hours, I crouch on the hillside buzzing with shock and relief over how quickly and easily the plan worked. It came together almost exactly how I envisioned it. I hope that's a sign that the rest of the night will go just as smoothly.

As the guard rounds the building, I silently get to my feet. I meet up with the demolition team, which now includes Gus and Marcus, in the dark where I left them.

"Everything is going perfectly to plan," I whisper.

Pierre hands me the tools to pick the lock.

"We know what to do, so let's go," he says. "Good luck to us."

THIRTY-SEVEN

The sky at our backs bursts into color and light. Effects of the catastrophic explosions catch up to us as we flee across the field. The ground trembles beneath our feet.

The plan to destroy the factory has gone off without a hitch.

Our victory can't be celebrated until we reach the farm, but Pierre slips his arms around my waist in a spontaneous hug that sweeps me off my feet.

In my ear, he says, "Thank you, Adele."

We run the rest of the way back to the truck, and the distance seems half as long on the return trip. I feel remarkable, so full of energy. I could run until morning.

Denise's cheerful march alongside her bicycle slows considerably. "Pierre, I see the truck way up there. See the reflection off the bonnet?"

"I know where the truck is," he says.

"What is that other reflection then?" She leans forward. "And that one?"

"I don't see what you're—"

In the split second before I identify the sounds of gunfire and bullets piercing trees, I think we've been invaded by wood-peckers.

The starbursts of muzzle flashes give away the position of two shooters. I return fire, giving Denise and Pierre the opportunity to run.

When I catch up, Pierre says, "Go. I'll hold them off."

The forest offers the most cover. We sprint in spurts across uneven ground. On our last go, Denise and I reach the scrubby brush surrounding the tree line.

Alone in the field, Pierre fires toward a muzzle flash that has been steadily gaining on him.

"Denise, I have to go back," I say. "I can't leave him."

"And I can't leave you."

"Ride to the farm. Warn them about this. For all our sakes."

"Bloody hell," she whispers, climbing aboard her bicycle. "Be careful."

She gives me the V for Victory sign as I scramble to find cover in a low area. When I look again, she's gone.

Pierre's arm jerks back. His Sten tumbles, butt over muzzle. He crumples in a way that doesn't look at all natural.

Not bothering to dodge and weave, I run to him. "No, no, no."

"Adele, I'm hit," he wheezes.

I fire a shot from the hip, emptying my cartridge. Hear a grunt as it hits its mark.

"I'm getting you out of here." I prop him up. Slip my arms under his armpits. "Can you walk? Use me as a crutch."

Gulping air, he says, "Leave me."

"I will drag you if I have to, but I will not leave you here."

My hands interlock, a slippery grip that threatens to release if I give it all I have. I haul Pierre along the ground. He cries out in anguish each time my arms apply pressure to his ribs.

Another round of bullets sprays the air above my head. Instinctively, I duck. With a fiery snap, my ankle gives way. Pierre's weight sends both of us to the ground. I fight cold sweat and nausea that accompanies the burst of pain.

"Adele, go." The plea gurgles from his throat. "Remember why we do this. Please tell my mother I love her. Tell her again how sorry I am for Father."

"No, you tell her. I can get us out of this. I'll fight them off."

"You are a good person, Adele." His whisper fades away with, "I'm glad for our time . . ."

Pierre's body goes limp in my arms. I press my face to his shoulder, hugging him against me. Warmth has soaked his shirt and wet my hands.

"Pierre, no," I sob. "Don't go. I can save you."

His breath slowly leaves him. I cling to his body, bewildered. This isn't supposed to be happening. I don't understand. In an instant, I've fallen into a nightmare I can't wake from.

I lay my cheek on his chest. It's so very still without his strong heartbeat. I hug him until my arms shake, breathing in his smell. I don't want to let go. If I let go, I will never see him again.

I raise my head.

The soldiers are close enough now that their shapes clearly stand out. I count six.

They can't have Pierre. They can't have me.

I reach to the bottom of my pocket. Between thumb and finger, I pinch the small but deadly object I've carried with me since day one. My cyanide pill is so well wrapped, even swallowing it won't kill me. I have to bite down on it, hard. To die from a cyanide pill is no accident.

A voice comes from the darkness. "You are surrounded. Lower your weapons."

With a backhanded toss, the pill—evidence I was trained by the SOE—flies to an unknown spot in the scrubby field.

Heavy tears blur my vision as I change the magazine of the Sten. I don't know who killed Pierre, but if I shoot all six soldiers, I will get him. I aim at the middle one first. I squeeze the trigger. And the metal weapon does what it does best.

It jams.

Thirty-Eight

In the car, in the light of early morning, one of the two soldiers escorting me to Paris turns to inspect the backseat. His gaze roams my body, head to foot and back again.

When he resumes small talk with the driver, I imagine myself diving over the seat to slice his throat open. They confiscated my knife. I lock my stare on the back of the driver's head. Can he feel it boring through his skull like a red-hot poker? I can crash the car if I want to and kill them both.

They fought over who deserved credit for shooting Pierre. Whose bullet took him down? They wanted bragging rights for it. "Is that your boyfriend's blood on your sweater?" a soldier asked, laughing.

I won't let them see me cry. I stare out the window. The smudged landscape streaks past.

"Girl, you want a cigarette?"

I turn farther away from him, holding fast to my breathing while he watches me.

"Girl, has the cat got your tongue?" He faces front, muttering, "Saucy bitch."

My hand slides down my worsted wool pants. My fingertips reach the cuff. For the better part of the trip, I patiently work at the seam. Once a tiny pocket forms in the heavy fabric, I slowly but surely move my charm bracelet from one pocket to a safer one, stringing it through the opening and along the tunnel of the cuff.

The car pulls up to 84 Avenue Foch. Gestapo headquarters.

The driver cuts the ignition. He steps out of the car and opens my door. The wildness in my eyes must be clear. "Don't be foolish and try to fight me," he says.

The soldiers lead me by the arm to a guard room on the fifth floor. I lower my head, ashamed to be inside the notorious building.

While I wait, seated alone at a table, I steel myself for interrogation.

Behind me, the door opens. I draw my fear inward. Imagine it a small, crumpled wad.

Just then, I smell the aroma of freshly brewed coffee. Not the ersatz coffee I've been drinking for weeks. This is what real coffee smells like. And if real coffee tastes as good as it smells, then it must taste like heaven. I breathe it in for all I'm worth.

Will they bind my hands and cruelly draw the coffee beneath my nose?

"Excuse me, miss?"

I slide sideways on my chair. Someone's gray-haired grandmother stands where my interrogator should be. I stare at the tray in her hands.

Bread, butter, jam, coffee, sugar cubes.

"I have brought your breakfast."

Is she one of the "friendly nurses" we were warned about,

who will offer good food and comfort, or apologize for rough treatment, or seemingly look out for my well-being? No one can be trusted. Whatever happens here is all part of their bigger plan to wear me down.

My chest rises and falls quicker and quicker, pumping my lungs like bellows. As much as it pains me, and as hungry as I am, I have to turn down the brief chance to revisit normal life.

"No thank you."

"It is not a trick, miss," she says, a German accent marking her fluent French. "Please eat. You are quite thin."

I refuse until the woman gives up and leaves the room.

A grand chandelier hangs from the ceiling outside the office on the fourth floor, dangling crystal daggers over my head.

Guards lead me into the room. The mahogany desk in the center of the office dwarfs the slight man seated behind it. He must be important and high ranking, but he wears civilian clothes rather than a uniform. I figure it's his tactic. A tactic I'm not about to fall for. He isn't my neighbor. He isn't my friend. No ploy of his can win my trust.

The window next to the desk shows an expansive view of the yard. An officer decked out in full riding gear gallops by on horseback.

"Adele, please sit," the man behind the desk says.

He knows my alias. I swallow the swelling lump in my throat.

"There is no reason to stand. You may sit," he says in broken French, forcing me to piece together what he said.

I sit in one of two studded leather chairs.

From a side entrance, a woman enters the room with a typewriter, her wide hips straining the limits of her skirt.

"I am Joseph Krieger," he says. "Senior counterintelligence officer." Like a marionette the woman jumps after he speaks, to translate for him.

He stands, extending his hand. I remain seated.

"I am told you refused breakfast. Would you prefer a sandwich?" he asks.

Ironically, when he speaks German, I understand him better than when he speaks the language I'm *supposed* to know best. I focus my attention on his translator as she repeats the question to keep up my cover.

I haven't eaten proper food in ages. It physically hurt to turn down the food they brought me earlier. Now offers of sandwiches are coming at me in multiple languages.

I shake my head.

"Come now, I'm sure you are hungry," Krieger says. He points to a wall chart. "There is no point in keeping the charade going. We know much more than you think. See for yourself."

Gut instinct tells me to ignore him. But it might help me to gather as much of their intelligence information as possible. I look at the chart.

What a kick in the teeth that proves to be.

They have a hierarchy of names, all of SOE senior command, drawn up to the letter, in addition to detailed information about the training schools. Until that moment, I've been tight-lipped by choice. Each name on the chart hammers me deeper into silence. My gaze returns several times to my section head's name. For a few seconds, I worry I might become sick to my stomach.

What is so goddamned secret about us secret agents then?

"I don't know what this is I'm looking at," I say.

Krieger waits for the translation. When at last he understands, he smiles. "You do know what it is, Adele."

"I'm afraid I do not."

"No, you do. There is no sense in keeping quiet. In what way does that benefit you? Don't you see? We know. It would not be wise for you to prolong our discussions."

"I'm sorry, sir. I don't know what you are talking about."

Krieger drums his fingers on the desktop. To the soldiers, he says, "Take the girl to her cell."

For a week, I stay in one of twelve attic rooms on the fifth floor, above Krieger's office. The hallway leads to a bathroom at one end and the guardroom at the other. The conditions may be far cushier than I imagined possible, but cushy doesn't mean easily escapable.

Several times throughout the week, Krieger invited me to his office to eat with him. I declined, baffled by his attempts to treat me well. On the third day, I picked at the delicious sausage and cheese in the guardroom. If they really are attempting to poison me, I thought, at least I'd go out on a full stomach.

I enter Krieger's office this mid-June afternoon, as I have every day since my arrival to Avenue Foch, to be questioned. His interrogation methods seem based on the premise of catching more flies with honey than with vinegar; a surprising tactic for him to take, but it has obviously helped him win over agents in the past. He knows too much for that not to be true.

"Good afternoon, Adele." When I'm seated, he says, "I have a question for you. What do you think of Churchill?"

Krieger's inquisitiveness extends beyond the workings of the SOE to all things British. He asks some peculiar questions, and only in part to dupe me into talking with him. His interest in the answers seems genuine.

"Still not talking to me?" he asks. "I am trying to be honorable, don't you see? It is not you, or agents like you, that I want. I must stop arms and supplies from reaching the Maquis bandits in the woods. Certainly you must agree that is a worthy goal."

I stare blankly at a point over his shoulder.

Krieger sets a photo on his desk. "Do you know this girl?"

I glance only briefly. But of course I recognize her.

Krieger's civilian clothing and easygoing attitude might have lulled other agents into a false sense of security. Those same things make me think he's as fallible as any other regular person. I want to grab him by the collar. To scream in his face that he has to keep Denise out of this. That if he hurts her I will kill him. But the best thing I can do to protect her is to not acknowledge her at all.

"Come now, Adele. You put up a good fight, however, the game is up. We know everything. You may as well answer my questions."

Liar, I think. *If you know everything, then why the hell am I sitting here?*

"I am a patient man. Some of my friends are . . . not so patient."

A nub of skin has formed in my mouth from near-constant chewing. I pull at it with my teeth.

"Talk to me now and treatments at the house prison will not be necessary. You are a clever girl. Why put yourself through that? Why suffer needlessly?" he says. "I ask you once more to cooperate."

I shake my head.

Thirty-Nine

Near the end of June 1944, on a cool, misty morning, I'm moved from my cell in the Avenue Foch mansion and transferred to a solitary confinement cell within the nearby Gestapo prison, to begin "treatment" for my unwillingness to talk.

When I shuffle into the interrogation room, the first thing I see is a large vat of water.

My feet lock in place, refusing to move forward. Please, no, not this. Anything but water. An anguished whimper escapes me. There is nothing I can do to restrain it and nothing I can do to take it back.

To each other, the interrogators smile.

With brute strength that easily overpowers me the men force my rigid body onto a chair next to the vat. One interrogator holds me down. The other secures my wrists and ankles.

I struggle to free myself when I'm released from their rough clutches, violently rocking, pushing, and pulling until my stretched muscles and joints scream in agony.

The shackles binding my arms and legs to the chair scour my blistered skin to a bloody mash.

Firm hands clasp my hair and forcibly lower my head.

Ice water envelops my face, eagerly flowing up my nose. Devouring my head whole. A thousand pinpricks of pain spark across my raw cheeks. Panic wrings the air from my lungs, and it climbs my throat, claws of desperation sinking deep.

Fingers wind tighter through my tangled hair, raising me to the surface.

Above me, my interrogator shouts in French, "You are a spy! You are an agent of the Special Operations Executive! You are the American, Betty Sweeney!"

"*Non,*" I gasp, catching my breath. "*Je m'appelle Adele Blanchard.*"

"You worked with the British agents Denise Langford and Timothy Bishop! Where are they?"

"*Je ne connais personne de ces noms.*" *I know no one by those names.*

"You do! Who is assisting them?"

"*Je ne sais pas.*" *I do not know.*

My head plunges, displacing jagged chunks of ice. The sting becomes excruciating, as if my face has been turned inside out.

"You do know them! You will give us their locations! You will tell us where the weapon drops take place!"

I spit a mouthful of water on the floor in the direction of the shiny pair of army boots I see there. I draw a long breath. Down I go again.

Garbled voices bounce back and forth above me.

I strain against the chains, screaming on the inside. Fear eats what little oxygen I have left.

I am about to drown. There is nothing I can do about it.

Take a breath.

Just when I come to accept my fate, they pull me back for more. It goes on that way for over an hour.

I sit on the floor of my empty cell, wracked by violent shivering and bouts of coughing. My head feels stuffed with cotton batting. I hug my legs to my chest and lock my chattering teeth against my knees.

In the moment, it seems as if interrogation will go on forever. The trick is to stay lucid enough to remember the pain will eventually end, when instinct takes over and every part of me wants to fight back, run, scream.

Time in my cell gives me the chance to rest, but on edge every moment, never knowing when to expect another go-round with Krieger's bully boys. In these quiet moments, I think about the Allies. I picture them marching across the country, rolling over the Germans with their tanks. They're coming. They're coming for me. It's only a matter of time.

To keep from going stir-crazy here, I combed my memories from the past weeks and spliced together the good bits to create mental film footage I can watch whenever I close my eyes. Right as I settle into the movie, I hear faint tapping against the wall of the neighboring cell. My eyes pop open. I scoot taller against the wall, deciphering a definite rhythm. Someone is forming words in Morse. To talk to me.

I am Lisa.

I scramble around the floor, desperate to find a rock. I snatch one up as if it's a diamond and tap the message, *Adele.*

How long?

Four days. You?

Three months.

I lower my rock, unsure of how to respond to this blow.

Food delicious, Lisa says.

I can't believe she's able to poke fun at her situation after three months.

She asks, *Enjoy games?*

Sometimes.

Sing song. I guess.

When Robbie asked for a song to play on the piano, my mind went blank. I have an even harder time of it now. I hum the tune to "Someone to Care for Me," imagining Robbie's long fingers effortlessly gliding across black-and-white keys.

Lisa taps out the dots and dashes of her guess. *"Danny Boy"?*

No. Played this way, the game is too difficult. It needs something extra. *Your turn. Give clues.*

Take long way there.

I rub a filthy finger across my forehead, confused, until I realize Lisa gave a clue. I smack my rock into the wall to shout, *Long Way to Tipperary!*

Hurrah!

In that moment of shared victory, I picture Lisa, a complete stranger, as clearly as if I've known her all my life. We smile to each other through the concrete divide.

Your tu . . . The dots and dashes that follow make no sense. Then the tapping stops altogether.

I wait for a very long time, fearful that others now listen in on our game, before I silence my rock.

I curl up in the corner to sleep.

"Wake up!"

A boot heel slams into my ribs. I didn't move quickly enough to convince the soldier that I'm already awake. I stagger to my feet. Agonizing pain wallops my side, pulsating through my chest, as if I've been kicked again. I double over, gasping for breath.

Two guards lead me from my cell. At the door to the interrogation room, I limp, expecting to go inside. They carry on. I drag my feet. I don't recognize the guards. Maybe they're new and don't have directions to the interrogation room.

Soon nothing looks familiar. The temperature drops. Sound reverberates differently through the halls. The hair on my neck stands on end when I reason out the purpose for moving me outdoors.

I step through the open doorway. Golden strands of dawn stretch across the courtyard walls. The air smells and tastes like freedom.

"Go to the wall," one of the guards commands.

"Please, no." I force my feet backward, shackles scraping my bruised ankles. "Don't do this. Please, I beg you."

A rifle butt to the kidneys sets me in motion. Another knocks me breathless to my knees.

I kneel before the stone wall. A numbing sense of peace grows out of my fear.

I wish my father happiness in his new life. I say good-bye to Denise. I pray for Robbie's safety. I kiss Pierre and hug Madame LaRoche. I ask for one more day with my aunt. I plead for liberation to come.

Behind me, in the middle of the courtyard, rifles are readied.

Will I hear the gunshots before I die? Will I feel pain? Or will everything just end with silence?

Snide laughter penetrates my last thoughts.

"Rise!"

I lurch forward onto my hands, heaving hot rancid bile into the dirt. I swing my shackled legs around and stand, dizzily watching yellow liquid trickle down my legs and pool at my feet.

Without a word they march me back to my cell. I clutch at the wall, moaning away an intense urge to vomit.

One of the guards sneers at my filthy legs. "You are a disgusting animal. This place is too good for you."

He shoves me to the floor, where I collapse in a heap. He locks the door behind me.

I curl on my side, feeling broken and brittle as a dried cornhusk. Nothing makes sense anymore. Nothing at all.

———————

After two days without word from Lisa, the dots and dashes return.

I limp to the wall. In my excitement, I forget to take shallow breaths. A jolt of pain spikes my ribcage.

Lisa?

Tina.

In slapdash tapping, I ask, *Where Lisa?*

Her answer confirms my fears. *Cell empty. Your name?*

Adele.

I'm crushed, Adele.

We will get out.

Lonely. Pain too much.

Outside of prison, being alone meant something different to me. I wasn't alone at all. There were ringing telephones, playing radios, children running past open windows. A dog barked or a neighbor's car pulled up to the curb. Ordinary everyday connections I took for granted my whole life—I can't put into words how much I crave them now.

I bring my hand to my chest when she asks, *Will we be all right?*

I can't afford to hesitate with my answer.

I quickly tap, *Yes!*

Thank you.

I untangle my hair with my fingers. Straighten my blouse.

Tina. Like to play games?

fORTY

At the end of June, Krieger's men finally give up on me. I'm put in a van and driven to Fresnes, the massive prison on the outskirts of the city.

I've always assumed that the first time I bared my body completely would be with a man I love, in a romantic setting. Not with two frosty German women in a chilly room under the unflattering glare of fluorescent lighting. I leave the full-body search sore, humiliated, and on the verge of tears. But what matters is that they didn't find the bracelet in the hem of my pants.

A beefy prison matron in a pale-blue uniform wordlessly leads me from the search room to a long, high-ceilinged room. We pass several numberless doors until we come to an open one. The cell isn't much more than a dark hole.

"Go inside."

My reputation as an uncooperative prisoner sure hasn't done much to improve my living quarters. I enter the cell and the matron bolts the door behind me.

Three straw mattresses are stacked upon the one and only cot in the room. I heave the two extras to the floor and lie down. There isn't much else to do but sleep.

———————————

The door to my cell opens with a bang loud enough to jolt me awake and get my heart racing.

"Bread and coffee," the matron says, her flattened mouth never showing more emotion than disdain.

I carry the bread and bowl of coffee to my mattress without spilling even a drop. I take a cautious first sip. Not only is the liquid not hot, it could only be called coffee by some wild stretch of the imagination. And the mushy bread tastes as if it has been soaking in that liquid. I gag down the bread, helping it along with great gulps of the coffee.

I've barely finished eating when the door is opened again, this time by a different woman.

This matron knows how to smile. She says, "Come with me, please."

I follow her with no sense of where I'm being taken or for what purpose. There's no point in studying my surroundings for clues. Everything about the place looks the same: windowless hallways, numberless doors, metal and concrete.

The uniformity breaks when we reach a long, broad hallway. The din of many voices reverberates throughout a nearby vast space.

At the end of the hallway, I slow behind the matron. This is prison as I've imagined it, as it's portrayed in movies.

A massive sunlit corridor towers four stories above me, each balconied level lined with jail cells. At both ends of the lengthy room, monstrous floor-to-ceiling windows allow a glimpse of the outside world. The cells themselves are completely segregated one from the next; concrete boxes with solid metal doors rather than bars.

The commotion in the room is god-awful, with guards and matrons everywhere, shouting to be heard and calling names from clipboards. The abrupt switch from silence and solitude to the bustle and barrage of echoing noise batters my senses.

The matron directs me past a line of female prisoners waiting to hear their names. I take a long look at the sun through the bars on the window as I climb the staircase to the third floor. At room #347, the matron inserts a key in the door, unlocks the bolt, and pushes the heavy door open.

A blond woman sits cross-legged on the floor beneath a small barred window.

"*Bienvenue,*" she says with a wave, as if welcoming me to a party. She motions for me to join her.

I scan the small cell as I enter—metal chair and cots secured to the walls, an open toilet, and not much else. When the door locks behind me, I become secured to the room like everything else.

When I sit next to the woman she says, "My name is Christina."

We shake hands. Despite her slightness, she has an assured grip.

"Hi, I'm Adele." I hold on to the handshake well beyond the point dictated by proper etiquette, shocked to have been given a cellmate. "It's too bad we couldn't be meeting under better circumstances."

Christina stands. She must catch me staring at the summery

nightgown she wears in the middle of the day, because she says, "The cells are unbelievably hot and muggy. You'll soon despise those heavy wool pants of yours."

My legs immediately begin to itch. "Oh."

"Don't worry. I came here when personal parcels were still allowed. I have an extra nightgown you can borrow. And a toothbrush."

I run my tongue over my teeth. It's been far too long since they've known the luxury of a toothbrush. "Thank you, Christina."

"I'll give you the grand tour," she says. "The best part is there's no need to get up. You can watch it entirely from where you are sitting."

I laugh.

"This is the chair. It's not nearly as comfortable as iron typically is. These are the smelly blankets and mattresses we sleep on." Gesturing to the door like a poised model in a magazine advertisement, she says, "Once in a while this door will open. Sometimes the reason for this will be good, such as the twenty-minute walks they permit us to take in the courtyards twice a week. More often than not, the reason will be bad, for instance when the soup cart rolls around. And occasionally, the reasons will be quite bad."

I don't want or need her to elaborate on the "quite bad."

Moving on, she says, "Here is the dish of water I catch fleas in. And the toilet with its imaginary privacy screen." At the window, she offers a hand to help me up. "I saved the best part of the tour for last. The peephole."

A portion of the wood casing around the window has been cut away. If I peer through at just the right angle, I can see over the prison walls.

"We can spy on the guards as they make their rounds," Christina says. "And watch the wing where they keep the men."

"Fantastic. You made the peephole?"

"Yes. I smuggled in my tiny nail file, in my hair."

Studying the window, I say, "Do you still have it?"

"The matrons will find it eventually, but I have it for now."

"See this bolt that holds the window shut? If we use the file to the remove the screws here and here, we can prop the window open a few minutes a day to let fresh air in."

Christina shakes her fist with excitement. "Adele, that's brilliant!"

My curiosity draws me back to the peephole. I smirk when a guard strolls into view. Without his knowledge I stalk his every move.

The Fresnes guards wasted no time getting to interrogations, questioning me about fellow agents—some I know, but most I don't—and SOE headquarters, and weapon drops, and whatever else they have their cold hearts set on knowing. They seem almost desperate for information about Denise, grilling me relentlessly about her whereabouts, her radio, and her codes. Part of me is glad for this. It means she's still alive.

Sometimes I wonder if they're pulling questions out of thin air whenever it suits them, as an excuse to torture me more. To draw them away from the parts of my body that hurt the most, I cry out when they beat me where the pain is manageable. Still, no matter how bad it gets, no matter how close I get to cracking—and I've seen the final seconds before my breaking point—I tell them nothing more than they already know.

I don't want to give up hope that liberation will come, but too much time has passed. I have so many unanswered questions. Why are the guards still interrogating me for information? Where are the Allies? Did the D-day invasion fail? Are we losing the war? And then there's the one question I almost can't bear to consider. Have we already lost?

In the three weeks at the prison, the movie I've been creating from my memories has become a real spectacle worthy of Hollywood, with the help of some substitutions. The role of Louis is now played by Clark Gable, and Madame LaRoche bears a striking resemble to Marlene Dietrich. Even Rat hasn't escaped scrutiny. I replaced him with Roddy McDowall.

I lounge on the mattress, compiling a list of places to visit before I die. None of my lists are set in stone, they change with my moods. Surprisingly, "Top Ten Films of All Time" gave me the most grief. "Twenty Foods to Eat When Freed from Prison" was easy as riding a bike.

I hear movement outside the door. I pick up the mug of soapy water a female guard brought me. When Christina enters our cell after interrogation, I'll be there to wash whatever wounds they inflicted on her, just as she does for me.

There's a knock on the door. "Adele."

I recognize the voice of Greta, the kind guard. I run to the door, saying, "What is it?"

Key. Bolt. Open door.

A paper-wrapped bundle appears through the opening. "This has come to you. I wouldn't ordinarily accept a bribe to smuggle gifts to prisoners. I will for you, but only this once. I cannot afford to lose my job."

I grab the parcel from her hand. "Who is it from?"

"I'm sorry, I don't know. A guard in the men's wing received it from an acquaintance. He passed it on to me."

The door and bolt close with their familiar metallic rhythm.

I carry the parcel to the mattress and rip into the paper. Two of my fingernails were extracted the day before. I let the package tumble from my hands, lightheaded with pain. Sparks of white light dart before my eyes.

I open the package the rest of the way with my good hand. Inside, I find two biscuits, two squares of chocolate, cheese, and salted meat. I clutch my throat, overcome with joy, savage hunger I can no longer ignore, and the fear that if I look away even for a second the food on my lap will vanish.

Someone put himself in danger to smuggle food to me. That reconnection to the outside world boosts me as much as the food.

I hide the package beneath the mattress, to share it with Christina.

A short while later she weaves through the door when it opens.

I guide her to the mattress, careful not to put pressure on her back, chest, or upper arms.

"Oh, Christina, what have they done to you?"

She makes several clumsy attempts to lie down. Even with my help, the slightest movements send spasms shooting through her.

"Adele, I think someone gave me up. Until now they've never questioned me about anything I had legitimate ties to. Today they knew about my fiancé. They did what they could to make me talk, but I will go to my grave before I breathe a word to them about Thomas." Shaking her head, she says, "They burned me. What's next? I won't talk. Not ever. It will only get worse." A tear rolls down her cheek. I wipe it away before it reaches the open cut on her lip.

"We will get through this," I say, showing her the food. "I have something for you."

"I don't think I can eat. I've lost a tooth."

I break her portions into bite-sized pieces and feed them to her, as if she's a helpless baby bird.

———————

I wake after a fitful, nightmare-filled sleep.

Pierre and Robbie visited me while I slept. Overjoyed, I ran to hug them both. "Pierre, you're alive!" I cried. But he held me at arm's length, saying, "No, Adele." Deep red bloodstains oozed across his chest like blooming roses. "We are dead." I looked beyond Pierre to Robbie, who stood alone in a field, next to a fiery downed plane. He silently backed away, disappearing into ethereal white smoke. I tried to follow, desperate to tell him that we're meant to be together, but I couldn't move or speak. I could only watch in agony as he left me forever, with the words "I love you" locked behind my lips.

I keep my eyes shut and turn on my side, craving more rest.

Far below my bedroom window, my cousins run giggling through the yard with Biscuit happily barking after them. Off in the distance, I hear my aunt call, "Boys, time for school. Off you go now." Once the boys are out of her hair, I'll join her for tea.

During the night I wedged my whole body against the wall. I roll over to avoid whacking my head on the sloped ceiling. My mattress feels unusually firm this morning. I try to settle into a comfortable position, but no matter which way I move, the mattress has no give. I'll have to tell Aunt Libby there's something the matter with my bed. She'll know what to do. There's no point in trying to fall back to sleep now anyway, with the rock-hard mattress doing its best to wake me up.

My heart sinks with a sudden and crushing despair.

I can't bring myself to open my eyes. I'm not at my aunt's house. I silently sob into the crook of my elbow.

Key. Bolt. Open door.

"Adele."

I raise my head, convinced I heard my mother calling me.

Next to me, Christina sleeps, curled into the fetal position. I watch the gentle rise and fall of her ribcage.

"Be quick, Adele. I have news."

I hobble to the door. My bruised and battered feet cry out with each step.

On the other side of the door Greta says, "I heard the guards talking about you. They are transferring you to Ravensbrück. One of the camps. In Germany."

She whispers "camps," as if it's a secret word she is not permitted to speak aloud.

I lean against the wall, feeling faint. "When?"

"I don't know. I will try to find out."

I nod, too downtrodden to do much else.

"I thought you might like to know that many of the guards hold you in high regard, Adele. They respect your strength and honor."

What does it matter to me that they respect my strength when they're about to ship me off to my death?

"I appreciate everything you've done for me, Greta."

Sometime within the last day, my legs took it upon themselves to support me for only two minutes at a time. I shuffle back to the mattress before time runs out and curl up beside Christina.

I know precisely why they're moving me like a chess piece.

They will see to it that if, or when, the Allies roll into Paris, not a single prisoner will be found.

———————————————

"Seahorse. Seee-horse."

Christina awakens from her nap to give me a lethargic evil eye.

"Is that a real word? Seahorse?" I stretch it out again. "Seeee-horse. That's a strange word. A horse that lives in the sea?"

I rub my finger along the dried flakes crusted over my lips. I pry one loose and it comes off in one satisfyingly intact piece. I draw my hand away from my mouth. It blurs in and out of focus.

"How many of my hands do you see here?" I ask, but Christina has already drifted off again. "I'm holding up one, I'm sure of it. I see two."

The hands swim before my eyes, rippling like waterlogged rubber gloves. They flap at me, open, shut, open, shut.

Two guards storm into the cell. I watch them come at me, slow to react. They seize me by the arms.

"No!" My heart feels shrunken to the size of a pea. It trills furiously in my chest. A sudden burst of energy comes over me. I crack one of the guards across the face.

They drag me from the only friend I've known in over a month.

"You can't take me! I won't go!" My scream comes out a hoarse murmur, as if my vocal cords turned to dust in my throat.

My head droops. Strength drains from my legs. I float down the hall between the guards, neither a ghost nor an angel.

Intense white light fills my vision. I shut my eyes against it, blinded.

Death snuck up on me. Snatched me when I wasn't looking. It shouldn't come as any surprise that Death is devious. He says, "Where is Ahren . . . supposed to . . . in the van."

I go forward, bathed in the warmth of the light.

The support beneath my right side falls away. I hear a heavy thump. My eyes open to intolerable light. Another thump. I lurch forward into nothingness, shielding my eyes.

The guards lay on the ground before me. One has a bloody hole for a third eye.

A car speeds toward me. I slide one foot in front of the other, every movement a battle of wills with my twitching muscles. The white light returns. Through a pinpoint I see the car pull up. A door squeals open on dry hinges. Another door opens. Men come at me. I claw the air, aiming above the flurry of shadowy arms and legs. My arms whirl to fight the men off.

I won't go to the camp. I won't!

"We've got you."

FORTY-ONE

I wake little by little, wrapped in a soft cocoon of blankets.

My eyes focus on Denise sitting at the edge of the bed, surrounded by a golden aura of candlelight.

From my arm, a small tube travels upward to an intravenous bottle.

The room drifts in and out of focus.

"Where am I? Am I dreaming?"

She holds my hand. Real and true and not a figment of a dream, she says, "Dr. Devereux had a hard enough time getting that liquid into you, don't waste it on tears."

I struggle to hold on to the vague image of her face. It blurs to nothingness. I lose it.

"Go back to sleep. You're safe."

———

When I wake next, Dr. Devereux has taken up Denise's vigil in the chair. Sunshine stealing through the partially drawn curtains has replaced the candlelight.

I look around the prettily decorated room. I've been here before, when Dr. Devereux allowed me to spend the night in his home.

He pats my hand. "How are you feeling?"

"As if I slept for days."

"That is no coincidence. And you have more bed rest ahead of you." Checking my IV, he says, "It's a miracle Bishop and I found you when we did. The state your body was in, under shock and dehydration that severe, another day and it would have been too late."

Too late. My heart aches for Christina and whatever fate lies ahead of her.

I've swung from one extreme form of security to another without a link between them. As horrifying as prison was, it became my life. Now, surrounded by comfort and freedom, I don't know what to make of the change.

"This seems unreal," I say. "I don't want to sound ungrateful, but I'm confused, Dr. Devereux. How did I get here?"

"I imagine your rescue must feel as overwhelming as it does a relief," he says. "Let's save the discussion of details for a later time. For the time being, know this: you have many friends who are willing to do just about anything in the world for you."

From the door, Denise says, "One of them happens to be the best shot I've ever seen."

"You shot the guards?"

"Adele, do you know of anyone else who can shoot like that? The kicker is I used a Mauser we stole from a crashed German truck. They probably didn't bat an eye when they heard shots fired from one of their own weapons. Brilliant how it all came together." Grinning, Denise says, "Did you know we were coming for you?"

I shake my head, confused. "No. How was I to know?"

Dr. Devereux briefly stops taking notes on a clipboard to ask, "Did you receive the parcel we sent to Fresnes?"

The overwhelming emotions of that day come flooding back. "Yes, I received a parcel."

"It was a sign from us," Denise says. "We found out where you were being held. We were working on a plan to free you. Did it give you hope?"

At the time, I thought only about the food, not what its arrival should have signaled to me. I can't explain that to them, though, without having to relive a moment of savage hunger I'd rather forget.

All I can say is, "Thank you."

"I'll leave you two to talk," Dr. Devereux says.

"Is that a new skirt?" I say, as Denise passes the end of my bed.

"New skirt? Why, it's a whole new outfit. One of the bedroom closets is overflowing with women's clothing. I could live in it quite happily."

Laughing, I say, "I bet you—"

I bite down on my quivering upper lip. The roof of my mouth hardens like a tortoise shell, until the pressure is too great. I bring my pillow out to hide behind it, breathing a fusty bouquet of medicinal scents. If I don't grab a hold of myself, Denise will have to watch me crumble to pieces.

"I'm sorry," I say.

She lowers the pillow from my face. "It's all right."

Once the tears start there is no stopping them. For every sad memory of what is lost there's a joyful one for what remains. Denise smooths my hair, not seeming to notice or care that I'm sobbing huge patches of tears onto her blouse.

"François told me I nearly died at the prison. I wasn't in my right mind. I wouldn't have even known. If not for you, Denise, I would have just been . . . gone. I don't want to die at seventeen."

Denise sets her hands on my shoulders and gently puts some space between us.

"Wait." She positions the pillow behind my back for support. "What did you say?"

"I lied about my age to come here," I say. "Just like Robbie did."

Denise's face crumples and she turns away on the edge of the bed. She stares at the street below through the window.

"When I saw you collapsed in the backseat of François's car, it scared me half to death. He showed me the horrific wounds they left. I can't believe what they did to you." She turns back to look at me, her eyes brimming with tears.

I clasp my hands, pale from months without sunshine, on my lap. "I'm sorry I lied," I say, sniffling back tears. "People trusted me. They were relying on me. I abandoned them."

"You abandoned no one. Your courage and silence allowed Resistance activities to continue. It saved many lives, including mine. Do you have any idea how I feel, knowing"—she covers her face—"what they must have put you through to find me and my radio? Please don't tell me I'm right, I couldn't bear to hear you say it, but I know that I am. The thought of you being tortured and near death, protecting me all the while—"

Denise buries her face in my blanket, sobbing uncontrollably. After what feels like an eternity, she lifts her head. Crying has washed the prettiness from her pale-gray eyes. Her sunburned nose looks as if it's been rubbed to a scalded shade of red.

"I thought this was supposed to be a happy reunion." Denise

passes one of two handkerchiefs on the bedside table to me and contains her sniffling with the other. "These things are terribly unhygienic. How I miss disposable tissues." Behind the kerchief, she mumbles, "Blasted war."

I pat my eyes dry, saying, "Denise, between my capture and now, I haven't heard a thing about the invasion. It was like living inside a bubble. Hasn't Paris been liberated?"

"No, not yet."

"But I was about to be moved to a camp in Germany. The Allies must be close?"

"They are."

"What about Bishop, and Madame LaRoche, and—" When I think of Pierre, I struggle to say, "Pierre's men?"

"Bishop is Bishop, invincible as ever. Madame LaRoche is holding on, but Pierre's death hit her very hard. Her daughter, Elise, has gone to live with her." Denise folds her kerchief into a neat square on her lap. "And the agents Cammerts introduced us to at the café before we returned to the farm? Both are feared dead."

I close my eyes to take in the gravity of all that has happened since that night at the factory. How could I have been thoughtlessly smug about those agents meeting a bad end?

"Within hours of Pierre's death, his men armed themselves and joined forces with other circuits to attack an elite Panzer tank division on its way to Normandy. They hounded it for hundreds of miles, doing everything they could think of to slow it down or stop it. Firefights, grenades, you name it. They fought until their ammunition ran out. Big Edgar and Marcus were quite proud of their idea to fell massive trees across the roads and hide anti-tank mines beneath them. They tied up hundreds of tanks and thousands of men for fifteen days. The entire Panzer division didn't reach the beaches in time to do much more than twiddle their thumbs."

I think back to the day Pierre introduced us to a ragtag group of men at the camp, and how little faith I had in them. "Really? They did all that?"

"They did. Bishop believes that was crucial to the success of the Allies' advance after D-day. Men you trained did that, Adele. They were willing to fight to get their country back, but you helped make it possible for them." Holding my hand in hers, Denise looks me straight in the eyes. "Don't you dare feel guilty about a thing, my friend. You are a hero."

FORTY-TWO

Denise and Marie embarked on a mission to nurse me back to health. There was no talking them out of it. It took a while for me to realize Denise was doing some healing of her own. Even though she wasn't responsible for the torture I endured, I could convince only her mind of that. Not her heart. If she needed to help me, I owed her the chance to do it.

In the weeks I grew stronger and healthier, Paris weakened, as its occupiers packed up and pulled out. By the middle of August, the Metro no longer ran at all, electricity became available only for an hour or two each day—and then during the middle of the night when hardly anyone needed it—restaurants closed up for days at a stretch, and the city fell into a state of chaos and fear, with firefights between the Resistance and remaining Germans taking place in the streets.

But during that time, normal life began to return. On daily walks like the one Denise, Marie, and I are about to set off on, we saw hundreds of children playing in the Seine to cool off in the summer heat and a couple eagerly prying apart the makeshift wooden signs that relabeled the streets in German.

"You look good today," Marie says. Cradling my face in her hands, she rotates my head left and right. "The sun has put some color back into your cheeks. Did you take your vitamin supplements this morning? Did you eat every bite of your breakfast?"

I squirm free. "Yes, I did. Denise tried to force-feed me the last time I didn't."

Overhearing me as she steps outside and closes the door to Dr. Devereux's home, Denise laughs.

"I will do whatever is necessary to have you looking like your old self again," she says. "Protruding hipbones and sunken cheeks will never be in fashion."

The two months I spent away from a mirror has given me a distorted sense of my self-image. Looking down at my body in prison, I saw slimmer arms and legs. I ran my hands over bony bumps and ridges that used to be comfortably padded. But I assumed I looked pretty much the same as always, just a little thinner. Nothing could have prepared me for seeing the girl who gaped back at me from the gilded mirror in Dr. Devereux's upper hallway when I got the go-ahead to leave my bed. Her gaunt face, sinewy neck, and dead stare repulsed me. She's a stranger. I don't want to be her.

It feels as if my interrogators still maintain a hold over my life, a stranglehold at my throat. I was freed from prison, but I'm not free from what they did to me there.

"Last evening, there was a firefight at the end of our avenue," Marie says as we walk. "The Resistance shot two German soldiers dead. From my bedroom window I saw their bodies, lying in the middle of the street where they fell. Two women ran over and stole the boots right off their dead feet, to sell on the black market, I guess. The fighting was so close a stray bullet hit the stone lion that guards the entrance to our building. Poor Gustav. He has only one good ear now."

We jump back to the safety of the sidewalk when a truck speeds around the corner. It rounds another corner so quickly I barely have time to make out the faded mark of the French Forces of the Interior on the truck's side.

"The truck was transporting women," Marie says. "Why do you think that is?"

"Let's find out," Denise says, striding away.

It seems like only yesterday I had athletic abilities to take pride in. I fall into an uncoordinated run, determined to keep up with Denise and Marie.

By the time we catch up with the truck a boisterous crowd is already gathering around it. Through a separation between two onlookers, I watch a man wearing an FFI armband raise a pair of scissors into the air. He shows the long blades of gleaming steel to the crowd. A cheer goes up.

People emerge from all directions to join the crowd. Denise, Marie, and I work into places at the outskirts of the group.

Another member of the French Forces jumps into the back of the open truck. Above his head, he shakes a battered paper sign that reads *LE CHAR DES COLLABORATRICES*.

The women in the truck collaborated with the Germans.

Whenever the crowd shifts, I glimpse the four women, lined up and on display for all to see, covering their faces with their hands in shame.

The wielder of the scissors waves a fistful of chestnut-brown hair. The crowd roars. They hurl insults. When he has chopped the length of the woman's hair until nothing but stubble remains, he moves on to the next woman. The taunting continues.

The brutality of being roughly shorn like some farm animal resonates through me. A terrible wave of nausea sweeps over me.

Men press against me to get a better look, closing me in, tapping my feet out of the way with their boots. Elbows jostle for space. I feel the tension budding in the air, eager to bloom into violent bedlam.

A man in the crowd cracks one of the women on the back of her head with his hand. I tremble, unable to catch my breath, listening to her cries.

Denise lays her hand on my shoulder. "Adele, maybe you shouldn't be watching this."

As Denise directs me by the arm, the woman who was shaved first lowers her hands from her face. Our gazes connect and lock for an instant. Her expression is one I wished to never again see on another woman. I have to look away.

Crying, Marie says, "Those poor women. Someone should do something to stop that."

"No!" Denise says, and her vehement retort makes Marie cry even harder. "Women like those four sent fellow countrymen and women to abysmal prisons. To German camps. To starvation and slow, agonizing deaths. Women like our Adele. Traitors are what they are, the lot of them. So they could be wined and dined and knock boots with a German officer? For God's sake, it's only hair. It will grow back. They're getting off lucky, if you ask me!"

Denise storms ahead of us, swiping at her eyes. She stops abruptly in the middle of the street and waits for us to catch up.

She hooks her arm through Marie's and says, "I'm sorry. I shouldn't have lashed out at you."

"I understand." Marie blushes, unable to look Denise in the eye. "And you're right. It is only hair, after all."

Yes, it may be only hair. But without hers, Dr. Devereux's wife isn't nearly as pretty.

———————

From my bed, I listen to Denise's footsteps padding down the hallway. Her distinctive tiptoe usually returns to a chipper march once she's passed my bedroom, but this time she doesn't go beyond the partially closed door. My afternoon nap will have to wait.

"Adele, are you awake?" she whispers.

I roll onto my back. "Yeah, come on in."

Denise slowly enters the room, smiling, but something about her expression is off.

"Denise, what's the matter?"

"I have news. It's big news. I wanted to make sure you're in the right frame of mind to deal with it. You know, with the chest pain and palpitations you've been having."

Between her pastiness and twitchy smile, I can't read her expression at all. What is she trying to tell me? Part of me wishes she'd just come out with it, and part of me wishes she wouldn't.

"So, are you feeling all right, Adele?" she asks.

After a night crammed end to end with nightmares that seemed truer than life, I've taken a big step backward. Dreams of the night Pierre died in my arms always leave me feeling numb and beaten up and exhausted and ready to cry at the drop of a hat.

I imagine myself standing alone on the brink of a seaside cliff, engulfed by bleak, stormy skies. If I fall to the jagged rocks beneath I won't care. I fought to survive in prison. I could've given up plenty of times. And now that I'm safe, on days like today, I'm apathetic about dying.

"I feel okay. What do you have to tell me?"

"I have news about Robbie."

I practically fly into an upright position. My heart can't take any bad news. Not today. I don't want to know.

"What about Robbie?" I ask.

"Adele, he never left France."

Unable to speak, I vigorously shake my head, as if that might make Robbie's death untrue. How could he not have made it out of France? Why couldn't they get him home safely? I want to scream at Denise to take it back.

She runs to my side, crying, "No, no, no!" She lifts my chin, forcing me to look at her through tears. "He hasn't died! He's still here in France." She hugs me to her, patting my back. "My God, what have I done to you? This is exactly what I didn't want to happen. Couldn't you tell the big news was happy news from my ear-to-ear smile?"

"So"—I choke out—"he's alive?"

"He is." Denise raises her eyebrows, frowning with nervous uncertainty. She has more to say, but her big news announcement didn't go the way she planned. Now she's not sure how to continue. Finally, she blurts, "Would you like to see for yourself?"

I take a ragged breath, sniffling. "What do you mean?"

"He's here. Downstairs in the front lobby. He came to find you, Adele."

My mind reels. Robbie is here. Downstairs. A single floor away from me?

I look down at my weakened arms. The two unsightly fingernail nubs on my right hand. The nightgown I wear so often it must smell as bad as the grubby blanket my youngest cousin totes everywhere.

I don't want Robbie to see me this way. Dr. Devereux removed the large gilded mirror from the hallway outside my room, but once in a while I accidently spot my reflection in a storefront window or Denise's round makeup mirror. I know what I look like.

"Denise, I'm scared." I grab my handkerchief from the nightstand. "I do want to see him, but it's been months. What if everything's different?" My voice catches in my throat. "Everything *is* different."

"Would you rather wait until you feel healthier?"

"No, I want to see him," I say. When Denise turns to leave, a rush of panic compels me call her back. "Wait, Denise. Would you comb my hair for me?"

She spins around. "Of course!"

She runs the comb through my hair again and again, easing out the tangles until shiny waves fall past my shoulders. At least one part of me has returned to normal.

"Sit tight," she says. "I'll go get him."

The next minutes of waiting give me more anxiety than I felt some days in prison.

Heavy footsteps slowly climb the staircase. Is he as nervous to see me again as I am to see him? The footsteps quicken. He's running now. I almost can't stand to keep my eyes open. And then, there he is, and I can't look away. Within the past four months, the boy I was expecting has been replaced by the tanned, rugged man who stands in the doorway.

"Hi," he says.

"Hi." I smile so hard I fear my face might break. "You look so . . . different."

"You look just the same. I've thought of that smile every day. I knew I'd see it again."

He might look more rugged, but underneath he's still the same sweet boy.

"Come here. Come sit down," I say, excitedly waving him over to the bedside chair. "How come you didn't leave France?"

"It's a crazy story, Adele. You probably won't believe me." He sits in the chair and leans forward. "My handlers got an urgent message from London that the invasion was close. All evacuation plans had to be stopped immediately. The Resistance had more important things to do than transport guys like me who had the bad luck to be shot down. So they took me to a camp. Do you know where Freteval Forest is?"

"Yeah, sure I do. I stayed at a farmhouse near there."

"That's where I spent the last few months, along with more than a hundred and fifty other downed pilots. We lived in the woods, right under the noses of the Germans."

My mouth drops open. "But that area must have been swarming with Germans after D-day. You lived in those woods without being seen or heard?"

"I guess it was the last place the Germans expected anybody to hide, right inside the lion's den," he says. "And we had two strict rules. Never make a break to get back to Britain on your own, and never raise your voice. The camp was smack-dab between German ammo caches. Patrols went past every fifteen minutes. Some days, none of us dared speak above a whisper."

I shake my head in awe. "Those must have been frightening months, for all of you."

"What we were doing was dangerous, but believe it or not, we were bored. We spent a lot of time lying around in the sun, swapping stories and jokes. Then, in the middle of July, a couple of the guys came up with the great idea to start Freteval Country Club, so we got busy whittling golf clubs and balls. We had tournaments and everything."

"C'mon," I say, playfully smacking his arm. "Now you're really pulling my leg."

With the boyish grin I love so much, he says, "I swear to you, Adele, every word is true. I know I called it a camp, but it was much more than that. We had our very own secret village in those woods until the Allies liberated our camp on August thirteenth. That day was one of the happiest of our lives, let me tell you."

Robbie's fascinating story trails away. His healthy tan seems to fade from his face.

"Robbie, what's the matter?"

"Here I am babbling like an insensitive jerk about how much fun I had living at Freteval. God, I'm sorry, Adele."

"Robbie, no, I want to hear all about it," I say, reassuring him with a smile.

"Denise told me what happened. It just about killed me to hear how those men hurt you. They hurt *you,* Adele, the most wonderful girl I've ever known—" His voice catches as he says, "And there's not a damn thing I can do about it."

His arms engulf me in a hug. He brought the warmth of the sunny summer day inside with him. I cling to him with all my strength, not wanting to let go. I think about Robbie hiding out in a forest camp, like Pierre and his men, forced by war to live in seclusion and fear. The seclusion and fear was what brought

Pierre and me together. We gave each other security and understanding at a time when we needed them above all else. But as Robbie holds me in his arms right now, I feel more anchored than I have in months; like if he came into my life for good, I might finally be able to let go of my past and move on.

"I've missed you so much," he says in my ear. "Not a day went by that I didn't think of you."

"I've missed you too." The words I wanted to say months before outside the Commodore come back to me. "Robbie, please don't leave."

"I don't want to leave, I really don't."

"Then stay here with me."

"There's nothing I'd like more," he says. "But I have to go, Adele. The other fellas from the camp are waiting for me. I snuck away because I had to see you again."

With his supportive arms around me, my body doesn't feel weak and fragile, and when we separate from the hug I immediately long for another. Robbie hasn't left yet, and already I've started missing him. I understand why he has to go, but what if after he walks out my bedroom we never see each other again? I don't want this day to be our final memory.

He gently brushes strands of hair from my tear-streaked cheek. "I was hoping to get your address, so I can contact you when life settles down. If that's all right, of course."

"I don't know where I'll be, but please write to me." I jot my aunt's address on a slip of notebook paper and tear it free. "My aunt will make sure I get your letters."

Robbie tucks the folded paper in his pocket. "Thanks, Adele." He leans over my bed to kiss my cheek. He picks up my hand and holds it for a moment. "I guess this is good-bye again."

I bite my lip, fighting tears. "Bye, Robbie."

At the door, he turns to wave.

"This isn't the last you've seen of me," he says with such confidence I let myself believe he'll do whatever it takes to find me again. "That's a promise."

FORTY-THREE

Denise lowers the book I'm reading by candlelight.

She brings her hand out from behind her back, balancing a small flat box on her palm. "A belated birthday gift."

I mark the page with a turned-down corner and put the book on the table.

She sets the gift in front of me. "Open it."

I slowly lift the top of the box. "But it's my charm bracelet."

"Have a better look," she says, dangling the strand in front of my face.

New charms have joined Uncle Edward, Aunt Libby, Philip, and Paul.

My gusty laughter almost extinguishes the candle. "The handbag! Is that you?"

"However did you guess?" Pinching the next silver charm, the Eiffel Tower, she says, "This one represents your friends in France."

"What about the heart charm?"

"I think you know it's the boy who holds your heart."

Fingering the final charm, I say, "And the acorn. Who is that?"

"Well, that's you, of course."

I fixate on the charm Denise chose for me. Why the acorn? The answer is probably so obvious, but it just isn't coming to my mind.

Tilting her head, she says, "Do you not see? Everything the small, unassuming acorn needs to grow into a mighty oak is within it."

Like an acorn, I fell to earth. I landed in the right place at the right time. The charm represents transformation and the potential for greatness. I sit taller, smiling, puffed up with pride, straightening the silver strand on the tabletop to line up the charms. Two heartfelt gifts have come together as one. There are people who care about me deeply enough to believe I deserve such a gift.

"Thank you. I really love it."

"I'm so glad. I hope it wasn't presumptuous of me to add to your family like that."

My family.

I go so far as to shake my head and say, "No, Denise—" before I realize there's no reason at all to correct her. I smile at the tiny trinkets. "No, Denise, it's perfect."

She begins to sit on the chair next to mine, but then springs into the air.

"Listen!"

Somewhere in the city, church bells ring. The distant clanging is music to my ears.

Denise clutches the sleeve of my nightgown, tugging on my arm as she bounces in place. "Do you know what that means?"

"The Allies. They've made it. They're approaching the city!"

Holding hands we jump in a circle, like kids playing a high-spirited game of ring-around-the-rosy.

I drop into my chair short of breath but laughing. Denise dances the jitterbug right out of the room. In moments she's back, carting a bottle of champagne and two glasses. She fills both glasses to the brim.

I raise my glass. "I never thought we'd share another glass of champagne together."

"Well, my friend," she says, wiping her smile clean with the back of her hand. "There's plenty more where that bottle came from. Dr. Devereux hid a secret stash from the Germans."

I watch my champagne swirl round and round. Who knew the prospect of leaving would feel this bittersweet.

"It won't be long now before the Allies have freed Paris. We'll be off for home," Denise says. "But don't worry, we will keep in touch."

"I hope so, Denise."

"Call me Sarah."

I glance up in surprise. When I look at her face, it's as if I'm seeing her for the first time all over again. "Your real name. It's Sarah?"

"It is. But if you know Denise, you know Sarah just as well. We're astonishingly similar." With a laugh, she adds, "Sarah has better shoes."

"Sarah. The name suits you, but it might take me some getting used to."

"And you, Adele? Who are you really?"

"Betty."

"Betty." Denise draws my name out, trying it on me for size. Judging by her cockeyed expression, it fits about as well as an old sack. "No, no, you're my friend, Adele."

I tip my glass toward Denise's. "Here's to Denise and Adele."

Our glasses meet with a melodious *clink*.

Friends till the end.

EPILOGUE

"Here they come!" Denise bends to catch her breath. "Adele, I may toss my cookies."

"I can't believe this is truly happening," Marie says, clutching the bars of chocolate she brought as gifts for the most handsome soldiers.

I squeeze my body through a break in the crowd to look down the Champs Élysées. I have a clear view all the way to the Arc de Triomphe. It seems the entire city has come to welcome the Allies.

Army jeeps and tanks, loaded down with soldiers, roll through the avenue. A cheer erupts from the crowds, the joy deafening.

The tears streaming down Marie's cheeks set off some waterworks of my own.

"At long last, liberation has come," she says, and I vow to always remember how purely happy she sounds. "We are free."

A look passes between Denise and me.

"We are free," she says.

I hold my breath when a column of soldiers at least twenty men abreast, spanning from one side of the avenue to the other, marches into view. Row after row, they seem to go on forever.

When I clap alongside Denise, silver charms jangle at their rightful place about my wrist—my mischievous cousins, my loving aunt and uncle, my friends in France, and Denise and Robbie.

I came all this way, searching for my place in the world, believing that I was stranded and alone. That I had no family. Nothing could be further from the truth.

At the beginning of our journey together, Denise asked me what I would do once I got back to regular life. Where would I go from here?

I still don't know the answer. But I do know one thing for certain. My place in the world doesn't matter nearly as much as the people who open their hearts to me while I'm there. And wherever I am, as long as they're by my side, I'll be home.

Acknowledgments

The idea for this book came from my husband, Steve. Throughout the seven years of research and revision that followed, I occasionally cursed him for planting that idea in my head. Now, I thank him from the bottom of my heart. I also owe a huge debt of gratitude to Steven Chudney for never giving up the faith. He put the book into the hands of its perfect editor, Mary Kate Castellani. Many thanks go to her, Stacy Cantor Abrams, and the entire team at Walker.

Writing novels can be a lonely experience, and I'm so grateful for my wonderful friends in the online writing community. Their encouragement and understanding kept me from throwing in the towel. A special thank-you goes to my sister, Andrea, who read several drafts of this book and loved it from the get-go. Thanks to Shelley, Adam, Brian, Kiri, Bailey, Ken, and Mom for your excitement and support. And, of course, thank you to my biggest cheerleaders, Kate, Erin, and Brenden.